Bride of the Blaine

SEQUEL TO A GAME OF SHADES AND SHADOWS

Bride of the Blaine

SEQUEL TO A GAME OF SHADES AND SHADOWS

ROBERT A. G. ERICKSON

BOOKS IN THE FLUKE FAMILY SERIES:
Fluke Family Fortune
Fluke Family Hero
Fluke Family King
Fluke Family Assassin
Fluke Family Sorcerer
Fluke Family Curse

BOOKS IN THE WIZOR FAIR SERIES
The Wizor Fair
Shadow Hunters
The Last King of Eskeling
The Wizard of Seattle
The King of the Whelfs
The Dawn of the Whelfs
A Game of Shades and Shadows
Bride of the Blaine

OTHER BOOKS BY THE AUTHOR:
Homindroid: Marzian's Martians
Homindroid: Far from Heaven
The Waifs of Trove
Diary of Fear

DEDICATION

I thank my wife Barbara, who was invaluable in editing the book and to family and friends who encouraged me to write. I also digitally created and rendered the cover art.

CONTENTS

CHAPTER 1

BLAINE KAMP

Sixteen-year-old Lenny Conklin materialized within the oak forest next to Kings Keep, but he was barely aware of having done so. Although the stone turrets of the castle curtain were clearly visible above the treetops, he paid them little attention. He was so lost in thought that he had nearly forgotten that his fraternal twin sister, Cassy, had traveled through the magic ether with him from the Whelf Fen until she spoke.

"We're here, Lenny," she reminded him. "Do you have any idea of how lost you look right now?"

The Queen of the Whelfs' wings billowed in the wind like a great bird of paradise. To bring them under control, she folded them neatly around her body, forming a pink traveling cloak with black pinstripes. The bright glow from her protective whelf bubble was the last to vanish as she took on her beautiful, fully human appearance.

Lenny leaned wearily on his gnarled wizard staff. The steel ball, held in the grip of a goblin's claw, still glowed from the magic energy that brought them here, but becoming aware of it, he extinguished it.

"This is so unlike me," he said. "I suppose that I can compare my feelings to yours when you discovered that you couldn't just destroy all of your whelf friends in the fen even though they would return as neophytes anyway. That's where Night Shadow had you over the barrel. It took both of us to resolve that battle satisfactorily, but I'm concerned that there's no hope for me. I'm torn between Zada's love and Jenna's."

"I'm sorry that I can't help you with affairs of the heart, Lenny," she replied, "but contrary to popular belief, queen whelfs are not all-powerful. The best I can do is make you forget that you love anyone, which I'm sure is not what you want."

Lenny stared hopefully at her for a moment, but then he nodded and replied, "You're quite right, of course, Cassy. I suppose that it's best if we did what we came here to do."

Cassy smiled and took his hand. "I'll take us the rest of the way, Lenny, and inform everyone that we're coming."

They appeared inside the castle hospital room in the next instant. Prince Symon who also served as the court physician eagerly greeted them with a quick bow.

"I'm glad you're back," the young physician said. "You'll be pleased to know that my patients are recovering very well."

By his patients, he meant the twin's mother, Marge Conklin; Zada, Lenny's girlfriend; and Skeldon, their mutual friend. Also visiting were their father, Jim Conklin; and Jenna who threw her arms around Lenny and kissed his cheek.

Lenny was glad that Zada as well as the other patients appeared to be asleep and did not witness the exchange of endearment. All three patients had magically aged but were now recovering, courtesy of the sorcerer Scapita's strange youthening potion.

"I'm so glad that both of you are safe," Jenna said. "I know that Night Shadow could not have treated you very well in the Whelf Fen. I couldn't get past the barrier to find you."

"It's best that you couldn't, Jenna," Lenny replied. "I've never seen such a horrible battle as in Night Shadow's *Game of Shades and Shadows*. It was not just a game. It was for keeps. If we hadn't managed to trick her into our trap, none of us would have returned as we are. We would have been changed into whelfs forever."

"Goodness, is that true?" Jenna asked, glancing at Cassy.

The Queen of the Whelfs somberly nodded. "That was the only other option to win the game, but Lenny fortuitously showed up and helped me win it. I was at my wit's end until then."

Lenny grasped Zada's right hand and squeezed it, but she did not respond. He noted unhappily that her shriveled hand seemed to belong to an old woman rather than to the young girl he doted on. Leaning closely, he felt her warm breath on his face, which reassured him that she was indeed alive. Her face appeared ashen, and her hair still bore an off gray tinge from her usual black.

"She's improving," Prince Symon said. "All of them are. You would know that if you had seen them yesterday. It just takes time for the potion to counter the magic that created the problem to begin with."

"I understand, Prince Symon," he replied. "I suppose I'm somewhat responsible for that since it was the destruction of two of my wizard staffs that created the aging problem."

He noted that Skeldon seemed to be in a similar condition as Zada, but his heart went out for his mother. She still resembled an eighty-year-old woman, which was twice as old as she should be. Her hair was virtually white but slowly reverting to a streaked gray. He knew that in time it would return to the sleek auburn color that was her norm.

"She doesn't look so good right now," Jim Conklin said from behind him. "I've been here the whole time. She looked like a wrinkled old witch yesterday. I promise that I'll stay here until she fully recovers, though. You don't need to concern yourself with that."

"I know," Lenny replied, "but I can't help but be concerned. The past few days have been hard on us all. Sometimes I regret having come to the Kingdom of Duscany or even discovering the portal that transported us here from Seattle. If it weren't for Zada and my friends here, I would go home and never return. You understand what I'm talking about, don't you, Dad?"

"You know I do, son, but I doubt if leaving and not returning is an option. Your mother and I have made friends here too. I would not enjoy leaving them behind if I had to go."

"It doesn't seem fair that Cassy and I will have to attend school the moment we return to Seattle," Lenny said. "That doesn't give mom or the others much time to recover."

"You don't have to worry about that," Cassy said, joining them. "I guarantee that no time will have passed since we left Seattle when we do return through the portal. We can stay here as long as we must to recuperate. Believe me, I need some time off too."

"Still, I would like to find a way to speed up their recovery," he replied. "Zada and Skeldon have loved ones too who need them. Cassy, you must have some sort of idea of how to achieve that."

"I'll give it some thought, Lenny," she replied, "but it was your magic that aged them after all. Perhaps we can work something out together."

"I'll help," Jenna chimed in. Her head dipped and her smile faded when the twins suddenly stared at her. She didn't like the look on Lenny's face in particular. "Well, I think I can be useful. I'm not exactly helpless."

"You aren't helpless at all, Jenna," Cassy grinned. "Of course, you can help. We'll just have to prepare a plan of attack is all since this problem is not an easy one. We may have to search the new magic archives for a precedence."

"Perhaps Uncle Scapita can help," Jenna interjected. "He's an archive of magic in himself. Did you know that Guena and Uncle Scapita are getting married?"

"I find that hard to believe," Lenny replied. "Isn't he something like four times her age?"

"Well, his youthening potion did remove a lot of years from his appearance," Jenna replied. "Come on, and you can see for yourself."

"Go on and we'll be fine," Jim said. "I'll let you know if anything happens."

"I suppose you're right," Lenny replied. "I want to hear Scapita's take on how my wizard staffs created the aging effect in the first place. That might be the key."

Cassy took Lenny and Jenna's hands and said, "Let me transport us together. I'm not looking forward to climbing that long flight of tower stairs."

"I hear you," Lenny said, but they were already gone.

Appearing on the landing outside of Scapita's apartment, they waited only a moment before Guena opened the door. She was a sorceress in her mid-forties. Normally, she wore her dark brown hair in a high bun tied up with thin leather strings, but today she wore it down below her shoulders in large curls that made her look years younger.

Smiling sweetly, she asked, "What kept you so long? Scapita and I have been waiting for you to come for some time."

"Well, we did make a stop at the hospital first," Lenny said, as she ushered them into the living room of the apartment.

Scapita sat in his usual rocking chair with a comforter thrown over his legs. They were astounded to find that he had lost at least half of his two hundred years of age. Even his hair was brown in the back, but his face was brimmed with long strands of white hair as was his belly length beard.

Scapita, however, was not alone. A dark-complexioned man in his mid-thirties rose from his chair and bowed to each of them.

"My name is Kamp," he said. "I'm the Blaine of Stroop Town. I have a problem I hope the great Scapita can solve for me."

Cassy whispered into Lenny's ear, "Blaine Kamp is like a mayor in our world, but Stroop Town is a suburb of Kings Port. He works for the governor of that city."

"I swear, Cassy," Lenny complained. "How do you know this stuff?"

"It's like osmosis," she replied. "It kind of seeps in unbidden on the ether, a perk of being a whelf, I suppose. You could do it too since you're the King of the Whelfs. All you have to do is listen."

"I guess I'm just too sleepy to do that right now," Lenny said. He would have to investigate whether that were true or not later.

They assisted Guena in setting out more chairs and arranged themselves appropriately about the room. Guena dropped a log in the fireplace and stirred up the coals until the fire crackled warmly.

"Blaine Kamp was about to tell me about his problem when you three arrived," Scapita said. "He is one of the best Wizors I've ever tutored and now a strong sorcerer in his own right. I suspect that you'll be interested in what he has to say. Go on, Master Kamp."

Kamp glanced at the three newcomers and smiled. "First, I would like to introduced myself to your guests, Master Scapita. I believe that the young lady leaning on your shoulder is your niece, Jenna. I was astonished when I saw her perform at the last Wizor Fair and win it hands down. I've never seen such strong magic performed by such a young Wizor before."

"You're quite right," Scapita agreed. "Jenna has surpassed all my expectations. I've begun to wonder if there is anything left that I can tutor her for, but for now, Guena is seeing to her wizor education. Jenna is also the Wizor to Prince Leonard."

"I'm eager to see how you turn out, Princess Jenna," the Blaine replied. "As for this second beautiful woman, even I have heard about the gorgeous Queen of the Whelfs. I never saw a grander entrance made at the Wizor Ball, and I was even more flabbergasted to see her astonishing exit. I thought you were much older than you now seem, My Lady."

"Just call me Cassandra, Master Kamp," she replied. "The Queen of the Whelfs can look as young or old as she pleases. If you knew me, you would know that there is little that I can't do within the realm of my powers. The real power in my family, though, is Prince Leonard, my brother and the Wizard of Seattle."

Cassy turned her blushing face toward Lenny to divert the Blaine's interested eyes from hers.

"Of course, I've heard much about the Wizard of Seattle," Blaine Kamp replied, "but I've not seen you perform. Perhaps I'll have that privilege should you decide to work with Scapita on my request."

Lenny glanced brutally at his sister, but then he pulled his thoughts together. "I'm not at all certain that I will, Master Kamp," he replied. "We've just been through a particularly tiresome ordeal, and frankly, I need some rest."

"I doubt if this request will be that trying, Prince Leonard," Scapita said. "Please, Master Kamp, enlighten us."

"I suppose that this scrap of parchment is the starting place," he said. Reaching into his breast pocket, he extracted a folded piece of parchment and passed it to Scapita.

Scapita merely scanned the few words written inside and passed it to Lenny who looked at it as if it were poison. Finally, he warily accepted it and read the flowery content for himself.

My dear heart of my hearth,
I am now far away, but my
Love still burns for you.
I so much hope that you can
Rescue me from this dreadful place.
    Leanne Mellot

A hand drawn rose followed the simple note.

"Well, what does it mean?" Lenny asked. He passed it to his sister who passed in on to Jenna without opening it. Jenna seemed just as perplexed after reading it.

"That note is the last word I heard from my dear Leanne," Blaine Kamp replied. "We were very much in love. We were betrothed to wed on the day when she simply vanished leaving only that note behind. This is nearly the tenth anniversary of her disappearance. I searched for an answer, but I've finally come to the realization that my magic is not nearly enough to solve the puzzle left by that note. I want you to help me solve the puzzle and rescue my beloved. If I understood the note, she's been abducted and hidden away in some dreadful place. As you can see, she begged me for rescue, but I've failed her. Your prowess as a sorcerer is foremost in the land, Master Scapita. That's why I came to you. I'm prepared to pay you a thousand gold pieces if successful."

"That is indeed a goodly sum, Master Kamp, but since I'm preparing for my wedding, I must decline your request." His eyes joined Guena's across the room, and their lips uplifted in a bright smile.

"But you must accept," the Blaine replied. "I have no one else to turn to. You're my last hope."

"I cannot accept your offer, Master Kamp," Scapita replied, "but there are three very competent magic users here who can. This is your opportunity to shine, Jenna. Perhaps you can encourage your friends to help you solve this mysterious disappearance."

Jenna gaped in surprise. "Uncle, I've never done anything like that before. I don't see how I can help."

"Considering the myriad of problems you and your friends have solved over the past few months," Scapita said, "I believe that you are more than capable of bringing home Master Kamp's betrothed. I admit that ten years is an inordinately long time, but I think there are adequate clues to go on. Don't you think so, Queen Cassandra?"

"But she didn't even read the note," Jenna objected. "I tried to hand it to her, but she refused to take it."

Cassy smiled. "I don't need to read the note with my eyes to know what it contains. I do sense that a clue is hidden within those lines, however."

"Here we go again," Lenny replied. "Cassy, what clue could there be in that simple note other than that she might have been abducted?"

"Lenny, you've read all of the classic Sherlock Holmes books, haven't you?" she replied. "Well, put on your thinking cap while I point out an obvious issue. My first question is for Master Scapita. Have you heard the phrase *heart of my hearth* before?"

"Not at all, Queen Cassandra," he replied. "Have you, Guena?"

"I'm sure I've never heard of it before," she said.

Even Blaine Kamp shook his head no.

"Lenny, I'm sure that you of all people can recognize something in it, can't you?" Cassy asked.

Shrugging, Lenny replied, "Zada did call me her *hearth heart*, but so what? What does that have to do with the abduction?"

"Even you should note the difference, lamebrain," Cassy said. "Since Zada is a Bugoward, one can assume that perhaps Leanne is too, don't you think?"

Blaine Kamp suddenly brightened. "Yes, she did say that she had lived in a tree prior to working for me. She had run away from home not long before I found her in Kings Port. That's where my home is. Since only my grandmother lives with me, I allowed her to stay in one of the empty rooms and to help me in my grocery business. In time, we fell in love and planned to marry."

"Don't you think that's a clue that can be followed up on, Lenny?" Cassy asked.

"Smart ass," Lenny whispered to her, but then he covered his lips and embarrassment with a hand. "You're quite right, Cassy," he added. "Perhaps Elder Wolsa would know something about her."

"Exactly, but the phrase suggests another meaning," Cassy said. "You know that the proper phrase is *hearth heart*, meaning a loved one at home. However, she purposely wrote *heart of my hearth*. Suppose she meant it as a phrase to be questioned, perhaps suggesting that something could be hidden there meant just for Blaine Kamp's eyes?"

Lenny's eyes brightened. "Well, we do have a member of the family who can think," he agreed. "Maybe I do need a break from working on that old castle. Every time I start on that chore, something dreadful happens."

"Oh, I want to help!" Jenna cried. "I do enjoy working with Prince Leonard. Are you going to help too, Cassandra? It sounds like we could really use it."

"I will as much as I can, Jenna," she replied. "If I'm called back to the Whelf Fen for queenly business, you'll have to proceed on your own until the problem is resolved."

"I'm so glad that you accept," Blaine Kamp replied. "I'm certain that I couldn't be in better hands." Handing another piece of parchment to Lenny, he said, "That's my address in Kings Port. I'm leaving for there now since I have a grocery to manage. If you want to start your investigation from there, let me know, and I'll inform my grandmother. Please make yourselves at home. There's plenty of room."

The Blaine enthusiastically excused himself, and Guena showed him out.

CHAPTER 2

THE QUEST

Lenny leaned toward Scapita. "Now that he's gone, perhaps I can get some straight answers on how and why my staffs exploded. I never meant for anyone to suffer because of me."

"Don't beat yourself up over it, Lenny," Cassy said. "I'm sure that it wasn't because of anything that you did out of the ordinary."

"Perhaps, I should offer my observations, Prince Leonard," Scapita said. "I admit that I am curious about how your wizard staff works such marvelous magic, but I was trying to recover my niece from wherever she had been sent. I believed that if I found her, I would also find you."

"I'm sure they understand the motive for our investigation, Scapita," Guena said. "I want to assure you, Prince Leonard, that we were only doing what we thought we had to do to understand where you had gone off to. Isn't that right, Scapita?"

"I couldn't have said it better, Guena," Scapita replied. "Prince Leonard, I carry as much guilt over the damage I caused your mother and friends. I don't understand how or why the staffs exploded any better than you do, but it was my decision that caused them to be brought here for examination. All I know is that one of the staffs was quite dead, but the other was still viable. Zada and Skeldon were indeed successful at extracting some of what we required from it, but unfortunately, not enough. The extraction somehow caused the metal balls on your staffs to draw together and explode. I don't know what force could have done that. It's beyond my experience."

Listening carefully, Lenny glanced at Cassy and replied, "Perhaps I can offer a kind of explanation. Cassy, you remember learning about magnetism in science class. I believe that the electrical connection between the positive and negative poles of the steel balls on the staffs drew them together. That produced a kind of short circuit that blasted them to pieces." Except for Cassy, who understood him, the others wore blank expressions. "Well, it is a scientific explanation. That works here too," he said. "I couldn't have predicted that would happen, though."

"It wasn't your fault, Lenny," Cassy interjected. "Your explanation seems perfectly plausible to me. Master Scapita, do you have any of those metal pieces left from the explosion. I would like to analyze them myself."

"So do I," Lenny added.

"You may have all the pieces," Scapita replied. "Guena, if you would, fetch them, please. We'll assemble at the table. Since dinner is not far off, I think it would be more comfortable there anyway."

They had no more than sat down when Guena arrived with a small leather bag and placed it before Cassy at the table.

"I hope you can make something of it, Queen Cassandra," Guena said "As you can see, there's not much left. Be careful of how you handle the metal pieces. That's what poisoned your mother and friends."

Reaching into the bag, Cassy withdrew piece after piece of the charred remains of the wooden shafts and arranged them on the table. She added a few of the larger pieces of the metal balls that once fitted on the head of the shafts.

Lenny closely scrutinized one of the wooden pieces before replacing it on the table and taking another. He did the same with all the other wooden pieces before he sat back and sighed.

"There's no magic left in them, Cassy," he said. "Do you detect anything? Your whelf magic is more sensitive than mine."

"I doubt that, Lenny," she replied. "I agree that there is nothing left. I hoped to find a recording that we could examine, but there's nothing."

"I have a suggestion," Scapita said. "Since I was here when the staffs exploded, my far-sight recorded everything. Perhaps I can replay precisely what occurred here."

"Go for it," Lenny said. "Show us everything."

Scapita nodded then closed his eyes and leaned back in the chair. The space above the table began to glow and thicken until the original staffs were displayed on the table. Everyone who was present at the time also appeared.

Lenny was disconcerted when he realized that he sat where Skeldon sat during the experiment, and Cassy sat in the same location as where Zada sat.

"Maybe we should vacate the table until the projection has finished," Cassy said, rising from her chair and stepping back. Lenny did the same, but Scapita and Guena remained where they were since their counterparts in the projection sat in the same locations.

The projection revealed how Skeldon and Zada handled the staffs to draw out their own projections of how the charred staff had been damaged. The power in the undamaged staff soon began to vibrate, producing an electric glow in the orbs of both staffs. Suddenly, the orbs crashed together and exploded in a blinding light.

The projection ended the moment that Scapita opened his eyes.

"As you know," he said, "the metal pieces wounded your mother, Zada and Skeldon. Although your mother received fewer pieces of metal, she was affected just as much as the others. I cannot show you that part because the explosion temporarily blinded my far-sight. That's how powerful it was."

"If I had sat anywhere else," Guena said, "I probably would have been hurt too."

"What protected you, Uncle?" Jenna asked. "You were closer than anyone to the exploding orbs."

"I never take unnecessary risks, my dear," he replied. "I activated a protection charm the moment we began the experiment. I had a feeling that I could come to harm at the time. I always listen to my feelings."

"You were quite right to do so," Jenna said. "I'll do the same from now on. I learn from my mistakes too, you understand."

"Good girl," Scapita said with a smile. "Now if we're done here, I must inform you that supper is on the way. Guena, if you will, please remove this trash from the table."

"I'll take the pieces," Lenny said. "They are my property after all, and I might be able to extract something else from them."

"As you wish," Guena replied, handing him the bag, "but I advise you to be extra careful. I'm sure that everyone would hate for you to suddenly grow old like your mother. There's only so much youthening potion left, and the victims require that."

Lenny touched the bag with his staff and grinned as it vanished. "I've sent it to a safe place," he replied. "No one will suffer from my mistakes again. I'm working on a way to keep that kind of explosion from happening again even now."

Because he had his mind set on the patients in the hospital, Lenny picked at his meal. When he realized that the others had finished before him, he concentrated on wolfing it down.

"You really didn't have to eat it all if you weren't hungry," Cassy said. Even though she didn't need to eat in whelf form, she did so as a matter of courtesy.

"Actually, I am," he replied. "It's because I'm very tired after fighting that war against Night Shadow, but you should be exhausted after spending days in that swamp sparring with her. Why is it that you still look like a million bucks after all that?"

Cassy leaned back, crossed her arms and smiled. "It's because I'm also the Power of the Fen. I can freely renew my energy at will, but you seem to struggle with that when you don't have too. You're the King of the Whelfs. You can do the same without constraints of any kind."

"Actually, that's not the power that I'm thinking about, Cassy. I know I can renew my energy that way, and I sometimes do. The point is that Zada, Skeldon and particularly mom are soaking it up as fast as I can renew it."

"Lenny!" Cassy cried. "Stop it! You don't have to transfer any of your energy to them. It won't help them any better than it'll help you. All you need do is sit back and let the healing potion do its job. All you're doing is replacing it with your own strength."

Lenny's eyes suddenly lit up. "I didn't realize that until now,

Cassy. Thanks for pointing it out. I think that the problem now is that I feel such empathy for them that it happens automatically. I think I simply have to go home and get some decent rest. You can do the same by spending your time in the Whelf Fen, but I don't have a real function there. I guess that I'm just bored with all of the whelf attention and adoration I get when I'm there. You seem to just soak it up."

"Lenny, I just enjoy being among my thousands of friends in the fen. I understand how you feel, but I do have a function there. I think that I would welcome becoming a full-time whelf when that time comes. I know that the whelfs welcome your presence just as enthusiastically whenever you visit them. You needn't worry about their acceptance no matter how you feel about it."

"I admit that I enjoy the whelfs when I am there," Lenny replied. "I guess that the constant adoration just makes me self-conscious, that's all. Since there's still some time left in the day, I suppose we should visit Elder Wolsa and inform him that Zada is doing well, and we can ask him about Leanne."

"Lenny," Cassy said, "even I can tell that you're less than enthusiastic about this quest. If you don't want to do it today, we can go tomorrow after you've rested."

"No, I promised Elder Wolsa that I would keep him apprised of Zada's health," he replied. "You know that I keep my promises."

Silent until now, Jenna replied, "Then we better go now. You know I'm pumped after hearing Blaine Kamp's story. I want to know what became of Leanne too. The name, though, doesn't sound like a Bugoward name."

"It does sound like a human name from my world," Lenny replied. "Many names here are like that. I wonder if there was some sort of mutual connection between the worlds long ago that since faded out."

"There's only one way to find out," Cassy replied. "There's no point in sitting here discussing it any longer. We better go, Lenny, if you want to get some decent sleep tonight. The mystery of not knowing might keep you awake otherwise."

Lenny stood up and extended his staff. "Jenna, touch me or the staff and we'll be gone. Cassy will probably beat us there anyway."

The portal opened and closed the moment that Jenna touched his hand. All three youths suddenly vanished into the eerie glow.

"I wish I could do that, Scapita," Guena said. "It would certainly save a lot of time in getting around in this dreary old castle. They're right about those stairs. They're far too long for my weary bones."

"You're still a spring chicken, Guena," Scapita replied. "That youthening potion has taken quite a number of years off you too in case you haven't noticed."

"Oh, I've noticed all right," she replied. "I'm just as light on my feet as I was in my early years. Now, Scapita, I know you don't want me to ask this question since you've been flattering me far too much for a man of your years."

"Why shouldn't I, Guena? After all, you agreed to marry me, didn't you?"

"Of course, but that's half the problem anyway. You used it as an excuse to pass the Blaine's quest onto Jenna, and the others. Now why did you do that? Our wedding plans have long been decided."

"You're quite right, Guena. You are very perceptive. Actually, I thought that a very weary young sorcerer and his Wizor could use a distraction."

"You mean Jenna and Prince Leonard? Why, I don't see what you mean. All they need is a decent amount of sleep, and they'll bounce right back. Oh, you're talking about them being together!" she cried, suddenly seeing the light.

"I figure that the longer they're together," Scapita explained, "the better for Jenna. She loves him, you know, in spite of Prince Leonard's betrothal to Zada. A betrothal is breakable after all."

"So now you're saying that this deception is for Jenna's sake?"

"I couldn't have said it better myself, Guena. Now if you'll toss another log onto the fire, perhaps we can make use of our alone time together."

Guena laughed and replied, "Only if you promise to lend them a hand if they need it, Scapita. After all, a ten-year-old mystery surely won't be easily solved in a day."

"But of course, Guena, I had no other idea in mind."

⊷ ⋯⋯⋯⋙⋘⋯⋯⋯ ⊶

When Jenna and Lenny appeared inside of Elder Wolsa's tent located in the forest not far from Leonard Castle, they found Cassy waiting for them.

"Show off," Lenny whispered.

Cassy merely grinned as Elder Wolsa's wife set some cups of steaming resoberry juice on the homemade table set up in the middle of the tent.

"Thank you, Mola," Cassy said as everyone sat at the table.

"It's nothing," she replied. "Drink up. There's plenty more if you want seconds."

"Is Elder Wolsa here?" Lenny asked. "We need to ask him something."

"He'll be here soon," Dame Mola replied. "Perhaps I can help you if you tell me what the problem is."

"First, Mola," Cassy said, "Zada is recovering nicely, but it'll be a few more days."

"I know that she's in good hands," she replied. "Prince Symon keeps us apprised. Now let me help you with your problem. I can see the question quivering on your lips."

"I would like to hear it too," Elder Wolsa said, stepping beneath the flaps of the tent. "I just came from Leonard Keep. I wanted to inspect the progress we made today and plan on tomorrow's work. You'll be happy to know that repairs to the castle towers are nearly complete, but there is still some outside curtain damage that must be repaired. Some more deep cracks in the mortar have developed."

"I really appreciate your help," Lenny replied. "Perhaps tomorrow, Jenna and I will repair the hole in the floor Night Shadow created and make whatever repairs are necessary to keep the place from falling down around our ears. I know that there is still plenty of work to be done inside the keep, but I'm really not in the mood to put much time into it right now. Besides, Scapita volunteered us to solve a missing woman cold case. Have you heard of a person named Leanne Mellot? We suspect that she might be a Bugoward."

"She was indeed," Dame Mola replied. "She was just a little girl when her mother died in our alternate Bugo world. One of our families adopted her when her father became ill and couldn't care for her. I don't think that she had ever traveled through the portal before. She must have been about sixteen when her adopted parents passed away. She vanished only a couple of years after that."

"Somehow she ended up in Stroop Town at the home of a sorcerer named Master Kamp who is also the Blaine of the town,"

Cassy explained. "Do you know anything else about her, Mola?"

"Not much," she replied. "Leanne seemed happy at first, so I'm uncertain about what caused her to leave in such a hurry. It was like she was trying to escape from someone. Since the great tree belongs to her now, we've sealed it until her return. We can give you access should you want to inspect it for your investigation."

"We'll keep that in mind," Lenny said. "I was concerned that she or her parents had come from my world."

"That's not possible, of course," Mola said. "She was quite adept with Bugoward wood and stone magic, which is unusual in itself. A Bugoward is usually adept at one or the other form of magic rather than both."

"You're quite right," Lenny replied. "We have to rule that possibility out."

"There is still the clue the Blaine found," Jenna suggested. "I think that we need to follow up on that first."

"You're right, Jenna," Lenny replied, yawning, "but my next stop is my bedroom. It's all I can do to stay awake."

He stood up but Cassy caught him before he toppled over asleep.

"He wasn't kidding," she said, shaking him awake. "I'll put the poor boy to bed. He's had a very trying day."

"Goodnight, Leonard," Jenna said, longingly. "I'll wait for you at your castle tomorrow morning. I'll look it over for you and let you know if there are repairs that can't wait."

Lenny covered a yawn with his hand and replied. "Thanks Jenna, I know you're capable. I'll try to be as early as I can, but I am really sleepy. I don't know what's the matter with me."

"I do," Cassy whispered to Jenna. "He's over extended himself again. He could solve the issue by going to the Whelf Fen and soaking up the magic he needs, but he's too proud." Then to Dame Mola she added, "I'll come visit soon, but I have some things I must do first."

The twins were gone almost before she finished speaking.

"I worry about him sometimes," Jenna giggled, "but he'll be fine."

Lenny awoke the moment he toppled from Cassy's arms onto his bed in the Conklin residence in Seattle. Wide eyed, he didn't seem to understand where he was until Cassy nudged his foot with one of her own.

"You're home now, silly," she said. "I'm sure you can manage to get dressed for bed. I have some queenly business I must take care of in the fen, so I'll see you in the morning."

"Yeah, sure," Lenny replied, sitting up, but Cassy was gone before he could respond properly. "Goodnight," he uttered to the air, but he heard her ethereal reply.

Good night, Lenny!

Wearily pulling off his clothes, he sat back down on the bed and fell backwards, instantly asleep.

CHAPTER 3

CLUE

When Lenny awoke, the sun beat hotly through the bedroom window. Somehow, he had managed to climb beneath the sheets during the night, but he had no memory of having done so.

Rolling over onto his back, he suddenly stared into Jenna's bright eyes. She wrapped an arm around his neck and kissed him passionately. He weakly responded at first, but then his strength returned, permitting him to push her away.

"Jenna, you shouldn't be here," he complained. "It's not appropriate."

"Listen, Leonard," she replied, "I know it's not appropriate for Jenna to be here, but I'm Jen. I'm all magic, and not human at all, so I came in her place through the portal in Cassandra's bedroom."

"That's still inappropriate, Jen. Jenna can see and feel everything you do."

Jen laughed. "Isn't that convenient, Leonard? I know that you love her just as much as she loves you. We're worried about you too. You over extended your magic yesterday. We want to know if you've recovered enough to work on castle repairs. Jenna says that she can work on them alone if you need to rest another day."

Lenny glanced at the digital alarm clock on the nightstand beside his bed and cried out, "Geez, it's eight o'clock already. You better go, Jen. I have to get up, and I'm not wearing much under here."

"Whatever you say, Leonard," she replied. She took a step back and vanished as if she had never been there.

Lenny waited a moment to make certain she meant it before rising out of bed. Donning a robe, he hurried to the shower and bathed. Dressing in clean clothes afterwards, he bounced down the stairs to the kitchen.

He found, Mare, making breakfast. He was taken aback with her presence at first. Mare was very much like his mother, but she was actually Marge's magical twin. Everyone in this family had one.

"Good morning, Lenny," she said. "I decided to stay home from work today. I know how you like to sleep in, but I've prepared some eggs, hashbrowns and a slice of ham for you for breakfast. I heard that you need nourishment."

"I am hungry, Mare," he said. "I almost called you mom."

"I wouldn't have minded if you did," she replied, setting a plate on the table for him heaping with the promised breakfast. "I have her feelings and memories, you know."

Lenny's eyes grew wide. "Don't you think you overdid it, Mare? There's enough here for the whole family."

"Cassandra said that you really need to eat it all," she grinned. "She told me not to listen to any complaints."

He whispered, "So the word has gotten around. Well, it does look good."

It took time to consume all of the food plus drink three glasses of milk. He felt bloated, but then his abdomen shrank as he concentrated on magically assimilating the food, replacing the nutrients in his body that his magic usage extracted when he fought Night Shadow in the Whelf Fen. He realized that he would have to find a better way to manage his energy replacement or else suffer the consequences.

"I told you how," Cassy said suddenly from across the table. "You can replace the energy you expend by allowing the Power of the Fen to feed you. You just have to spend the extra time there, but you were in too big of a hurry to leave."

"You need to stop reading my mind, Cassy," he replied. "It irks me. Besides, I had to see that mom, Zada and Skeldon were okay for myself."

"I know, but I only do it for your own good," she said. "I'm your twin sister, and I love you. If you would only volunteer your feelings, I wouldn't have to resort to magic."

"Well, you do have a point, Cassy," he relented. "When I saw mom lying there like she was on her deathbed, I freaked out. Can't you do something to help her?"

"Not any more than you can, Lenny. The youthening potion can't be hurried. It's not as simple as healing wounds or broken bones. Besides, by the time we find the Blaine's bride, they should be their old selves. We just have to be patient. I think that this case is the perfect distraction for all of us, myself included."

"I see that you're worried about mom too."

"Of course, but I know that she and the others are in good hands. Prince Symon will let us know if there is a turn, but they'll be fine. Now what do you say, dear brother? Are you ready to find out who and where the bride of the Blaine is? I admit that I'm quite curious, but I need more facts before I can apply my whelf magic to the problem. I think the same exists for you too. Am I right?"

"You're always right, Cassy," he replied. "If you have something to do, you better do it. I'm going to meet with Jenna at my castle and make some necessary repairs before we check out the clues."

"I'll be doing some checking on my own, Lenny, but if you need me, just shout. I'll come running, okay?"

"Get out of here, Cassy," he replied. Touching the miniature staff on his lapel, he duplicated it and expanded the duplicate to full size. It was his way of making sure he had a working staff to fall back on.

"I think you just want to impress people with that huge staff," she said. "I know you don't need it that big."

Before he could respond, she was gone. Glancing at the staff, he grinned and made it much larger, which made it unwieldy. Giving up, he shortened it to use as a walking cane and turned the ball into an artistic dragon grip with purple eyes that gleamed in the sunlight.

Tapping the butt of the staff on the floor, he teleported himself to the great oak tree in the courtyard of Leonard Castle.

Jenna waited there tapping her foot impatiently, but then she grinned and rushed into his arms.

This time, he didn't push her away. "I still think of you as Crosia," he said. "I thought it was the love potion that made me love you,

Jenna, but Cassy said that it wore off long ago."

"I know, Leonard. I've felt your love all along. I just wish it was me that you promised to marry instead of Zada. She's a wonderful girl, and she deserves you, but I really can't help the way I feel about you."

"I can't either about you, but I have no choice," he responded. "I'm betrothed to her. I made the Bugoward promise. You know that I keep my promises."

"I know," she said. "Love is so unfair. Maybe we should take an antilove potion. I'm not sure how much longer I can stand not being with you."

"I can't take one," Lenny said. "It would only keep me from loving anyone. I would lose both of you, and I couldn't stand that."

"Then let's get to work and not think about it anymore," she said, marching to the entrance to the great hall. "I've examined every floor, Leonard. There's plenty of cosmetic work to do, but the castle is physically in good shape. When the floor collapsed under us on the fourth floor, it caused cracks to travel up to the roof. I think those are the only necessary repairs we have to make. I've already loaded up my wand with wood and stone."

"It shouldn't take more than an hour or two then," he replied.

He followed her up the tower stairwell to the fourth floor. Staring down the hole in the floor created by Night Shadow, he realized that the collapse had left considerable debris on the floor beneath it.

"I think I'll start by cleaning up that mess," he said, levitating himself down to the third floor with his staff. He quickly vacuumed up the gravelly chunks of stone and broken wooden supports into his wizard staff. "I'll make the repairs to the floor down here while you fill in what I've missed up there. This shouldn't take long. I'll meet you up there."

He began to reform the vaulted ceiling as the stone sprayed from the staff like water from a hose. Jenna did the same from her viewpoint until the hole was covered over with new stone, which blended in perfectly with the rest of the corridor. She had just begun to fill in the cracks running up the wall, when Lenny's sudden appearance startled her.

"My, you do that so well," she said. "I wish I could get around like you can."

"You can if you just concentrate. If you recall, you did much the same thing during the Wizor Fair that you won. What I did wasn't any different than that. In fact, that's where I got the idea from."

Giggling, she replied, "I never thought you would admit that you learned something from me. So far, it's been pretty one-sided."

"You're a very talented Wizor, Jenna. You might even qualify as a full sorcerer now. In case you haven't noticed, you're capable of doing much more than many of the sorcerers in the guild. Even I would hate to duel you to find out who is the strongest."

"Now you're teasing me, Leonard," she replied. "I can't do even half of what you can. I learn something new from you every time we work on this castle. I think I can repair almost anything now."

"If you can repair it, you can create it anew, Jenna. The method is no different for anything existing or imaginary. You just have to believe in yourself, that's all."

"I wish I had your confidence," she said, finishing the repair of the long crack that climbed to the overhead. "There, I think we've done what we've come to do."

"I believe you're right," he replied. "The roof is sound, and I know the supporting walls are sturdy. I think that the castle can withstand anything mother nature can put out now."

"Mother nature?" she giggled. "You say the strangest things, Leonard."

"It's just another metaphor from my world. I'm sorry, but they just pop out of my mouth without thinking."

"I really don't mind, Leonard. I enjoy your world too. You know that I would gladly live in it with you."

"I know, but it's not possible," he replied, but his mind seemed elsewhere. "Most of the rooms in the keep aren't livable yet, but they'll wait. Let's get Cassy and look into the clue left by Leanne Mellot. I admit that I'm curious now."

"I'm ready," Cassy said, suddenly appearing and holding out her hands. "The Blaine's grandmother is waiting for us."

They took a hand each and instantly transported with her to the great room in a large stone house in Stroop Town, which was a suburb of Kings Port. They were immediately enraptured by the beauty of the masonry and rich decorations.

The grandmother jumped in surprise as they appeared, but then a smile creased her face as she curtsied and welcomed them. Although gray-haired and matronly overweight, she seemed otherwise in good health.

"Welcome to my home," she said. "My name is Karta. I see by your expressions that you're somewhat surprised. I take it that my grandson didn't prepare you beforehand."

"Not at all," Lenny replied. "This is a very homey house. I love the very old historical feel to it."

"My family has indeed lived here for generations," she replied. "Oh, Cassandra has already filled me in on who you are, and I am indeed glad to meet you. Kamp said you were coming, but I didn't realize your importance until Cassandra arrived. Kamp is a good sorcerer and gets many calls for help, but he can't do what you've just done by popping in here like that. I don't know anyone else who can either."

"I think we're probably the only ones who can in Duscany," Lenny replied. "Let me introduce myself."

"You are Prince Leonard, Master Sorcerer, and King of the Whelfs," Karta replied. "Queen Cassandra informed me, and you, my dear, are Princess Jenna, niece of the great Master Sorcerer Scapita. I've certainly heard about him. I was there when you won the Wizor Fair. You were simply wonderful. I rooted for you the whole time."

"You're making me blush, Karta," Jenna replied. "You needn't make such a fuss over me. Prince Leonard and Queen Cassandra are the heroes here. I'm just following them around."

"Don't let her fool you, Karta," Cassy said. "Her magic is quite formidable. I'm sure she could give any sorcerer a run for his money."

Jenna blushed and replied, "Why don't we just get on with why we came here. I'm sure I'm not worth all of this praise. Please, Karta, where did Blaine Kamp find the note?"

"Oh, we might as well get started. Perhaps when we're done with the investigation, you can join me at the table for refreshments. I've made some delicious cookies that everyone just loves. There's a choice of cow's milk or goat's milk if you like."

"Cow's milk would do nicely, Karta," Cassy replied, "but we would like to know where the note was found and how long was Leanne gone before it was noticed."

"Well, I can say that I'm the one who actually found the note on the fireplace mantel while dusting. I had just started my housework for the day. I know that Leanne went to bed on time the night before, but when I checked on her after I found the note, she wasn't in the house. Kamp had already gone to the grocer to stock his shelves with produce from the morning delivery. It isn't far, so I immediately showed him the note. He muttered something and magically examined the note, but he seemed out of sorts when he learned nothing, the poor dear. I know that they were very much in love. That's why I found her disappearance so disturbing."

Cassy strolled to the fireplace and began a systematic search for magic signatures, but she frowned when she found none. Lenny joined her and held his staff out to sniff the air. He detected nothing new.

"You found the note right here?" Lenny asked.

"Yes, right under that blue stone on the mantel. It was a gift from her to Kamp. It's interesting that it seems to have a face on it, don't you think?"

Lenny removed it from the mantel to inspect it more closely, but he suddenly lost control of it. It fell onto the hearth and shattered into several large pieces.

CHAPTER 4

BUGOWARDS

Scooping up the pieces in both hands, Lenny cried, "I'm sorry! I don't know what happened. It just fell."

"Oh dear," Karta replied, "I'll get the dustpan and clean it up. I'll be distraught to have to dispose of it. It's such an unusual stone."

"It's alright," Cassy replied. "We can fix it."

Inspecting the pieces in Lenny's hands, she whispered, "You just didn't drop it, Lenny. I detected a strong magic signature that forced you to drop it."

"It's Bugoward stone magic and something else," Lenny said. "Leanne must have made that face, but with it in so many pieces, I can't make it out."

"Then you should be the one to heal the stone, Lenny," Cassy said. "If I do it, it could change the signature. Perhaps you can keep it intact for study."

"I'll give it a try." Hovering his hand over the pieces, he began to analyze the signature. "I think I have it now. I'll record the signature in my staff in case I mess up."

He shaped his fingers into a claw and slapped the pieces. They suddenly spun about and joined in proper order before the stone leapt into his hand whole.

"Goodness, that's powerful magic!" Karta cried. "I felt that from way over here."

"You needn't be alarmed, Karta," Lenny said. "The stone is whole now, and it still holds the same signature that created it. Have you heard of Bugoward wood and stone magic?"

"I've heard all of the old stories about the Bugowards," she replied, "but I've only heard that they were very good wood carvers. Are you saying that they actually used magic to shape wood and stone?"

"Exactly so, Karta," Cassy said. "This stone was indeed shaped by Bugoward stone magic. This face is no accident. Did it remind you of anyone?"

"Not at all. Kamp said he thought it was his face, but I really doubt that. I felt that the resemblance was only superficial."

"Tell me, Karta," Lenny said, holding up the stone to her, "is this the same face you saw on the stone?"

She glanced at the serpent like face and shuddered. "Goodness no, I remember a much gentler face, much more childlike, not that ugly monstrosity."

"Did you look at the face when you found the note, Karta?" Cassy asked. "Was it the childlike face or the monster then?"

"Why, I don't know. I didn't look at it because I expected the same face to be there as before. I never suspected that it could change."

"I'm wondering," Lenny said, "if the owner of this face is the same thing that took Leanne."

"It must be," Jenna added. "She could have left it as another clue."

"I'm more interested about the clue she left concerning the *heart of the hearth*," Cassy said. "Let's check the fireplace for a secret compartment, perhaps a loose stone."

"It seems too obvious," Jenna said, but she went to work double checking every stone for the secret compartment but soon gave up.

"I detect nothing," Lenny said. "Maybe the note wasn't referring to this hearth."

"Then what hearth?" Jenna replied. "How many could there be?"

"Only one other," Cassy added thoughtfully. "We need to check the one in her Bugoward home."

Lenny smiled at Karta and said, "I think we're ready for your refreshments. Oh, if we may, we would like to take this stone with us. We'll be glad to return it after the investigation is done."

"Oh, you're welcome to it," she complained. "I don't want that monstrosity in my home. I'll explain it to Kamp. I'm sure he'll agree. Now, if you please, follow me to the kitchen, and we can get started on those delicious cookies. Don't be shy. Everyone enjoys my cooking. You can have as many cookies as you want. If that's not enough, I'll bake some more."

Once everyone gathered in the kitchen, Karta opened a ceramic container revealing the large cookies.

Lenny selected one, but he looked it over before biting into it. His smile widened when he tasted the distinctive flavor. "This is really good, but I don't recognize the flavor. It reminds me of walnuts but more flavorful."

"It is a special nut," she replied. "Kamp magically modified the tree. It's growing out back if you want to see it."

"Sure," Lenny replied. He took another cookie before he finished with the first one. The others did likewise

They followed her out the back door to the extensive yard, which was surrounded by a tangled hedge. The tree grew wide and tall in the center. It did resemble an Earth walnut tree. The nuts dangled from the branches in thick, green husks. A few ripe ones had split open, spilling the seeds over the ground.

A short swarthy man was busy raking up the nuts and dropping them into a wicker basket.

"The nuts just keep on coming," Karta explained. "They grow like that no matter what the season. That's why I decided to make cookies just to get rid of the mess, but I was pleased when they sold so well. I use the husks and shells to fuel the oven. They do burn nicely. Now I'm considering adding the nuts to bread."

Lenny levitated one into his hand to examine more closely, but realizing that Karta had not witnessed it, he slipped it into his jacket pocket to analyze more thoroughly later.

"They look like walnuts," he said, "but they do have a distinctive aroma about them. I wonder if one could make a perfume from the husk."

"It would be interesting to find out," Jenna said, snapping off a trio of green pods from a low-lying branch. "I love the smell."

"I doubt if it's necessary," Karta said. "I carry that smell on me wherever I go just from harvesting the ripe ones. Put one in your pocket and you'll smell like that for weeks. Leanne loved to crack open the nut and eat them raw, but I prefer to add them to my baking. I sell all my baked products at Kamp's grocer. He says that he could make good just on selling my cookies alone. He's thinking of adding a bakery to the store, but I won't let him do it just yet because I have to teach him how to bake. It would be a full-time job for me if I don't. Leanne was a fine baker, though. I wish she were still here."

Jenna dropped the pods she picked into the pouch in her skirt where she kept her wand. The comment wasn't wasted on Cassy either, but she magically placed several into a transparent bag she conjured out of the ether and vanished them.

"I don't think I want to smell like that all day," she whispered to Lenny. "The idea is worth following up on, though."

"I agree," he replied, "but I'm more interested in knowing why this tree looks so much like a walnut tree from our world. I've never encountered a walnut tree anywhere else in the Kingdom of Duscany."

"I admit that I haven't either, but that doesn't mean that there aren't any here, Lenny. After all, oaks, elms, ashes of all types, and so on exist here in abundance. I really doubt that your observation is relevant, but keep it in mind. You could be right."

Karta led the trio back inside her home, but they filled up their pockets with cookies when they expressed the need to continue the investigation elsewhere.

"You're welcome back anytime, children," she said, waving to them as they departed.

The short, swarthy man appeared next to her and demanded, "Who are those kids, Karta? I don't want them here."

"Hush your horrible mouth, Tallis," Karta replied. "I don't understand why Kamp insists on keeping you on, but I'm telling him about this when he comes home. I'll insist that he discharge you immediately. I'll take over for him in the store while he's working for the governor if I have to."

Tallis grimaced, then followed the children from the property. He trailed them until they turned around the block, but then he lost sight of them.

"Impossible!" he cried, but he quieted when an old woman walking the opposite direction glanced disapprovingly his way.

Tallis hurried down the block and up two more until he entered Kamp's grocery. He waited until Kamp finished with a customer, but he grasped his shirt in strong hands and shoved the grocer against the shelves.

"What did you do, Kamp?" he cried. "You were supposed to convince Scapita to come, but three nosey kids showed up instead."

"Back off, Tallis," Kamp replied indignantly. "I've given you free rein up until now, but if you touch me again, we'll see who's the strongest. There's nothing weak about my magic."

Tallis stepped back, but he furtively kept an eye on Blaine Kamp and the front door. He didn't need witnesses at a time like this.

"Just tell me what went wrong, Kamp. Why didn't Scapita come himself? What's the point of sending three kids instead?"

"Look, Tallis, I asked for Scapita to come," Kamp replied, "but he was too busy making preparations for his wedding. That's when he volunteered his niece, Princess Jenna, and the others. They're all fine sorcerers."

"Sorcerers you say," Tallis replied doubtfully. "I was there when Jenna won the Wizor Fair without mixing any wizors. I've heard that only Scapita himself could boast of doing that when he won it. I admit that she's capable, but who are the other two? They look like any other kid in Stroop Town or elsewhere for that matter."

"I was doubtful at first," Kamp replied, "but I've heard about those so-called kids. They're fraternal twins. Prince Leonard is a Master Sorcerer perhaps stronger than Scapita himself. His sister is Cassandra, Queen of the Whelfs. There's no sorcerer stronger than her in all of Duscany. I suggest that you watch your mouth before calling them just kids. I'm serious about finding Leanne, and I'm convinced that they can do it."

"Look, you fool, it's important that Scapita comes himself. I've set the trap for him."

"What are you talking about, Tallis?" Kamp replied, appalled. "Did you mean him harm?"

"Uh, not at all," the swarthy man backpedaled. "I'm preparing a special bachelor party for him, is all. Now that the planning is all messed up, I must do something about it."

He paced the floor for a moment deep in thought, but then he departed without another word.

"Don't come back, Tallis!" the Blaine shouted after him. "I don't need your kind of help around here!"

An elderly woman customer ambled into the store and smiled brightly at him.

"Do you have any more of those delicious cookies?" she asked. "Everyone just loves them."

"Don't worry yourself," he replied. "I have a whole barrel of them."

"Good, I'll take four dozen for now," she replied. "I'm holding a birthday party for my granddaughter."

———————————

Dame Mola was surprised when the young trio appeared in the Bugoward tent next to her.

"Oh, you're back so soon!" she cried. "I'm just tidying up here before we have to start cooking for the noon meal. Will you three be joining us?"

The three glanced at each other guiltily, but Lenny spoke first. "Perhaps not, Mola. We're quite full of Blaine Kamp's grandmother's cookies. They really are quite filling."

Jenna cried, "And oh so good! Oops, sorry, I got carried away. She makes the most wonderful cookies. I would really like to know the recipe."

"All of you do have a different smell about you," Dame Mola replied. "I'm sorry, but I don't recognize it."

"It's from the cookies," Cassy replied. "She uses a special nut she grows in her back yard as flavoring. She says that Blaine Kamp invented it, but I think it's just part of the mystery of why Leanne Mellot disappeared. We're here because we want to enter her old home in the Bugoward Forest. Can you let us in or does Elder Wolsa handle that?"

"Oh, I can do that," she replied. "As you know, I can travel through the tree portals, but I know that you can get us all there faster, Queen Cassandra. We can do it now if you're ready."

"We're ready all right," Lenny replied.

Cutting him off, Cassy instantaneously transported them there through the ether world.

They appeared just outside of Mola's home in the Bugoward forest. Although their arrival startled the children playing about the great trees, they recognized the visitors and eagerly greeted them.

"You'll have to take it from here, Mola," Cassy said. "I could probe the village, but I want to be polite. I don't want to take anything for granted."

Laughing, Mola cried, "So well you shouldn't, Queen Cassandra, but you're welcome here as one of us. No one would turn you away. As for Leanne Mellot's home, it's only a few trees away in that direction," she said, pointing.

Everyone followed her lead with the Bugoward children happily following along behind. The great tree was as large as Dame Mola's home, but it seemed dark and forlorn while all the other great trees had an inner glow about them.

Dame Mola touched the tree portal entrance, but she had to stroke it in a specific way before she could enter.

"You can come inside now," she said, entering through the portal.

The inside of the tree was dark at first, but then it began to brighten as the interior came to life.

"It's always like this when a great tree is abandoned even temporarily," Mola explained. "Our ambiance seems to fill the tree, which recognizes us as family. The tree wants to mother us now if that explains it. I don't know how else to say it."

"We understand," Cassy replied, strolling about the kitchen area.

The dining area was simply a separate part of the room. A partition in the center of the room contained the hearth where the mistress of the house would do her cooking chores. The partition was also open on each side of the hearth and admitted them into the living room. Twin ladders climbed the walls to the upper levels, one up, the other down. The male and female bedrooms were divided up in a similar way as the living room, kitchen and dining area.

"The hearth looks quite ordinary," Jenna said, rubbing a slim hand over the casing. Although constructed of wood, it was as dense as stone and just as fireproof.

"We're looking for some sort of secret hiding place," Cassy said, running her hands over the wooden mantel and down the casing to the stone floor. "I'm not detecting anything, though."

"What about that stone with the face on it?" Jenna asked. "That must mean something."

Cassy removed the stone from her frock pocket. "Yes, it must. Have you seen this stone before, Mola?" she asked, pushing it toward her.

Mola reached out to take it, but she immediately withdrew her hand. "No, but there's something terrible about the feel of it. I don't want to touch it."

"That's interesting," Cassy replied. "We suspect that Leanne created this face on the stone, Mola. It's also possible that the face was different at first. That's why I wanted your opinion. Did you ever see a stone like this one in Leanne's possession before?"

"I have to answer yes but not just one stone. She brought home many pretty stones and crafted faces in them of all kinds. She even gave me one. It's sitting on the mantel in my home."

"I wonder why there are none on this mantel," Cassy said. "If I were Leanne and wanted to display my artwork, I'd have them all around the house."

"Don't forget that the fireplace extends into the living room," Dame Mola replied. "Let's check the mantel there."

They quickly strolled into the living room to discover the fireplace mantel covered with stones with faces on them.

"There are stones all over," Jenna said, examining them one at a time. They all had realistic faces of Bugoward members. "The faces look a lot alike."

"Except for this one," Lenny said, taking it from the stone hearth. "Do you recognize this face, Mola?" he asked, holding it up for her to see.

"I'm not sure," she replied. "I don't recall anyone resembling that face ever living here, but he could have been a visitor. I recognize all these other faces, though. These two are Leanne's adoptive parents, and this one is Leanne herself. All these others look like the Bugoward children as they were years ago."

Lenny examined the stone with Leanne's face up close, turning it over and over in his hands. It had a distinctive magic signature, but it was unlike that of the signature on the stone with the unknown face. "She couldn't have made the face on this stone," he announced. "I can identify her signature on all of these other stones, but this one with the unknown face is different. It doesn't feel like Bugoward stone magic either."

Suddenly, he dropped it, but unable to catch it as it fell, it struck the hearth and shattered into hundreds of pieces.

"I'll fix it," Lenny said.

He knelt on the floor and hovered his hands over the pieces, but they refused to pull together. Instead, they simply dissolved into smoke that curled up through the flue of the fireplace.

"I don't get it," he said. "That shouldn't have happened."

"Look, Leonard," Jenna said, "the stone cracked the tile on the hearth. That didn't happen naturally. I'm sure the magic caused it."

Lenny touched the broken tile, but it was loose. Sliding it free of the hearth, he found a hidden compartment beneath it. "I think there is something inside of it," he said.

Reluctantly, he inserted his hand, expecting a trap, but he encountered a folded parchment at the bottom. Withdrawing it, he unwrapped it to reveal another note.

"It's the same handwriting," he said, "but the note makes the same sort of sense as the other one did. Listen to this …"

If anyone finds this note I'm probably
Dead or very nearly so. I thought I had
Outrun the horror that stalks me, but
It's followed me even here. The only choice
I have is to find a hiding place where it
Can't find me.
　　　Leanne Mellot

"There's no date or anything that suggests when this note was written," he added.

"I would think that the note was written before the other one," Jenna suggested, "unless she came here from Stroop Town. Mola, would she have been able to enter this tree after you and Elder Wolsa locked it down?"

"I doubt that she ever returned," Mola replied. "I suppose that she could have, though, since the tree would remember her. That would be also true of anyone the tree accepts."

"That means that she could have come here," Lenny said, gazing into the opening in the hearth. "There's something else in there."

Reaching inside, he extracted a dry walnut and held it up for all to view.

"It looks just like the nuts Karta used in her cookies," Jenna said.

Lenny sniffed it and shook his head. "There's no smell. It's just a plain walnut like the kind grown on Earth. Cassy, do you suppose that she gave one of these to Kamp? It would explain a couple of things."

Cassy took the nut and applied her Whelf senses to it. "It's not from Earth, Lenny," she replied. "The signature isn't the same. It's not viable either. It's very old and won't grow. Mola, you said that Leanne came through the portal from your alternate Bugo world, didn't you?"

"Yes, that's where her parents adopted her," Mola replied. "I was there for the ceremony. Leanne seemed so happy to come here, but she refused to return to the alternate world when we did. She spent most of her time right here. Come to think of it, no one saw her go, but she did leave a note."

"Oh, do you remember what it said?" Cassy asked. "It could be important."

"I don't remember the actual wording, but it was simple. She stated that she felt like a prisoner here and had to go."

"It sounds like she was a troubled girl," Jenna said. "I sometimes felt that way when Uncle Scapita wouldn't allow me to play outside of the tower when I was young."

"The difference here," Cassy replied, "is that her imprisonment was voluntary if she never left the tree until she ran away. Obviously, her adoptive parents never forbade her to go out, and there are plenty of children of all ages to play with here. She was obviously hiding from someone very powerful, possibly someone who followed her from the alternate Bugo world. I think that's where we need to go next. We have to find someone who knew her there. Mola, can you help us with that?"

"Well, I don't have time to accompany you, but I can give you the name and address of someone in the alternate world who could help you. I have it in my tree. Give me a moment, and I'll fetch it."

"We'll wait here," Lenny said. "I think that we have a few things to discuss before we're ready anyway."

Glancing back into the hiding place in the hearth, he thought he spotted a pair of eyes looking back at him. Getting a closer look, he thought he saw a red eyed, serpentine image. Grasping his wizard staff, he illuminated the steel ball at the end and pointed it into the hole, but then he began to laugh. Reaching inside, he extracted a small square mirror.

"I just saw myself in the mirror!" he cried. However, he lost his smile when he examined the mirror. Although silvered on one side, the other side was a similar mirror but smokey. "I don't understand this. A smokey mirror has no purpose. I just see a silhouette of myself."

Shrugging, he absorbed the mirror into his wizard staff for later study and extinguished the light from the steel ball.

CHAPTER 5

TRAP

Jenna repaired the cracked tile and inserted it where it belonged on the hearth. It looked as if it had never been removed.

"There, that's better," she said.

Lenny examined the walnut he had found in the hiding place beneath the hearth. He soon realized that one side was smoother than the other."

"This is odd," he said. "Both halves of a walnut shell are usually a mirror image. This side looks like it has an image pressed into it like the stones."

"Let me see," Cassy replied, examining the walnut. "It does have a faint image of a young girl. It could be Leanne's. Each side of the walnut not only has a different feel to it but also has a different magic signature. The warped side has nearly no signature, but the image side seems to have more than is warranted from the presence of the image."

Taking a turn, Jenna carefully examined the magic signature of the nut. "You won't believe this, guys," she said, "but this shell has been opened before. It has the faint signature of a sixth level latch charm, a periapt. I think it was made to be opened but not by just anyone.

It's too strong for me, but Uncle Scapita might know how to do it."

Lenny frowned. "I could open it, but the charm might not survive my probing."

Dame Mola entered the tree only minutes later. "I wrote the address down for you," she said. "You don't have to return it."

"Thank you, Mola," Cassy replied. She memorized the address at a glance, and then passed the parchment to Lenny.

"I must go now," Dame Mola said. "I have to prepare the noon meal for the men working on the curtain wall of Leonard Keep. They'll be hungry. There'll be plenty if you want to join us."

"We may after we check out this address," Lenny replied. "We're really appreciative of your help."

"Any time," she replied, departing the tree.

"I don't recognize this address," Lenny said, straining to read Mola's hasty scribbling.

"Don't worry about it, Lenny," Cassy grinned. "I memorized the whole city layout. We can go there directly as soon as we're done here."

"The contents of the walnut may be key to this mystery," Lenny replied. "I'm going to open it."

"Careful!" Cassy cried, as he squeezed the shell.

The shell cracked apart in his hands; however, emitting copious smoke, it suddenly detonated in a flash of light.

Lenny felt the power of the trap instantly and absorbed it with his staff; however, it was a moment before he could see again. Glancing about, he realized that Cassy was missing, but Jenna lay on the floor unconscious.

He checked for a pulse first on her neck and then on her wrist. He gasped when he found none. Shaking her, he cried desperately, "Jenna, wake up!" However, she never stirred.

Noticing a tightly packed piece of parchment stuffed inside the surviving side of the walnut shell, he seized it. Touching Jenna's hand and tapping his staff on the floor, he transported both of them through the portal to Scapita's apartment in Kings Keep.

"Scapita!" he cried. "It's Jenna. She might be dead."

"No," cried Guena, "not Jenna!"

"Maybe CPR will work," Lenny offered. The others simply stared at him in confusion. "Oh, I'll give it a try."

Kneeling net to her, he gave her two quick breaths and pressed on her chest for several more before repeating the effort. He worked for several minutes before giving up. Jenna had not stirred. He emotionally explained what had occurred.

"Even Cassy was gone," he added. "She's the Queen of the Whelfs. Nothing can harm her. Maybe if Jen were here, she could help me sort this out."

Jenna suddenly groaned and sat up, staring incredulously at them.

"I'm right here," Jen said. "I don't know what happened."

"Jen," Lenny cried. "If you're here, where's Jenna? I thought you were her."

"I'm not sure," she replied as Lenny tugged her to her feet. "I came because I heard my name. I usually sleep until Jenna calls for me."

"That would explain why you didn't have a pulse," Lenny clarified. "Being magic, you don't need one. Now maybe you can help us find Jenna. Can you focus on her wherever she went?"

Jen seemed bewildered initially, but then she smiled. "She's with Cassandra in the Whelf Fen. Something peculiar is going on there."

"It sounds like it's time to lend a hand, don't you think, Scapita?" Guena said.

"Indeed," he replied, "but Prince Leonard can investigate this issue much faster than we can. If you would, young man, find Jenna and let us know what's going on in the fen."

"Gladly," Lenny replied, suddenly alert. "Do you care to come with me, Jen?"

"I'll race you there!" she giggled, vanishing before Lenny could follow her.

"Oh, I'm going to have to shorten this process somehow," he whispered, tapping the butt of his wizard staff on the floor.

However, he did not reappear in the Whelf Fen. Glancing about him, he found the familiar green magic atmosphere that only could be the inside of Bella the Dryad's tree, which was near the fen. The wizard staff he had placed in the center of the tree looked as if it had taken root, and the steel globe at the top glowed a soft blue.

"Bella," he said tentatively, "why did you hijack me?"

The dryad slowly formed from the ether of the tree before him. The process was always a little slow as she manifested naked as

Jenna, but Lenny had to remind her to add clothes. The dryad manifested what passed as clothing by filling in a defined area with the green atmosphere of the tree.

"Now Bella, what is this about?" he asked.

"Leonard saved my children," the dryad stated slowly in a monotone. It was always difficult for her to understand the question and make appropriate replies.

"You're welcome, Bella, but that was months ago? Why bring it up now?"

In *The Wizard of Seattle,* they had discovered the origins of the Bugos in ancient Eskeling, and in the process saved her children from annihilation.

Suddenly, the dryad stated, "Help you. Help Jenna."

"Oh, you mean as in reward?" he asked. "That's not necessary."

Bella smiled and slowly reached for him, but she never made contact. She simply repeated her last utterance.

"If that's all you wanted to tell me, Bella, then I've got to go. One last question, though. Do you know what's going on in the fen?"

She simply replied, "I will understand—going on."

"I doubt if it'll be anytime soon," Lenny laughed. "I've got to go. Goodbye, Bella."

He grinned when she stated, "Goodbye, Leonard," which was fast for her. At least she understood the words this time.

He instantly transported himself to the Whelf Fen where he appeared next to Jen and Jenna.

Jenna happily raced into his arms and kissed him deeply. "Oh, I'm so glad that you're not hurt, Leonard!" she cried. "What took you so long? Jen has been here several minutes."

Lenny explained how Bella had diverted him to her tree. "Bella said that she wanted to reward us for saving her children, but really that's not necessary. She's helped in other ways. I'm curious, though, how did you end up here, Jenna? I couldn't see after that blast for a moment."

"I was holding Cassandra's hand, but suddenly we were here. She said that the Power of the Fen yanked us here together, but she didn't say why."

"Where is she, Jenna?" he replied "I want to know everything that happened."

"Cassandra is over there in the swamp, checking something out," she explained. "She made me stay here. I can tell that she's worried about something."

Slapping away the buzzing marsh flies, Lenny headed into the swamp but stepped back when he began to sink into the mire. Concentrating, he levitated above the mire and continued into the worst of the fen.

"Cassy, where are you?" he cried.

Her reply came immediately. "I'm over here, Lenny. You've got to see this. It doesn't look good."

Lenny landed beside her on a firm mound of white rock stained red by the iron in the damp soil. He strained to see where she pointed without recognizing a problem until something mostly submerged moved.

"It's a crocodile or something, Cassy," he replied. "What's bad about that? The Okefenokee Swamp in Florida has lots of them."

"Not like this one," she pointed out. "There's another one under our feet, but crocodilians aren't natural to the fen or even Duscany."

"What?" Lenny cried, stepping back. "Oh, you're joking with me. There's nothing but stone under us."

"That crocodilian out there was made of stone too until a few minutes ago," she replied. "It's still waking up. If you look carefully, you'll notice that both of them are at least forty feet long, which is more than twice the length of a normal crocodilian. The Power of the Fen tells me that these have been here since before ancient Eskeling fell."

"That doesn't sound good," Lenny replied, scuffing the red soil from the rigid stone back. The distinctive scute shaped protrusions quickly became evident. "That suggests that these animals were magically created."

"That's why we must return to Eskeling and find out if they're normal crocodilians magically enlarged and encased in stone or something else altogether. I suspect that Mercilus and his monsters may be involved somehow."

"You're not going to leave us out, are you?" Jenna asked. She and Jen floated magically in the air hand in hand behind them. "We're just as curious about them as you are."

"There's no time to waste," Cassy replied. "These crocodilians could escape the fen before long if we don't go."

"I have a question," Jenna said. "Will we meet up with ourselves, or won't that be a problem?"

"In this case, it's not because we're going back five years earlier than last time we visited," Cassy replied. "I'm confident that we'll find the answers then."

"I hope you're right," Lenny replied. "Poking around in old Eskeling could be dangerous. I'm not in the mood to meet up with Mercilus or his son again, so how long will we be gone?"

"As long as it takes, Lenny. I'll inform your uncle Scapita of our plans, Jenna, if you're still interested in tagging along."

"As long as Jen is with me, I'll be fine," she replied.

"Good, then the message is sent," Cassy said. "I'm sure he won't be pleased, but we don't have time to await his reply. If you all are ready, we can go now."

"We're ready," Lenny and Jenna replied simultaneously. Jen merely grinned and blended back into Jenna's body to travel together.

"We're here," Cassy replied, seconds later.

They all stood outside of the Sorcerer's Guildhall next to the fountain that bordered the park. The guildhall itself was an imposing sandstone structure four stories high that filled most of the city block. Delicate limestone columns held up the decorative frieze that was lined with dueling sorcerers.

"I'm sure that you recognize the sprawl of the city before its destruction," Cassy added. "This is the year when Mercilus lost his wife to the monsters in the arena."

"I heard that they trampled her to death when they broke out of the arena," Lenny replied. "I suppose we're about to find out if that's true or not."

"In about ten days," Cassy verified. "This time slot is where the Power of the Fen sent us. It said that the problem started here when the Queen of the Whelfs of that time was captive but still alive. My job is to contact her and watch the events evolve from her standpoint."

"But what are we to do?" Jenna asked. "Watching Mercilus' apartment is pretty boring if you ask me."

"Besides that, your jobs are to stay out of trouble and purchase tickets for the show. I've filled your purses with Eskeling gold, so you should be able to do that. You'll have to find a place to stay too unless you want to sleep in the park. I wouldn't recommend it, though."

"Now you're just being silly," Lenny replied. "Now how can we reach you if we need to tell you something important? We obviously can't follow you wherever you're going."

She touched Lenny's staff and replied, "I've just installed a communications wizor in your staff, Lenny. We can easily keep in touch that way. Your wand, Jenna, already has a communications mode that I can use. Now if there aren't any more excuses, we can start."

Jenna glanced at Lenny and giggled, but Cassy had already vanished into the ether.

"Well, that hasn't changed," Lenny said. "According to the Power of the Fen, we're ten days early, but at least we're somewhat familiar with the layout of the city now."

"She did say that we would have to find someplace to stay," Jenna said, "and I am getting hungry."

"Let's follow that guy just leaving the Sorcerer's Guildhall," Lenny added. "Maybe he knows someplace close if he's hungry. That gives me an idea. I hate leaving things to chance." Tapping his staff on the cobblestone street, he grinned sardonically when the individual stopped and glanced about. Laughing, Lenny said, "He should be hungry enough now. Ah, yes, he definitely has someplace in mind to go."

They knew that Mercilus and his family lived in the apartment building to the right of the guildhall, but they occupied the whole building. The individual, however, strolled in the opposite direction and turned the corner.

Lenny and Jenna hurried across the street and fell into step behind him as he hastened along. They recognized the secondary entrance to the guildhall as they passed, which they had used to escape imprisonment before. The man continued across the next street and entered an eatery.

"Don't you think you should disguise that staff or something, Lenny?" Jenna asked. "It is a bit obvious."

Realizing that carrying a wizard staff in Eskeling might tip off the residents, Lenny changed its appearance to the gentleman's walking cane with a dragon handle before they entered the eatery.

Apparently, the man they trailed recognized someone sitting at a table and joined him. The children chose another table where they could listen in on their conversation.

They found the proprietor standing next to them wearing a frown on his face. "I don't give handouts to children. Move along."

Lenny placed a gold coin on the table. "We're not vagrants, sire. Bring us both the special of the day with whatever you have to drink. Answer our questions and you can keep the change."

The proprietor greedily eyed the gold coin and agreed as he pocketed it. He then took the stranger's order, and departed for the kitchen.

"That's a huge tip, Leonard," Jenna said. "Both of our meals will hardly add up to a silver at the most."

"I know," Lenny agreed, "but I want him to remember us as someone other than vagrants. He'll be nicer to us next time we come in here. At least I hope so."

"He'll certainly remember us," Jenna said, "but I'm not certain that's a good idea. After all, Mercilus and his sorcerer goons control this city. Perhaps the residents are so terrified of him that they'll turn in anyone who looks suspicious, and we most certainly do."

"I'm listening in on the conversation in the kitchen, Jenna. I bugged that coin."

"So that's why you gave him the gold coin," she replied. "You knew that he would take it."

Lenny merely grinned and lifted a finger to his lips as he listened. A moment later, he whispered, "He's discussing the issue with his wife. She just told him to shut up, take it and feed us. No one needs to know if the coin was stolen or not. He agrees with her, and she's preparing our order. The special includes lentil soup with a loaf of black bread and ale to drink for a starter. I think we're getting the works."

"I don't know, Leonard, I'm not that hungry."

"I'm not either, but at least we have a reason for sticking around. The conversation at the next table is just getting interesting. I think they're both sorcerers, so we don't want to attract their attention."

"Yeah, I've heard the news, Butkus," the sorcerer who arrived first said. "I hope that Mercilus knows what he's doing."

"So do I, Magus," Butkus replied. "If he's wrong, the citizens could be placed in horrible danger. I don't agree that creating more monsters to fight in the arena will make them happier. I think these contests are getting out of hand now."

"You better not let Mercilus hear that, Butkus. He's already cracking down on dissenters, and I don't want to be numbered among them."

"Nor do I," Butkus replied.

They quieted when the proprietor placed bowls of steaming lentil soup before them along with eating utensils.

Lenny and Jenna stirred strips of bread into their soup and glanced furtively toward the sorcerers who were doing the same.

"I wonder if those two could become allies at some point in the future," Lenny whispered. "We both know that Mercilus is as nasty a sorcerer as they come."

Jenna held a finger to her lips and continued to eat. The proprietor was already bringing out plates of boiled meat and assorted vegetables.

"All we have to drink is ale or red wine," the proprietor stated. "We don't have anything else."

"We'll take the wine," Lenny replied. He furtively nodded to Jenna who also accepted the wine.

"Before you go," Lenny said, "are there any apartments near here where we can rent a room for a few days?"

"Just keep walking around the block," he replied. "The rooms are expensive, though, but I see that you can afford it."

"Thanks," Lenny said, but he wished that the proprietor hadn't spoken so loudly. When the sorcerers glanced their way, the children knew that they had overheard him.

The sorcerers wolfed down their meals and asked for an ale refill. They talked for a few more minutes as they sipped the sparkling liquid.

The children leaned back in their chairs and put down their utensils. "I don't think I can eat any more," Jenna said. Her bowl of meat and vegetables was untouched, and most of the loaf of bread remained. "Perhaps we can take the rest with us?"

Lenny glanced at the remainder of the stew in his bowl and wondered the same thing. Positioning the handle of his walking cane near his plate, he siphoned the leftovers into it and did the same with Jenna's, but he noticed that the sorcerers had caught his trick.

"Oh, I wouldn't have thought about that!" Jenna exclaimed. "It's like sucking up wood or stone. I bet you can recreate it just as it is later. Am I right?"

"You know it," Lenny replied, "but let's get out of here before the proprietor gets suspicious."

She glanced at him and replied, "I bet he already is, Leonard. He's looking our way. You're right. We need to leave now."

They casually strolled from the eatery and down the street looking for the apartment building the proprietor mentioned. Although they cautiously glanced about, no one else seemed interested in them.

They quickly found the tall brick apartment building. A sign nailed to the door read ROOMS FOR LET in large red letters. The heavy door easily swung open when they entered. An elderly woman seated at a desk in a room just to the left called to them.

"You kids don't look old enough to rent a room here," she said. "Why have you come?"

"The proprietor at the eatery recommended you," Lenny said, placing five gold coins on her desk. "I'll pay in advance for ten days with no questions asked."

The old woman's eyes quickly bulged in surprise. Her feelings warred inside her as she weighed the coins in both hands. "I shouldn't," she said, "but very well, ten days with no questions asked. I'll still need your names whether aliases or not. I'm Munge."

"I'm Leonard," he said. "You don't have to worry, Munge. No one is looking for us."

"If you say so," she replied. "How about yours, young mistress?"

"It's Jenna. We really don't have anything to hide, Munge."

"Well, Leonard and Jenna, I only have one room on the second floor, but several on the fourth. It's more private up there if that matters to you."

"If a room on the fourth floor has a view of the street and close to the bath, we'll take it," Lenny replied. "We'll be in and out."

"Very well," Munge replied, "follow me."

Removing a key from a hook on the wall, she ushered them out of the room and closed and locked the door behind her. She breathlessly led them up the flights of stairs to the fourth floor. Unlocking the door on the left, she showed them inside.

"The room is clean as you can see," she said. "It's up to you to keep it that way. The sheets are new. They won't be cleaned during your stay, so if you want them laundered, you'll have to do it yourself. The room doesn't come with maid service."

Jenna turned down the sheets and inspected the pillows. Deciding that she told the truth, she replied, "This is fine, Munge. Now show us the bath."

"It's just next door, but you'll have to draw and heat the water yourselves," she replied. "As I said …"

"Yes, we know," Jenna whispered. "There's no maid service."

Once Munge departed the room, leaving them alone, Jenna turned to Lenny and said, "But there should be for that price, Leonard. You really should stop overpaying for everything here. Throwing around money like that just makes people suspicious. I saw the greedy look on her face. One gold coin would have paid for a month, I'm sure."

"I'm hoping it'll inspire some loyalty, is all," he replied. "Now that we have a place to stay, we need to find out how to get advance tickets for the show at the arena. Now that we've been here, we can travel by portal. That old busybody doesn't need to see us come and go."

"Suspicion, Leonard," Jenna replied, "what did I tell you about that? It won't hurt to walk down those stairs, but I already hate to walk up them. Why didn't you take the one on the second floor? It would have saved us a lot of steps."

"You forget that we can travel by portal anywhere we've been before, Jenna. That means we can do it anywhere along that path. We'll simply hop down to the first floor, walk by Munge and stroll out the front door. That should satisfy your suspicion idea, Jenna."

Laughing, she replied, "All right, let's get hopping."

They vanished instantly and appeared just outside of Munge's office. Entwining arms, they waved to her as they passed, but she ignored them. Outside, they vanished and reappeared just in front of the guildhall where they first arrived inside the city.

Chatting with the driver of one of the free city carriages that plied the streets, they discovered that advance tickets could only be purchased at the arena. All they had to do was to take the next carriage traveling in the opposite direction.

Waiting only a few minutes for the carriage to arrive, they climbed up and sat on one of the benches provided. Several other men and women climbed on with them, occupying all eight seats.

Butkus and Magas hurried down the stone steps of the guildhall to the curb, but the driver waved them off and snapped a whip over the horses' backs. The carriage instantly lurched away.

"I bet they're trying to follow us," Lenny said, glancing back. "We have to take great care now."

CHAPTER 6

CAPTIVE QUEEN

Cassy appeared just outside of the border to the Whelf Fen as it existed in this timeframe. It appeared cold and forlorn without a sign of another whelf in sight. She carefully listened but detected none of her whelf friends inside the border.

Taking a chance, she stepped into the Whelf fen and began to sink into the quagmire. Magically lifting herself above the ground, she floated further into the fen. She spotted several flitting whelf lights taking cover not far away, but she didn't feel their signatures. Taking another chance, she transformed into the brilliant globe of the Queen of the Whelfs and approached them.

They instantly joined her but then they suspiciously held back.

"You are not the queen," one of the whelfs said. "We thought she had escaped."

"You are Star Night," Cassandra said, reading her signature. "I was looking for Sunshine."

"We're awaiting Sunshine's return appearance as a neophyte," Star Night replied. "You are strong, but we can't read your name."

"I'm Cassandra," she replied. "I'm a future Queen of the Whelfs. I'm here to help save your queen and your futures. I couldn't help but to stop in and say hello. I believe that your Long Night is only a few days away, isn't it?"

"It is, Queen Cassandra," another whelf cried. "Please save our queen. You certainly appear strong enough."

"I will try," Cassy replied, but she knew that she could not this time. Their queen would simply die five years from now in the cage Mercilus crafted for her. When tears flowed down her cheeks, Cassy quickly departed the fen. She could do nothing for them now.

Homing in on Mercilus' signature, she located him climbing aboard a city carriage at the arena. She carefully reduced herself in size until she became a dot hiding in his shaggy beard. She tried to emit very little energy in case the sorcerer could detect her signature, but he gave no indication of doing so. He callously urged his driver to drive faster, but the horses only had one pace. The team merely strolled up the street no matter how much the driver urged them on.

"Very well, Alva," Mercilus said, "let them rest. I have a great deal on my mind."

"As you wish," Alva replied, stowing the horsewhip in a vertical holder. The team didn't change pace. "The horses know how to travel the route, sire. They could do it without me, but only I know the stops. That's horses for you. They only know how to do one thing at one speed."

Laughing, Mercilus replied, "How long have you been driving this route, Alva? I don't recall seeing anyone else driving in your place."

"That's because I have only been your driver, sire. I'm the only one who's been able to put up with your terrible temper."

"I do have one, don't I, Alva? Well, I've had to keep my sorcerers in line. I have the feeling that many of them don't agree with my methods, but my gold coffers are running over. I get richer with every bout my monsters participate in, and my sorcerers share in it."

"I've heard them complain that it's a meager share," Alva replied, but then he realized that he shouldn't have opened his mouth when Mercilus became sulkily silent. "I beg your pardon, sire. I misspoke."

"You're not at fault, Alva," Mercilus replied. "If you hear anything else, you'll tell me, won't you?"

"You have my loyalty, sire."

"Good, now leave me alone for a while, Alva. I have some serious thinking to do. The fair must commence on time in ten days."

Cassy carefully listened in on his subliminal thoughts but was appalled at all of the monster ideas that flitted through his mind. She was happy to discover, however, that they were still in the planning stages. His mind constantly raced to create the wizors he planned to use in their construction. The majority of them were level seven, but two were level nine, which were the crocodilians the Power of the Fen uncovered in the Whelf Fen.

She became so agitated that she nearly revealed her presence, but Mercilus, momentarily distracted by a darting rabbit in a thicket, quickly turned back to his thoughts.

Before long, Alva halted the carriage outside of Mercilus' apartment. Apparently distracted, Mercilus dropped down from the carriage without a word and entered through the dilapidated doorway.

Having been here in a future timeframe, Cassy didn't stir from her vantage point. The inside of the apartment at this level was heavily alarmed and entrenched with traps. She could only wait until Mercilus entered his laboratory where the present Queen of the Whelfs was imprisoned.

Mercilus instead climbed the magically boobytrapped stairs and entered the cozy apartment at the top. Cassy relaxed since the family residence itself was not alarmed.

She glanced about for Mercilus' three daughters, but they were not immediately evident. Barcelis, his only son, greeted him instead, but his face was clouded with disapproval. Although he was fifteen years old in this timeframe, he was just as handsome as she remembered him to be. She quietly sighed, feeling the same personal draw she felt from him five years into this future when last she visited.

"You really need to rethink your plans for this year's fair events," he said. "Mother is beside herself with worry. She forbids my sisters from going, and I don't blame her."

"The girls are your mother's responsibility, Barcelis, but you're a man now, and I require your help casting the monster wizors. You know that the people go crazy over bigger and better monsters. I won't disappoint them."

Attracted by the loud voices, Barcelis' sisters sprang through the door barring the adjacent room. Cassy became instantly alert, but then she remembered that she had last seen them five years into the future from this timeframe.

Gobie was merely a toddler of three now with Brena being ten and Shuma seven. Cassy's heart instantly went out to them even though she barely recognized the children at this age.

The grown woman who followed them could only be their mother. Although her name was never spoken by the children in their future, Cassy read it foremost in her mind as Rosina. Beautiful as her namesake, her auburn hair was braided twice around her head and clipped into place by a hair brooch, which contained a central clear blue stone with a dark silhouette that could have been Rosina or her mother.

She hovered protectively behind the girls without speaking, but the words quivered on her lips. Cassy knew exactly what she wanted to say to her husband, but she sensed a profound fear of backlash. Although she plainly loved her husband, she strained to hide a fear that his machinations with dangerous monsters would end in disaster.

However, Cassy gasped when she read the premonition behind the fear that ended in Rosina's death. Rosina was a talented clairvoyant, but she did not trust her feelings or her words while in the presence of her husband. He resolutely would not listen to the warnings that she had declared to him in the past and even violently punished her for not trusting him.

Suddenly, Cassy understood now why the children wanted someone to take her place after her horrible death, a death that would occur in a mere ten days. Indeed, there was nothing she could do to prevent it, no matter how much she wished it since it had already happened a thousand years into her past.

The emotions spilled out of Cassy along with a string of tears. Suddenly, Mercilus reacted, forcing her to pull herself back together. Mercilus glanced up and turned about as if he had detected someone else in the room but after a moment of silent searching, he gave it up and turned back to his family.

He gazed into Rosina's fearful hazel eyes for a long moment as if reading her thoughts before speaking. "Barcelis tells me that you don't want the children to attend this year's fair, Rosina. I've always granted you the responsibility of the children as you demanded, but you are my wife. I demand your respect. I need Barcelis' help with the creation of the monsters, but I need your support in the arena. You will accompany me during each of the three days of the fair. The public expects to see you in the VIP box with the others. They must not see the rift in your eyes that I see. Am I understood, Rosina?"

"That is your right," she replied cautiously. "I am your wife. I know I have no choice in this matter, but as you said, our children are my responsibility. The girls will stay safely here. That is my decision. They are too young to see that horrible spectacle you're planning to execute in the arena anyway, fake blood or not. It's just as bad as seeing the real thing. Those monsters are the substance of nightmares. I can't imagine why anyone would want to see them torn to pieces in the arena."

"You used to support me in my work, Rosina," Mercilus murmured as if he did not wish her to hear his words, but he saw the hurt cross her face just the same.

"That was before you became obsessed with creating such terrible monsters," she replied. "You wanted to improve the lives of people, but instead it's been a steady decline. You said it yourself that there are fewer sorcerers born every year. It seems to me that it's been in direct proportion to the number and power of your monsters. Look at Barcelis. I was amazed at what he could do as a child, but now he can barely activate the simplest of magic wizors. I've hated to speak my mind, Mercilus, but now I see that I must for the sake of our children. As you can see for yourself, the girls depend upon the sympathetic wizors you installed in the house. Otherwise, they're powerless. I hope I'm getting through to you, Mercilus. Sorcerer families usually have sorcerer children, but now we're the exceptions. There are more exceptions in this city now than ever."

"I sense the bitterness in your voice, Rosina," Mercilus replied, "but you're speaking nonsense. Magic is like an ocean wave. It always rises and ebbs. In time it'll return. Our children will be the sorcerers they were born to be. I promise you."

Mercilus bent to touch Gobie's cheek, but she shyly hid behind her mother as did the other girls.

"They know the truth too," Rosina said. "They don't have to be told. If you had bothered to listen and play games with them, they wouldn't think of you as a stranger in our home. The man I married was gentle and kind with grand ideas that I believed in. Stop this evil magic, Mercilus, and come home to us. I believe that it is our only hope for a normal life."

"You're wrong, Rosina!" Mercilus cried.

"Go play, girls," she said, hurrying them away. "This conversation isn't over."

ROBERT A. G. ERICKSON

Mercilus withheld his voice as they departed, but his anger mounted when she stepped closer in defiance.

"Rosina, I've always held you and the children in high regard," he replied, visibly attempting to control his trembling emotions. "I've also given you your head, but I see that you've withheld something from me. I want to know what that is!"

"Everything you desire is within plain sight, Mercilus. Beware or else you'll lose everything of importance. Shouting me down will only drive us further apart. I hate to say it, but you've created all of your problems yourself."

Mercilus angrily raised the back of his hand to her, but then Barcelis stepped in front of her.

"If you must strike someone, Mercilus, strike me. As you said, I'm a man now. However, you had best reconsider if you still desire my help."

Mercilus shamefully turned away, but he refused to apologize to either of them. "Come with me to the laboratory, Barcelis. Your mother has much to do."

Barcelis smiled at his mother who returned it, but she also gave him permission to leave with a furtive wave of the back of her hand. He followed Mercilus, who did not wait on him, down the stairs to the long corridor at the bottom.

Mercilus turned right and waited for the stone floor to vanish but left a long dark stairway. Magic sconces lit up the way as they descended to the bottom where a thick oak doorway with wide hinges and protective iron bosses lent it strength. Removing an iron key from his tunic, he inserted it into the lock and twisted it. The lock loudly clicked open, but it took both of them to tug the heavy door open.

Cassy, however, was waiting for this opportunity. Entering the keyhole with the key, she left a way for her to squeeze through in either direction, bypassing the defensive wizors already set in place. She would have no trouble entering or departing the laboratory now.

She waited until Mercilus and Barcelis magically ignited the light sconces and conferred at the laboratory bench in the rear of the room before pressing herself close against the large, dark ball set on a wooden cradle.

She easily sensed the presence of the whelf queen trapped inside, but she was weak from exhaustion. The queen immediately edged closer to the outside edge of the glass globe and gazed curiously at Cassy, but she did not speak.

"This is rather awkward," Cassy said. "You see, I'm the Queen of the Whelfs a thousand years into the future. We meet here as equals."

"Equals, no," the queen replied. "I felt your arrival in the Whelf Fen and your power. You're strong, but I do not understand your name, Cassandra, Queen of the Whelfs."

"It simply means Queen of the Whelfs," Cassy replied. "I know you have another name, but I'm curious as to why I can't detect it."

"It's a habit I've grown used to," the queen replied. "I couldn't allow that scoundrel, Mercilus and his son know it or else they would have the full power of the fen at their disposal. As long as I keep it from them, I can exert some control. I suggest that you hide yours too, Queen of the Whelfs from the future, or else you could fall beneath their control as well. I know that I'll never recover from my captivity, but I sense that you are many times stronger than I am or was at my best. You must know that your very presence adds to the power that keeps me bound here."

"I know," Cassy replied. "This isn't the first time we've talked. The first time was actually five years into this future timeframe. I know that you didn't escape your prison and perished along with Mercilus. Unfortunately, there's nothing I can do to make your captivity more comfortable for you now."

"It's comforting to know that this horror will end in so short a time, but you have a reason for coming now. Please reveal it to me. I'm sorry, but I don't dare say your name aloud because of them."

She made eye motions towards the pair working at the bench even though neither of them could see them from this vantage point.

"You're right, of course," Cassy replied sadly. "I'm sure you know that they're preparing the wizors they'll use to create more monsters to display in their arena. It's disgusting to create and destroy them for entertainment. I don't know how far along they are in their plans, but the Power of the Fen of the future informed me that the monsters that are awakening in that world were created here during the time of the Long Night. I hope that you can help me understand why."

"Why indeed," the queen replied. She fell away from the glass wall and danced forlornly about, but in time she returned and smiled.

"Most of the low-level monsters Mercilus wants to open the show with have already been created. As you must know, he increases the power of his monster creations for each of the three days of the fair. He saves the most powerful for last. I have read it in his mind what the monsters will be. He's creating one of the wizors now, but once he activates it, it'll take several days to mature to full power. There are four level nine monsters in all, but it'll be difficult for him to control them."

"Let me guess," Cassy said, "two of the monsters are forty-foot crocodilians with saber length teeth strong enough to chew through solid stone. Am I right?"

"I assume that those are two of the monsters that are awakening in your world," the queen replied. "Since I cannot communicate with the Power of the Fen, I cannot look very far into the future, but I know that you can. Beware, future Queen of the Whelfs, I don't know how many of the monsters will escape Mercilus' control, but there are two more possible ninth level monsters to look for. He intends to pitch a pair of ninth level troglodytes against the two crocodilians. Please understand, future queen, that once he's created so many monsters, he'll become incapable of destroying them all. His power will weaken in proportion to mine. I suspect that your presence has already affected the future of this time. Whatever you do, do not return to the Whelf Fen. You've already encouraged the Power of the Fen to start the Long Night as scheduled. It's your power that the Power of the Fen is tapping into even now. Please go, future queen, and do not return. You cannot help anyone here, especially not the whelfs or me. Mercilus is coming. Hide before he traps you. Do it now!"

Cassy felt Mercilus' power as he approached, attracted by the fuss in the cage. The whelf queen was right. She had to keep as far away from him right now as possible or risk being captured. She cautiously shrank to the size of a mote of dust and found another hiding spot near the laboratory workbench.

Mercilus approached the whelf trap to investigate the peculiar power emanations he felt, but after verifying that the whelf queen was still ensconced in her cage, he grinned in satisfaction and returned to work.

CHAPTER 7

MONSTERS

Lenny and Jenna waited an hour before it was their turn to purchase tickets for the fair. A silver for each of the three days seemed steep for the highest twenty rows of seats, but they had no reason to complain. The lowest VIP seats next to the arena were set at five in gold, but the middle twenty rows were priced at a gold piece each.

Jenna stuffed her tickets into the pocket of her skirt which contained the wand she aways carried.

"Well, that's that," she said. "At least we've done everything Cassy told us to do. I wonder how she's getting along."

"Why don't you ask her," Lenny replied. "You have the power."

"So do you," she grinned. "I am curious, though."

Finding a secluded spot where she could talk in private, she removed the wand and spoke into the head. "Cassandra, we've done what you told us to do. How are things going for you?"

A tiny image of Cassy suddenly appeared at the end of her wand, but she didn't seem happy. "I'm fine, Jenna, but we've got big problems. Mercilus is planning something bigger than he can handle, and there's nothing I can do about it."

"Like what?" Jenna asked.

"I can't explain now, but I'll find you later. I have to go."

"Wait, Cassandra," Jenna cried, but she received no reply. "She's gone, Leonard. I wonder what's so important that she can't talk to me. She said we had big problems."

"I saw two of them," Lenny replied. "If the problems are bigger than that, then we're in for real trouble. It means that our time here over the next ten days is crucial."

"I'm worried about those ten days," Jenna replied. "What's happening in Duscany during that time? Maybe the crocs have fully awakened and have gone on a murderous rampage. What are we going to do, Leonard?"

Grinning wryly, he replied, "I'm sure my sister has a plan, Jenna. Let's not worry about it until it is a problem."

"All right, what do we do now?" she acquiesced.

"Head back to our apartment," Lenny said. "Our driver is waiting patiently since I paid him to wait. I think he's getting antsy about leaving."

Jenna glanced at the fidgeting driver and laughed. "We better go before he asks for another silver."

"Actually, I'm not quite done," Lenny said. "We still need the carriage until we're acclimated here, so I'll see what he wants for waiting a little longer."

"What could we do now?" Jenna asked. "It'll be dark in an hour, and the return trip will take half of that time."

"I want to see what's inside of the cage area beneath the stands, Jenna. If Mercilus has already created some of his monsters, that's where they would be. I want to know what to expect come day one of the fair."

"That's not a bad idea as long as we don't get caught," she said.

Lenny spoke with the carriage driver for a moment and handed him another silver. The driver merely grinned and sat back comfortably in his seat to wait.

"It appears that the city doesn't pay him a decent wage," Lenny explained. "He makes most of his money on special fares like this one, so he didn't complain."

"Well, you're the brains of this plot, so how do we get inside? All of the entrances are locked and barred until the first day."

"Just hold my hand," he said, holding it out.

"With pleasure," she replied, taking it.

Suddenly they were standing at the top of the stadium wall, starring down the many rows of seats to the sandy floor of the arena.

Glancing about, Lenny said, "The monsters have to enter the arena somehow. Hang on and we'll look for it."

The next hop found them standing just inside the arena floor. Although, the wall was at least forty feet high, there was an overhang over the last ten feet of it. Multiple gates lined the wall, but some of them were much larger for the biggest beasts to enter the arena.

They listened outside of one of the wooden gates for a moment before using Bugoward wood magic to walk through it into the dark passageway beyond. Lenny lit up the way with his wizard staff and glanced around at the lines of empty wire cages.

"Impressive," Lenny said. "The corridors must go under the seats all around the arena. These cages seem too small for the monsters I've heard about. I wonder if they fought nonmagical beasts in the arena centuries past."

"I wouldn't doubt it because many people have a morbid taste for blood," she said. Quivering, she huddled up closer to Lenny. "I'm scared. Let's get this over with quickly, all right?"

"Well, we aren't learning anything standing here holding each other."

"That's the part I like," Jenna grinned. "I just don't want to meet up with any sorcerers or monsters. This place is spooky."

They had followed the passageway only a few yards when they heard the throaty moan of an unidentified beast, which echoed morosely through the gloom.

"It sounded like it came from down there," Lenny said, following the corridor.

"I think we should go the opposite direction or even out of here," Jenna sobbed, holding onto him more tightly.

The way was soon blocked by a pair of thick oaken doors that spanned ten feet wide and twenty high. The great iron hinges appeared to open in the opposite direction but drawn by a complicated arrangement of ropes and pullies.

"Let's not go in there, Leonard," Jenna sniffled.

"Come on, fraidy-cat," Lenny laughed. "We won't find out anything if we leave now."

Bugoward wood magic carried them through the wooden doors without a hitch, but trouble in spades awaited them on the opposite side. The great room was filled with cages holding a variety of gigantic monsters created from the dark imagination of their makers.

A human sized rat hissed at them from the first cage, but Lenny did not shrink away as Jenna did.

"I hate rats," she whispered. "We know there are monsters here now, so let's go."

"No, we're not done yet," Lenny replied. "For instance, I'm sure that this rat was created by a level five wizor or perhaps six but no more. Those two headed wolves and all of these other monstrosities are no better. They must be here for the opening battles, kind of like a warm up. A good sorcerer would have no trouble in defeating any of them."

"Please, Leonard, let's go," Jenna begged. "The stench from all of these monsters is getting to me. I feel like passing out."

"All right, if it'll make you feel better, Jenna," Lenny replied. "Judging by the size of this space, there should be room for a lot more cages on the other side of these. The biggest problem is that there are still three more sides to the arena, plenty of room for even the biggest monsters."

"Come on!" Jenna said, tugging him by the hand back to the great door. It took only a moment to pass through it to the opposite side.

Lenny checked a tear that rolled down her cheek and apologized. "I'm sorry, Jenna. I didn't mean to scare you. I just find the monsters fascinating creatures, even though I know they're creations of magic. As for getting out of here, we could have done that at any time."

Dropping the butt of his wizard staff on the stone floor, they were instantly transported back outside of the stadium to the spot where they had entered it.

Passing the line of men and women who were purchasing fair tickets, they quickly found the driver, who waited for them, and climbed aboard the carriage.

"We're ready now, driver," he said.

The driver sleepily arranged the reins in his fingers and slapped the rumps of the horses. They seemed reluctant to leave the lush patch of grass on which they munched.

The return to the city was uneventful. The driver left them just outside of the Sorcerer Guildhall. He refused to take them to the apartment building where they were staying since it wasn't on his route.

While they were gone, a food vender had parked his cart near the fountain, which gave them the opportunity to choose a couple of chilled chicken sandwiches. They had talked about avoiding the eatery down the street while traveling simply because of the two sorcerers who stalked them.

Eating the sandwiches here also gave them the excuse to watch the front door of the guildhall and Mercilus' apartment building. Finishing up the sandwiches, they scooped up some water to drink from the fountain and walked the distance to their apartment.

They planned to use the same technique to keep Munge off guard, but the door was closed and the matron was nowhere in sight. Shrugging, Lenny transported them to their apartment.

Jenna collapsed on the bed and cried, "My this is comfy. I think I'll sleep like I'm in my own bed tonight." Glancing at Lenny, she added, "I suppose we better talk about the sleeping arrangements, though, since there's only one bed."

"We did it before without a problem," he replied. "Why should tonight be any different?"

"Maybe because we actually love each other?" she suggested. "I hate to admit it, but perhaps we should have taken separate apartments."

"It's too late for that now," he said, "but this rocking chair is comfortable. I can conjure another blanket and curl up here if you're worried."

"No, Leonard, you're the most honorable man I know. You promised Zada that you would marry her, and I plan to leave it at that, all right? I just wish that Cassandra would let us in on the big mystery she mentioned."

"Your wish is granted," Cassy said as she suddenly appeared inside the room. She bowed to her and broke out in laugher. "I'm sorry, but I'm not actually here. I'm still in Mercilus' laboratory listening to them create their monster wizors."

"My, Cassy, you seem real, though," Lenny said.

Jenna laughed with her, but then she became serious. "This really isn't a joking matter, Cassandra," she said. "There's a lot of things happening that we clearly don't understand yet."

"Right on," Lenny said. "Come on, sis, let us know what you found out."

"Nothing good, I'm afraid, Lenny," Cassy replied, nervously pacing the room. She explained everything that had transpired in Mercilus' lab. "Ehe whelf queen enlightened me on a number of points, but there are still many questions left unanswered. For instance, I still want to know what will actually transpire over the next nine days. For example, how did the monsters escape, and which ones will appear unbidden in the future? The crocodilians were frozen in stone, but how were they frozen? If we know that, it might be possible to return them to their hibernation permanently. Otherwise, it'll play hell to cage them up again or even harder to destroy them. Unfortunately, those are our only options."

"I had hoped that you would have some better news," Lenny said, but I hadn't thought about how we're supposed to fight the monsters. If Mercilus couldn't defeat them, then how are we supposed to do it?"

"I've been pondering that very question, Lenny. I only came because I needed to update you both of what's happening, but I must return to Mercilus' laboratory. They're still crafting wizors that will create the most powerful monsters. Most of the others are caged and waiting to be released on opening day."

"We know," Jenna replied. "We took a tour beneath the arena seats at Lenny's insistence. There are dozens of fifth and sixth level monsters caged there."

"I wanted to look through the rest of the spaces," Lenny said, "but Jenna is a fraidy-cat. We left before I could confirm the presence of any others."

"It's a good thing you left when you did," Cassy replied. "There are also seventh and eighth level monsters caged there. If you stirred them up enough to make them break out of their cages, you wouldn't have been able to stop them."

"See, I told you it was best to leave, Leonard!" Jenna cried.

Lenny flushed red but could find few words to say other than, "I'm sorry, okay? I thought I was only helping Cassy. She has more on her plate than either of us do. Besides, I'm bored."

Cassy gave him a sisterly hug and replied, "Don't get down on yourself, Lenny. You and Jenna are doing a very necessary chore for me. I really do need your eyes and ears open to keep watch over the city while I'm gleaning all I can about Mercilus and his family. I want to know everything suspicious that happens around you. Do you understand me, Lenny?"

"Of course, Cassy, but I'm feeling a little picked on. The only thing suspicious we know about is the two sorcerers we saw in the eatery around the block. They were talking like they didn't trust Mercilus to pay them what they were worth. They also tried to board the same carriage we did to go to purchase tickets at the arena. If they're participants in the fair, they definitely don't need tickets."

"Yeah," Jenna added, "they were quite put out about not being able to get on the carriage with us."

Cassy grinned cautiously. "Now that's the kind of information I want to hear about. You never know what will fit into the reason why the nineth level monsters escaped the arena. Now no more fighting, all right, Lenny, Jenna? I have to go, but my communicator is always open. Use it when necessary."

Cassy smiled brightly and faded into the ether.

"I guess she told me," Lenny said. "I'm sorry, Jenna. I really didn't mean to hurt your feelings."

Spotting Lenny's knapsack on the floor, Jenna tossed it to him. "I'm not angry with you, Leonard. Now why don't we dress for bed and get some sleep? I'm exhausted."

She removed the nightgown from her own bag and turned her back on him. Without waiting to know if he had done the same, she shrugged off her blouse and skirt. She paused for a moment in her underwear wondering if he were watching her, but she decided that she didn't care. Removing the remainder of her clothing, she pulled the nightgown on over her head and climbed beneath the sheets.

When Lenny didn't do the same, she rolled onto her back and glanced in his direction. Not only had he not dressed for bed, he had turned the rocker around and sat rocking in it fully clothed.

"Good night, Leonard," she said as a smile creased her face. This had to be difficult for him.

"Good night, Jenna," he replied. "Rest comfortably. Tomorrow will be an even longer day than this one."

He then extinguished the glow from his wizard staff, which instantly darkened the room.

CHAPTER 8

TRICKS

Jenna awoke with a start and glanced at the space beside her in bed. She had hoped to find Lenny there, but it was empty. However, she soon found him asleep in another bed on the opposite side of the room.

"Lenny?" she muttered. "Where did you get the bed?"

However, she grinned when she realized that he had magically conjured it and the blankets from the wood stored in his staff. Quickly pulling off her nightgown, she squirmed into her underwear, skirt and blouse.

Making certain that she was presentable, she stood over Lenny and watched him sleep. How he seemed like he was only a boy, but he was sixteen this year and eligible for marriage in Duscany if he wished. She only wished that he had chosen her over Zada.

Poking his shoulder, she cried, "Wake up, sleepyhead! It's a new day in Eskeling."

Yawning, he rolled over and glared at her. "I could use a few more minutes."

"You've had your few more minutes and more," she said. "We've both slept in. It's probably past eight."

"That late, huh?" He reached for his knapsack on the floor and opened the flap. Pulling out his wristwatch, he checked the time. "Ah, it's only seven-thirty."

"All right, before you go back to sleep, show me how to retrieve the food you stored in your staff yesterday. I want breakfast."

Sighing, Lenny replied, "All right, turn around, and I'll get dressed."

Giggling, she did as he requested, but she greatly desired to be closer to him. The love within her had grown stronger than ever without understanding why. Perhaps it was because they had grown closer whenever they were together on the road. She knew that he felt the same, but only Zada held him back.

"I'm ready," Lenny said. "Have a seat at the table, *mademoiselle* and I'll serve up your *petit-dejeuner.*"

"Mad mah zel and what?" she laughed. "Did some strange bug bite you last night, Leonard?"

Lenny touched his staff and drew out the steaming remains of the bowls of boiled meat, vegetables and the loaf of bread they had bought from the eatery and placed them on the table.

Sitting down, he said, "I wasn't bitten by anything, Jenna. Those are French words from my own world. *Mademoiselle* is an unmarried young woman like you, and *petit-dejeuner* means little meal, which is breakfast."

"Well, why bring that up now?" she asked breaking off some bread from the loaf. "Oh, we could use something to drink."

Lenny conjured two wooden cups filled with water. "I'm going to have to learn how to make real glass. It's primarily made from silicon sand. Anyway, I thought that it would be nice to kid you a little to lighten the day. I'm signed up for Spanish this year in high school, but I really like French. Unfortunately, it's not offered."

"That's nice, Leonard, but it won't do either of us any good here. Cassy already prepared us to speak the language spoken in old Eskeling in case you've forgotten. Why don't you just use magic to learn your Spanish or French or whatever? It seems easier."

"I'm still trying to figure that one out," he replied between bites. "Cassy can do it so easily, but I'm a neophyte next to her magic."

"And I'm a neophyte next to yours, Leonard. I'm blown away with what you just did by producing this hot meal. I might be able to figure out how to make the cup already filled with water, but the rest?

Listen, Leonard, you really make me think when you do magic. That's why I like being around you so much. I'm always learning something new. Promise me that you'll teach me the food trick, all right? You made it seem so easy."

Lenny finished his meal and sat back. "I suppose that it's possible to produce food without first storing it in my staff, but that's really advanced stuff. You already know how to store wood and stone in your wand, but food is no different. When we order next time, I'll let you do it. The recovery is just the opposite. I only added plates and warming wizors when I did it, simple."

"That's really easy for you to say, Leonard, but I have to be more deliberate in how I do things," Jenna said. "Now that we've eaten, we need to decide on how we're going to manage the day. I wish I knew exactly what Cassandra wants us to do."

"I think we should start with going to that eatery and maybe ask the proprietor an embarrassing question or two," Lenny replied. "I noticed that he wasn't comfortable about having us around."

"What if we meet up with Magus and Butkus?" she replied.

"That might not be as bad as we think. Come on. I'm getting my curiosity up. How about you?"

Smiling sweetly, Jenna replied, "Personally, I'm frightened out of my wits, but I suppose we better get this over with."

Lenny removed the staff from the center of the room and converted it to his dragon handled cane. He touched the duplicate miniature staff attached to his lapel to make certain that he still had his backup.

Lenny wasn't certain that he was doing the right thing when they arrived at the eatery. He glanced about them for any sign of being watched or followed, but seeing nothing, he led Jenna inside the eatery.

Although there were several couples eating at the tables, they spotted no one they recognized. When the proprietor didn't welcome them, they glanced into the kitchen where his wife labored over food preparation, but he was not evident.

When they turned back, they found him glaring over them.

"What are you two doing back here?" he demanded.

Lenny uncomfortably shuffled his feet, but he stilled his nerves and replied. "I wanted to ask you a question, sire," he said. "I'm sure you remember the two sorcerers who were eating here when we were. I want to know who they are."

The proprietor's face flushed. "Who wants to know? Who sent you two here? Was it Mercilus? You could be his children. They're the only ones who can do the magic I saw you do. Both of you, get out of here and never come back. I bet you're here without his knowledge anyway."

"Mercilus definitely doesn't know we're here," Lenny replied. "Come on, Brena, let's do as he says before we start something we can't finish."

Frightened, Jenna took Lenny's hand and strolled out the door with him. Outside, she asked, "Why did you call me Brena?"

"That's the name of Mercilus' eldest daughter," he replied. "I just wanted to see if it would provoke a response or not. Obviously, it did. Did you see the look on his face?"

"He looked like he wanted to kill us, Leonard!" she cried, as she pulled away from the eatery toward their apartment. "Please don't do that again. We were nearly killed the last time we were here, and I definitely don't want to take any chances this time."

"I'm sorry, Jenna, but we did find something out."

"What, like how much they hate us? I thought we were supposed to keep a low profile and our ears and eyes open. That's what Cassandra said."

"You're right, of course," Lenny replied. "I guess it has been difficult to do that, but we did discover that the eatery proprietor hates Mercilus."

"Listen, Leonard, I wouldn't be surprised if half the city hated him. Don't forget that he's responsible for the destruction of the city five years from now. I just don't want to take any more chances than necessary. That's all."

"I understand where you're coming from, Jenna, and I promise to consult with you and Cassy before I do anything like that again. Please, Jenna, I can't stand to have you mad at me."

Jenna grinned and replied, "I'm really not mad at you, but I definitely want a heads-up next time. Cassandra did tell us to use the communication wizor. I'm definitely taking her up on that and you better next time."

"I solemnly promise that I will, Jenna, so I suppose we should return to the apartment and regroup. Maybe Cassy has something new to tell us."

Jenna spoke into the tip of her wand and waited a moment, but hearing nothing, she tried again.

"She's not responding, Leonard!" Jenna cried. "What can we do if she's in trouble?"

"I'm not in trouble," Cassy replied, suddenly standing beside them. "I was distracted. I don't have much time. Mercilus and his son will arrive at the stadium soon to install their latest monster. I'm anxious to see how they do that. Now if there isn't something you have to tell me, I must go."

"I think Leonard pulled another stupid act when we visited the eatery around the corner from the apartment," Jenna said. "He passed me off as Brena to see how the proprietor would react. Man, did he get mad at us. I think we wore out our welcome big time."

"That's interesting," Cassy replied, "but don't do anything like that again without me there to back you up. Is that all?"

"Well, we haven't had time to get into any more trouble," Lenny replied. "It's still early in the day. I'm sorry, Cassy."

"If you feel that you must apologize, Lenny, then you're doing something wrong," Cassy replied. "Now be cautious, both of you. I have to go now."

Suddenly, she was gone. Although there were other people on the street, no one seemed to notice.

"She does know how to cover her tracks," Lenny said. "We're the only ones who noticed that trick. I would like to know how she did it."

"I would just like to know how to do it at all," Jenna laughed. "If there's only one thing I learn from this outing, it has to be that."

"I suppose we have nothing else to do while we're waiting on Cassy," Lenny replied. "Take my hand, and I'll transport us back to our room when we have a chance."

Jenna took his hand and glanced about, but she found herself inside the apartment with Lenny grinning at her.

"You're becoming a regular jokester, aren't you, Leonard? You knew that I wasn't ready for that transfer."

"It was on purpose, but it wasn't a joke," Lenny replied. "I just wanted to add a different perspective for your benefit. Making a transfer like that one is routine for me now, but you should have noticed a difference this time."

"I'm not sure," Jenna replied, sitting on the bed. She thought carefully for several minutes before she came up with an idea. "Leonard, I'm not sure, but there seemed to be a slight difference in the color of the aura when we transferred. Am I right?"

"Very good, Jenna," he replied. "You're quite right. I often use color to help me create sympathetic wizors. Now that you know that much, consider that making a transference like that one is very much like a wizor fair solution. How is it possible to go from the street, through the rainbow, and then to your destination in the blink of an eye? You actually did it on a small scale when you won the wizor fair yourself if you recall."

"Oh, I get it!" she suddenly cried. "I did it when I passed through the steel bars and blanket covering the cage without realizing it."

"That's right, but the intervening objects are a little different and further away. You can practice first by changing places here, but you have to do it with me in tow the second time."

"Talk about a tough teacher," Jenna said, "but I wouldn't have it any other way."

Concentrating a moment on transferring to the door, she suddenly found herself there but returned during the next thought. "It is the same, Leonard, isn't it? I actually saw the rainbow when I went through the ether in both directions. The colors were actually reversed, though. Why is that?"

"It's interesting that you noticed that, Jenna. If you saw a real double rainbow produced by the interaction of rain and sunlight, the colors are reversed there too. I think it's because the transference actually reverses your image. If you pay attention, you can tell the difference yourself, but it's most evident by looking in a mirror. That little beauty mole on your right cheek would be on your left and vice versa each time you transfer yourself. However, you will discover the biggest difference if you touch someone else. You'll feel a powerful electrical shock if you're reversed. It could harm you or even kill you or the other person under some circumstances. You can fix the reversal by simply making a short leap after you've transferred. I hope you take that one to heart. I discovered the problem by accident. Make certain you're normal if we transfer together next time."

"All right, then I should be normal now since I transferred twice, right? Let's do it together now. Is there something I should take into account first besides that?"

"You'll know if it fails," Lenny laughed, taking her hand. "You're in full control now."

Concentrating on making the transference to the door as before, she suddenly arrived there without Lenny.

"What happened, Leonard?" she asked, transferring back.

"You forgot to take me with you," he replied. "I'm serious, Jenna. You have to intentionally take me with you."

"Oh," she giggled. She took his hand, but this time they both arrived at the door. "I'm so happy. I told you that I learn something new every time I'm with you. No one else could have taught me that except maybe Cassandra."

"Now take me back," Lenny replied. "We are reversed."

"Oh, right," she said, doing it. "Now let's find that street food vendor. You can teach me how to suck up food into my wand and recover it piping hot. I'm really curious now."

"Fine, do you want to walk or pop over? It gets easier with practice."

"Would I be able to make it that far on my own?"

"You can go almost anywhere you've already been with some exceptions. We traveled by carriage to the stadium both ways to get the feel of the route or else the transference could get messy. Neither of us can enter a magically blocked room or travel through time."

"Do you think it's possible for us, Leonard?"

"Cassy can do it, and our magic is very similar. I don't see why not."

"Then there is hope for me too," Jenna replied. "I'll race you to the fountain."

Suddenly, she was gone. Following, Lenny appeared beside her. Although there were other people getting food, none of them noticed their sudden appearance.

"I have a theory," Jenna said. "I think they didn't notice because they know that what we did is impossible. It would destroy their world if they even considered seeing someone do it."

Laughing, Lenny had to agree as they waited for their turn behind two other men.

CHAPTER 9

KIDNAPPED

Mercilus arrived at the arena in a deep sleep, but he jerked awake when Alva vigorously shook him.

"Wake up, sire!" Alva cried. "We're here!"

Startled, he grasped the leather container strapped to his chest and glanced around. Although, he didn't understand where he was for a moment, he eventually stood up and climbed down from the wagon.

"I'll only be here an hour or so, Alva," he said.

He wandered as if drunk through the back gate of the stadium and ignored the guards' greetings. The guards simply grinned at each other knowingly. Mercilus was not one for amenities.

He found Magus and Butkus waiting for him in the sorcerer staging room. Although there were other sorcerers present, they were going among the fifth and sixth level monsters to quiet them. The monsters did not require material food like meat, grain, grass or water, but they still required magical feeding to keep them viable until the fair event.

"This is only the first one," Mercilus grumbled. "Let's get this over with. I still have a lot of work to do."

Magus and Butkus nodded and led the way across the arena to the corner staging area where the nineth level monsters would be caged after creation. Although the cages were composed of strong steel mesh, they were also fortified by magic to control powerful, otherworldly creatures.

Butkus pushed open the heavy steel cage door, but he leaned against it to rest. When Mercilus did not enter the cage, he said, "What's the matter, Mercilus? I thought this was the part you enjoyed most."

"It'll wait a moment," he replied, his lips spread into a broad sneer. "I want to talk to you both before I start. I've heard a lot of grumbling coming from you two concerning your wages."

"It's nothing," Magus said, staring at him. "We feel that we're worth more than we're getting, of course, but if it weren't for you, we would be paid nothing. Isn't that right, Butkus?" he asked, winking covertly at him.

"Uh, sure, Magus," he replied. "I guess we can't expect more than living wages. We're doing all right."

However, from the look that crossed Mercilus' face, he wasn't convinced of their sincerity. "I'm watching both of you. Try anything I don't like and you will join the monsters in the arena. Do you understand me?"

Butkus looked uncomfortable as he replied. "We already help you fight the monsters, sire. I'm not certain what you mean by joining them."

By the confused look on Magus' face, he didn't either.

"It means that I'll turn you both into monsters and let the bigger ones tear you apart!" Mercilus cried. Removing the leather tube strapped to his body, he opened it and removed a single ceramic container. Handing it to Magus, he added, "Now put this in the center of the cage and pull the leather cord. You know the drill."

"Yes, sire," he replied irritably, "we know what to do."

Joining him, Butkus whispered, "Careful, Magus, let's do this right."

While Magus held the container steadily on the stone floor, Butkus wrapped the cord around his hand and pulled hard but steadily until the wax seal peeled away. To Mercilus' amusement, they jumped back when white smoke began to fill the cage.

Immediately pushing the heavy door closed, they grasped a long lever that shoved three locking bars home with a loud clang.

The contents of the container popped and smoked for a moment before bursting in a torturous bang. The dark smoke, which filled most of the cage, began to coalesce into an opaque sphere that sprouted arms and legs but collapsed onto the floor in an amorphous mass.

"It doesn't look too dangerous right now, does it?" Butkus said, laughing.

"It's best to leave it as it is," Mercilus replied. "It's only an embryo now, but as it draws power from the fen, it'll grow until its twenty feet tall and stronger than anything you can imagine. This is only the first of two troglodytes. I plan to allow them to fight in the arena until one of them wins. We'll take care of the winner ourselves."

Suddenly the embryo twisted and assumed a more humanoid shape. A particularly humanlike wail suddenly split the air.

"Let's get out of here," Magus said.

Alarmed, Butkus headed down the exit tunnel into the arena with Magus close behind. Mercilus merely strolled ahead quietly laughing.

Cassy stayed behind to watch the embryo come to life, but after a moment, she realized why Mercilus advised them to depart so soon. Even she could feel the draw of power the creature pulled from her body. It would have done the same from the sorcerers as well.

Presently, now that Mercilus was unaware of her presence, she resumed her place in the dark tangles of his long, bushy beard, her curiosity satisfied.

———————◆◆◆◆◆———————

Magus and Butkus, however, only relaxed once Mercilus had departed for his laboratory. Finding a quiet area full of empty cages, they sat down on a bench and loosened their coats. The heat they felt was not entirely generated from the confined space.

"I have a mind to walk away," Butkus said

"So do I," his friend agreed, "but Mercilus would hunt us down and put us in the arena with the monsters just as he warned us. You know we've never had that option. We have no choice except to do as he says."

"He knows that too, Magus, but that makes me wonder why he bothered to threaten us the way he did."

"Well, it wasn't a gentle reminder of where we stand," Magus said. "That I have to agree on. He said that he's watching us too. I wonder how he's doing that? I think we'd know if he had his eyes on us. We're not neophyte sorcerers, and he knows that too."

"I think I'd notice if someone popped a far-sight wizor on me," Butkus agreed. "That reminds me of those two kids we saw in Bessel's eatery the other day. They must be two of Mercilus' kids. They're sorcerers, I tell you, and rich. Munge said they paid five in gold for that apartment. I don't understand why they would need that, though, so close to home. She said that the unusual names they gave had to be aliases although they denied it."

"That is curious," Magus replied. "We've only met his son Barcelis. We don't know how many children Mercilus has. He's alluded to more, but he doesn't discuss them. I wonder why."

"I think we should ask the kids," Butkus said. "Are you game?"

Magus stared him in the eyes and thought carefully, but momentarily he nodded. "It wouldn't hurt. If they are his, maybe we can hold them hostage long enough to keep Mercilus off our backs. We can hold them in the usual place. If not, well, too bad for them."

＊ ──── ＞＜ ＝ ＞＜ ──── ◂

Jenna sat at the table in the apartment concentrating on her wand. After a moment, she willed the chicken sandwiches she had purchased from the street vendor to appear appetizingly hot on a wood plate just as Lenny had done. Unfortunately, the result was a flaming mess that she rapidly squelched with a water wizor.

"I'll never get this right," she complained. "I'm hungry now, but I've just burned to ashes all the food I saved. Leonard, are you listening?"

Lenny, however, was highly absorbed in studying the crinkled parchment he had found wedged inside the walnut shell in Duscany.

"Hmm, what did you say?"

"I said I'm hungry," she replied, but then she saw what he was up too. "Haven't you figured that out yet, Leonard?"

"I might if I actually understood the traditional rules of wizor making," he replied. "It looks like some sort of wizor recipe, but I don't know for what."

Jenna sat on the bed next to him and examined the peculiar

scrawls on the wrinkled parchment. "It's like the ones I've seen in Mercilus' wizor books. Although I can read it, I don't understand what it says."

"That's what bothers me. I wonder if Cassy would understand it."

"I bet she could, Leonard, but I'm hungry. Let's find that street vendor and get some more sandwiches, lots of them this time, so I can practice."

Lenny laughed. "I would try producing the plate first, Jenna. You haven't tried that yet, have you?"

Jenna seemed startled as she glanced at him, but then she laughed with him and replied, "You're quite right. I need to practice each step first. I bet I could have produced the cold sandwiches without the plate if I had tried that."

Rising from the bed, she continued, "Now put that parchment away, Leonard, or else I'm going without you."

Lenny quickly folded up the parchment and vanished it into his wizard staff, which he converted into the gentleman's walking cane and followed her.

Walking around several blocks, they failed to find the same street vendor but discovered another one peddling roasted bits of meat strung on sharpened sticks.

Once the other customers departed, they confronted him and purchased all the cooked meat on a stick that he had prepared. Jenna carefully vanished them into her wand one by one while the vendor was distracted by stoking up the brazier to prepare more food.

"That ought to be enough," Jenna whispered. "Let's stretch our legs while we're eating. I've been shut up in that apartment quite long enough, haven't you?"

"I'll go along with that," he replied, "but I wish that Cassy had actually given us something to do."

"Agreed, but let's go sit in the park over there," Jenna suggested. "It's nice there, and we can enjoy the sun. If you recall, that's where you got the wood to make your wizard staff."

Lenny led the way through the gap in the stone wall lining the park and took her hand. "Of course, that's not something I can forget, Jenna. You know, this park is as beautiful as any city park in my world. That's one thing ancient Eskeling had going for it. Too bad Mercilus messed it up."

Finishing eating the meat on a stick, she stared at it a moment before absorbing it into her wand. It might be useful later.

Magus and Butkus spotted the children from the doorway of the Sorcerer's Guildhall across the street and stepped behind the stone columns supporting the frieze.

"It looks like they're hungry, the little devils," Magus said. "Perhaps we have an opportunity."

"I left the box wagon next to the park on the other side," Butkus replied. "Look, they're going into the park. How convenient!"

"Let's go," Magus replied.

They casually strolled across the street but entered the park through the southern entrance. Covertly working their way from one bush to another, they soon spotted the kids slowly strolling through the park.

"We better get the sacks ready," Magus said. "Come on."

Keeping out of sight, they found the wagon and removed two large, canvas sacks from the back. Finding a private hiding place behind a massive statue of a king riding a horse, they watched the kids strolling toward them but ducked back as they approached. Once they passed the hiding place, Magus pulled his sack over Lenny's head and Butkus bagged Jenna. A quick rap with a sap dropped them unconscious to the ground.

Slinging the sacks over their shoulders the kidnappers carried them to the back of the box wagon and secured them inside.

"That was easy," Butkus chuckled. "Now let's take them to our hidey-hole. They won't enjoy that place any better."

"Don't get too cocky, Butkus," Magus replied as they climbed up on the seat. He took the reins and snapped them over the horse's rumps. "They're both sorcerers, remember? Our goal is to find out who they are first. If they are who we think they are, we'll need them alive at least until after the fair. Mercilus won't need us after that until next year."

"Thank God for that," Butkus replied. "That'll give us plenty of time to disappear. I have some ideas about that too."

Arriving at their destination, they opened a warehouse door and carried the pair of sacks inside. It took only a moment to dump the children from the bags. Lenny's cane clattered to the stone floor.

"What's this?" Butkus asked, picking it up. Examining it closely, he stated, "It's just a cane. What should I do with it?"

"We can't leave it here, Butkus," Magus laughed. "It's a weapon in even their hands. That should be obvious."

"Well, it is quite stylish. The handle is shiny like silver and looks like some sort of monster, but I don't know. I think I'll keep it for myself, though."

"Suit yourself, Butkus, but let's get to our listening post. They'll wake up pretty soon."

Jenna stirred awake first and prodded Lenny's arm. "Wake up, Leonard. I think we've been kidnapped."

Lenny sat up and examined the spacious inside of the warehouse. "Yes, but for what purpose?" he replied, holding a finger to his lips. "I'm only missing my cane."

Taking a hint, she replied, "I'm not missing anything, so what do think happened?"

She carefully made running motions with her fingers and covertly pointing to the heavy door. Lenny realized immediately that she was suggesting a way to escape.

Lenny only grinned and stared intently into her eyes, but she jumped in surprise when she heard faint words in her mind.

We can escape from this place by blasting out the door, but that's risky, he said. *The warehouse is ordinary wood. I detect a strong magic containment wizor in force, but it'll take time to figure that one out. Our captors must be sorcerers, but they're not that good or that smart. I want to know who they are and what they want from us. Just play dumb for now. Your name is Brena for the time being.*

"I wonder who our captors are, Brena," he added aloud. "I'll bet it's those two creepy sorcerers we saw in the eatery. They didn't look too honest to me. Father did say that he couldn't trust his help."

"Really?" she replied. "He rarely talks to me. He's always too busy for us. Do you suppose he found out that we took that apartment just to get away from him for a while?"

That's good, Jenna, his silent reply came. *Let's see if we can draw them out. You called me Leonard when you woke me. That's a mistake, but I doubt if anyone knows who Mercilus' children are or their names. We're stuck with it.*

"He's pretty good at keeping tabs on us," he said. "It wouldn't surprise me if he already knows about our predicament."

"He won't find you here," Magus said as he and Butkus stepped from behind a blind. "I assure you that he can't look inside this warehouse. We've seen to that. Brena, you called him Leonard," he said pointing at Lenny. That's a strange name. I've never heard it before."

"It's just what I call him," Jenna replied, glancing at Lenny for help. "It's like a nickname."

Lenny immediately recalled a short version of Mercilus' ancestry. His son Barcelis was named after his fraternal grandfather. The maternal grandfather was called Leonus, and his wife was named Brena. It fit in nicely with his plan.

"My real name is Leonus after my grandfather," Lenny said. "I'm sure you've already met my brother Barcelis. He's the only one father trusts to help him in the laboratory. He says I'm too young, but I'm just as good as my brother."

"I sense a little resentment in your words, Leonus," Magus said. "To tell you the truth, you're here because we don't trust him either. He's threatened us once too often."

"Are we hostages?" Jenna whispered, grabbing one of Lenny's arms and scooting protectively closer.

"For now, yes," Magus replied. "If you behave yourselves, you won't be harmed."

Lenny placed a reassuring hand over Jenna's and replied, "We'll behave ourselves if you do. I'll do anything to protect my sister."

"I admire your brass, youngster," Magus replied. "We'll let you out of here in a few days if you cooperate with us, and no harm done. How about it?"

"I guess we don't have much choice, Magus," Lenny replied. He shrugged his shoulders despondently. "We'll do as you say. Now may I have my cane back? It helps me walk."

"You can have it back when we're done with you," Butkus replied. But he whispered to Magus on the way out, "It's a little short for me, but I'm keeping it. Maybe I can find a way to lengthen it."

Magus waved a hand over the door locking mechanism until something clicked. It clicked again once they passed outside.

"Lenny, what are we going to do?" Jenna cried. Frightened, she climbed to her feet with his assistance. "They're serious about this."

"We listen in, of course," he grinned, tapping the stickpin on his lapel. "It helps that they took my cane. We'll figure out how to escape this place eventually. You stored plenty of shish kabobs in your wand to last us both a couple of days. We won't starve."

"Shish kabobs?" Jenna asked seriously. "What's that?"

"Grilled meat and vegetables on a stick, of course," he replied. "That's what we call it where I'm from."

"Well, it sounds apt anyway," she replied. Holding her head, she added, "I have a headache from that blow they gave me. How about you?"

When Lenny touched the pin on his lapel, a small plastic bottle suddenly filled his hand. "This will help," he said, popping off the cover. He handed two tablets to her and kept two for himself before returning the bottle to the lapel pin. His next efforts produced two plastic bottles of water. "I packed everything in my wizard staff this time, a change in clothing and a lot of other things including my knapsack. They're easier to carry that way."

"Well, explain what these are," she said, holding out the tablets. "I've never seen anything like them before."

"Just medical magic from my world, Jenna. Wash them down with water, and they should take care of that headache."

"Amazing," she said, following his example.

Suddenly, Jenna jumped when they heard Magus and Butkus speaking as if they were standing next to them. They listened while they argued with one another for a moment.

"They're not saying anything much yet," Lenny said, "but I'm more interested in what they'll talk about when they meet up with Mercilus."

"Still," Jenna said, "it would be nice to see what they're doing too. Is there a way to do it? You're the wizard here."

Lenny glanced at her in surprise. "I wish I had thought of that idea. It's fantastic. Butkus has my cane, but the staff on my lapel and the cane are linked. I could call the cane back, but we're in serious need of information."

"Well, is it possible or not?" she asked.

"It should be," he replied. "All I need to do is create camera eyes on the cane, magical dragon eyes. They won't know the difference."

He removed the pin from his lapel and expanded it to the full-size wizard staff with the steel ball at the top. Setting the butt on the stone floor, he made sure it stood firmly before releasing it. He smoothed the steel ball into a large circular metal plate and stood back.

"Is something supposed to happen, Leonard?" she asked.

"If I've done this right, everything the dragon on the cane sees, we'll see in that plate. Ah, yes, here it comes now."

An animated closeup of Butkus' curious face soon filled the plate.

"Do you suppose he suspects something, Leonard?"

"Not likely," Lenny replied. "The camera is one way. I think he's just admiring the cane. Now that's done, let's examine our jail a little more closely. We know that it's protected by a magic wizor much like the cell we were locked in when we were here before, but we proved that sheer force was enough to destroy it. We're a little wiser now, so help me figure out a way to neutralize the wizor in case we want to leave without letting our two knuckleheaded friends know about it."

"I like the way you think, Leonard," she replied. "This is better than sitting around being bored."

CHAPTER 10

GRAVEYARD

Magus and Butkus flinched fearfully at the troglodyte's throaty roar. The creature was more than half grown now and frequently attacked the cage in their presence, but the magic shield instantly repulsed it. After several attempts, it sat sagely in the center of the cage and watched malignantly as Mercilus installed the second troglodyte in the adjacent cage. Once they sealed the cage, there was no need to remain any longer.

The pair casually followed Mercilus from the cage area beneath the stands of the arena and waited for him to depart altogether before they breathed sighs of relief.

"I didn't notice anything unusual in Mercilus' behavior," Magus said. "Did you?"

"Nothing, but you would expect something now that two of his children didn't come home last night. It doesn't make any sense unless he really doesn't care about them."

"I hope that's not the case," Magus replied, "or else we've done what we've done for nothing. This affair frightens me all to hell. I guess the only thing we can do is wait and see."

"I suppose," Butkus replied, "but what about the kids? We should feed them or something. There's no water or anything for them to eat in that warehouse."

"Let them stew it out for a couple of days, Butkus. We can't let them out of there anyway because they'll go straight to Mercilus. That'll be the end of us if we haven't finished our escape plan by then."

"That's what worries me. I still don't like this."

Lenny and Jenna laughed at their captors' dilemma as they chowed down on a shish kabob apiece and drank from the plastic bottles of water Lenny produced.

"Well, how long do you want to wait it out, Leonard?" Jenna asked. "The beds you made were comfortable and warm, but we still have to learn more than we have to be of any use to us."

Lenny tugged the last piece of meat from the shish kabob and absorbed the stick into his staff. The meat was chewy, which prevented him from answering immediately.

Finally, he replied, "I'm in no hurry, but you're probably right. We haven't heard from Cassy, so she's probably still observing Mercilus. First, though, I want to defeat the magic wizor that's holding us prisoners here. I could knock a wall down, but the roof of this flimsy warehouse could collapse on top of us. I prefer to play it safe for now."

"I have to agree with that," Jenna replied. "We're in no danger here unless Butkus and his partner return and try something awkward. From what we've just heard over your magic television, I know that's out of the question for now."

Lenny wiped his greasy hands on his pants and stretched. "I've been thinking about this old warehouse," he said, circling the walls. "It's a little larger than our double garage at home, but it obviously hasn't been used in a very long time. I wonder why that is."

"I think that we're not the first one's they've jailed here," Jenna said, finishing up her shish kabob. "It's just supposed to look like a warehouse to people who don't know any better."

Lenny had thought about that too, but he didn't want to frighten Jenna by bringing it up. Now that she had, he decided to do a little more investigating beginning with a pile of lumber and flagstones set at the front of the warehouse.

Carefully absorbing wood, stone and earth into his wizard staff, he watched for signs that something else was buried there. Several feet down, he found the dark brown skeletons of two persons one atop the other.

"Oh no!" Jenna cried, turning away in tears.

"At least we know they're serious about leaving us here to die," Lenny replied. Reversing the flow of materials, he returned everything until the area looked exactly the same as when he found it. "I'm sorry, Jenna, I didn't want you to see that graveyard, but I had to know what was buried there. There could be more victims if we looked for them."

"Don't worry on my account," Jenna replied. "I suspected as much. You just proved it, is all. It's just that no one can unsee what we just saw."

"It rattled me too," Lenny replied, "and I knew I'd find something I didn't like. One way or another, we can escape. I want you to keep that in mind before you start worrying."

She held him closely as she began to cry. "I know, Leonard. You got us out before, and I trust you, but please hurry up and find a way to neutralize that containment wizor. I just wish that I had done some research on it after we escaped the last time we were here."

"I forgot about it too, Jenna," Lenny replied, releasing her. "Come on and help me analyze the wizor. You're much better at it than I am. You know the wizor had to be made the traditional way."

Jenna admitted that it would be a good start. Stifling her tears, she waiting for Lenny to use his staff to probe the containment wizor, which released a rainbow image of its properties.

"It's weird," Jenna said. "I am detecting some very weak emanations, but I can't make them out. Can you amplify them with your wizard staff?"

"As much as you like," he replied, increasing the size of the aura.

Although the individual steps making up the wizor were now obvious even to him, Jenna understood the wizor making process better than he did.

"Oh my!" she exclaimed. "It's complicated and level six. It's beyond anything I can do, but your strength is above that, Leonard. You should be able to defeat this wizor easily."

"I'm glad to hear that," he replied. "Now that I can see the steps taken in its creation, I think that I can walk them back one step at a time. Now tell me, do you think that'll work, Jenna?"

"I don't see why not, but if we collapse the containment wizor that covers the entire warehouse, won't that signal Magus and Butkus that something is wrong?"

"That's smart, Jenna," he replied. "I think I can make a rectangular door on the wall here like so."

He drew the size of the rainbow down and aligned it against the wooden wall. Enlarging the rainbow within that marked area, he began the destruction of the sixth level of the containment wizor. It vanished in a loud bang that threw them both to the stone floor in a cloud of dust.

"Eek!" Jenna cried, coughing from the smoke generated. "We need to think this thing through some more. That hurt, and it's hard to breath in here."

Lenny absorbed all of the smoke and dust into his wizard staff and replied, "We made the mistake of standing in front of it." Helping her up, he said, "This time we'll stand over here, and I'll be ready for the smoke."

Making certain that she was out of the way, he set his wizard staff firmly upright on the flagstone floor and joined her. Since the rainbow shape that identified the containment wizor was still in place, he willed the staff to select level five. Protecting Jenna's eyes by holding her against his chest, he diverted his own and signaled the destruction of that stage.

Although the removal of level five produced a nearly identical explosion, he didn't wait to select the next one and walked them down to level one. The explosions reduced in proportion until only the last level remained. Lenny thought about that level for a moment before signaling its destruction. The rainbow pattern immediately blanked out. The containment wizor was now neutralized within that rectangle.

"That was interesting," Lenny said. "I now have a level six containment wizor in my repertoire. My staff recorded the properties of each level, so I know what they do. I can reproduce them one at a time or all at once."

"You can really do that, Leonard?" she replied, in amazement.

"Sure, I'll transfer the wizors to your wand if you want. You can use them too."

"Oh, I want!" she cried, eagerly digging out her wand. It took only a moment to transfer the wizors. Concentrating on her wand, she analyzed the wizors for herself and smiled. "You're right. Each level does something a little differently. The last level binds them together into a unit to create the strength of a level six wizor. I would have never thought of doing that. I think I've just learned something very important."

"So have I," Lenny replied. "Now that I know how, I'm going to analyze every wizor I find and store them in my wizard staff."

"Oh, Leonard, does that include monsters too?" she asked. "Mercilus is making some pretty nasty ones."

Lenny thought carefully for a moment before grinning. "I want to see how they're made, so I think I will. If there's a wizor I can use for something else, I'll record it, but I'm not about to tempt myself into making any of Mercilus' monsters. They're too destructive, but we might learn how to destroy the crocs we found in Duscany. That's why we're here, after all."

CHAPTER 11

Escape

To test their handiwork, Lenny and Jenna used their Bugoward wood magic to walk through the side of the wooden warehouse where they had neutralized the containment wizor.

"That worked wonderfully," Jenna said, glancing around to orient herself. "This doesn't look like a residential part of the city, though."

"You're right, Jenna," Lenny replied, doing the same. Using his wizard staff, he held it up and turned around once. The buildings around them appeared as if in x-ray vision. "The area seems largely abandoned. That's why those two lamebrains hid us here. It's doubtful if anyone would ever discover us alive or dead."

"Oh, I wish you hadn't put it that way, Lenny," she replied, folding into his arms. "You know, I really would like to retrieve the things I left in our apartment. I don't feel good about leaving anything there now."

Lenny touched her hand and transported them both to the inside of their apartment. "Your wish is my command, oh Princess Jenna."

"You don't have to be melodramatic about it, Prince Leonard," she said, stuffing her nightgown and other garments into the bag she had left on the bed. Working to make up the bed, she said, "You better get rid of that extra bed too. We don't want to alarm our landlord, do we?"

"Done," Lenny replied as Jenna turned around.

The extra bed was not only gone, but the room was also dust free. He had done an instant job of housecleaning.

"Well, it is our responsibility while we're here," he said.

Jenna sat down on the bed and smirked. "Well, now that we're here, what are we going to do? We need to come up with a better plan than what I've seen so far."

Lenny set up his staff in television mode in the center of the room and sat next to her. "I suppose we can watch those two jerks for a while and take our cue from them."

"Oh, why not," she replied. Taking her wand from the special pocket in her skirt, she absorbed her bag into it, a trick she learned from Lenny.

From the image generated, it soon became obvious that the nefarious pair were seated together in the back of a buggy behind the driver. They observed no one else present.

They had traveled this route before and even recognized some of the landmarks, but soon a familiar warehouse came into view.

"They're at the warehouse!" Jenna cried. "We have to go."

Lenny snatched his wizard staff and Jenna's hand. The next instant they were in the warehouse where he immediately removed the beds, shrank his staff into the lapel pin and attached it where it belonged.

They sat on some lumber they arranged as a makeshift bench and looked innocent.

Magus opened the door and entered while Butkus trailed after him. He intended to leave the door ajar, but Magus rebuked him for it. Sighing reluctantly, Magus closed the door, generating the usual magic click that signified the successful closure of the containment field.

"I'm going to figure out how to do that," Lenny whispered in Jenna's ear.

"Just watch yourself," she whispered. "We don't know why they've returned."

They stood up just as Magus and Butkus reached them. They didn't look happy.

"We think you've been lying to us," Magus said. "You're not

Mercilus' kids, are you?"

"Why did you say that?" Lenny replied, feeling them out.

"He hasn't complained once about missing you," Magus replied. "That's why. Don't you think that's a little strange?"

"Not if you know our father," Jenna replied. "When he's busy making monsters like he is now, we never see him. It upsets momma something fierce."

"She's right, you know," Lenny said, backing her up. "Father and Barcelis lock themselves up in that laboratory for days on end. He never goes home, so how would they know?"

"They have a point," Butkus said. "He's only around long enough to deliver his monsters."

"Maybe they do, and maybe they don't," Magus replied, unwilling to accept their words at face value. "Mercilus is tight lipped about where he lives, but just so happens I know. Tell me, big mouth, where that is, and I might just believe you."

Lenny and Jenna laughed. "Should I tell them or you?" Jenna asked.

"Well, he did call me big mouth, and I guess that's true," Lenny replied. "Very well, Magus, here's the truth. We live in the apartment building just to the right of the Sorcerer's Guildhall. The first floor is nothing but traps for anyone who doesn't live there. Now does that suit you?"

The youngsters grinned together, knowing that they had just confused their captors beyond hope.

"I reckon you're telling the truth," Butkus frowned. "Now what do we do?"

"Leave them here to rot!" Magus cried, angrily stalking away, but then he returned just as quickly. "Listen, you two brats, if you play it straight with us, we'll do the same for you. Once we get what we want from Mercilus, we'll open the door and you can walk away free. How about it?"

Grinning, Lenny replied, "So you don't want us to rot here?"

"Forget that part!" Magus replied, clearly coming unglued. "All you have to do is sit tight."

"We're hungry and thirsty, and it's hot in here," Jenna replied. "We could die first. What about that?"

"Damn it all to hell!" Magus cried. "All right, you've got us. Butkus, fetch that jug of water from the buggy. We'll get you some food later, kid. All you have to do is sit tight."

Butkus quickly retrieved the ceramic jug of water and left it on the floor. "Come on," he said. "There's no point in hanging around here now."

They walked quickly to the door without saying another word, but Lenny was ready. He touched his lapel pin and focused on the door where Butkus touched it. He recorded the opening and then the closing of the containment wizor as it clicked off and then on.

When the men were gone, Lenny setup his wizard staff to watch them depart in the buggy.

"Did you get what you wanted, Leonard?" Jenna asked.

"Oh yes, I should have thought of that first. I'll project it so you can see the wizor for yourself."

The projection opened up like another rainbow, but the colors were out of order, some close together and some further apart.

"What do you think, Jenna?" he asked spreading the colors apart to view them individually.

"Well, the gaps signify the levels as they were made," she replied. "It's definitely sixth level too, but the opening and closing parts differ only in the first level. That would make it simple to control if you knew how. That's the hard part."

"Actually, it's the easy part," Lenny replied. "I can open the door from here."

The door clicked and opened slightly, controlled remotely by Lenny's will. The door suddenly closed, followed by another click.

"Gosh, that's simple," Jenna said admiringly. "I wonder if anyone else knows how to do what you do so naturally."

"I doubt it," he replied, "or else there would be no point in making protection wizors. Don't forget that much of the control is broadcast by the sympathetic wizor Mercilus spread over the city to help make his sympathetic wizors easy to use. Anyone who knows those controls can use them."

"I did remember that from last time we were here," she replied, "but I didn't think it would be that simple."

"Well, it is. The containment wizor and controls are built into it. Mercilus turned it on, and he can turn it off at will. Levels one and two of these controls are actually how the overall wizor is connected to the sympathetic wizor if you can grasp what I'm saying."

"Oh, every word. Can I have those wizors too? I can't wait to see how they work for myself."

"Why don't you use your wand and see if you can do it yourself?" he replied. "Cassy created your wand to serve you. See if you can."

"Oh," she replied, removing her wand. "I don't know where to begin. You captured the open and close wizors when Butkus used them. Should I do it the same way?"

"I doubt if it's necessary, Jenna. You already have the containment wizor, which means that you also have the connection to Mercilus' sympathetic wizor that makes it work. Just focus your wand on the door and spread out the residue magic you find there. It's not very strong, but you should be able to amplify it with your wand, the same as I can with my wizard staff."

"All right, here goes nothing," she replied, pointing her wand, but she quickly realized that doing so was unnecessary. Her wand jumped at her command. The residue energy around the door opener became readily apparent as her wand focused and amplified the containment wizor until even she could read it.

"See, you've done it," Lenny said. "Now save it in your wand."

"I don't quite see, oh!" she cried. "Well, it happened as soon as I thought about it."

"That's the magic of the wand, Jenna," he said. "Didn't Cassy tell you that you could store any wizor you wanted in it and recover it on command?"

"Yes, but she said that I had to make the wizor first. This isn't the same thing. The wizor already exists and is activated."

"I suppose that was a poor choice of words on Cassy's part. The wand will absorb any wizor you can identify. Amplifying the residue energy permits you to do that."

"That is so easy," she said. "I wonder why I didn't think of it."

"You didn't because you thought it was something outside of your control. Trust me, Jenna, you can use your wand to do any magic you choose to do. Identifying the wizor like you've done is the first stage of the process to do just that. As you know, I've never closed my mind to any possibility in this world. I just wish it would work at home without me depending on the magic of this world. Maybe one day I'll figure it out for myself. Cassy does very well with it, but she keeps a connection open so that she doesn't lose control and revert to just a human being. She loves being a whelf too much. I admit that I enjoy the power too, but I do my best not to let it go to my head like Mercilus did. That's what eventually destroyed him."

"I was there too when it happened, Leonard," she said, sadly dropping her eyes. "I remember the chaos all too well."

"Well, something caused two of Mercilus' monsters to freeze into stone and sink into the Whelf Fen," he said. "I don't know if our two friends had anything to do with it, but their behavior may have distracted him once too often. Mercilus is using all of his power to create the monsters and to control them with nothing left over. I'm convinced of that. I hope that Cassy can verify it."

Suddenly Cassy's image appeared like a ghost before them. "You two don't look too comfortable in here," she said. "Do you need help in getting out?"

"You're too late, Cassy," Lenny said. "We've already picked the lock. Magus and Butkus shut us up in here, but we're not sure how they figure into this mystery yet."

Jenna giggled. "You should have seen Leonard work on breaking the containment wizor," she said. "It was simply beautiful. He's more talented than any sorcerer I know, including Uncle Scapita."

"I had my eye on you both," she replied. "I decided not to interfere unless asked. It's difficult to watch Mercilus at work and avoid detection too. I hope you both understand that."

"Yes," Jenna said, "but we're no closer to learning anything important. "What should we do, Cassandra?"

"What you've been doing," she replied. "Being nosey is part of the job description. Now I must go."

"Wait!" Jenna cried, but then she was gone. "Oh, I just wanted something to go on. We're two days into this mess, and we have nothing to show for it."

"Except for Magus and Butkus," Lenny laughed. "I wouldn't exactly call them competent murderers. We clearly have the advantage. Hopefully, we can force them to make a mistake with Mercilus."

"Let's not wait to see if they bring us any food or not," she replied. "Maybe we can find a different eatery or street vendor. Those shish kabobs were good."

"That's a great idea," Lenny replied, "but we need someone here to warn us in time should they return."

"What, you want me to stay here and wait for you?" she cried. "No way!"

"Not at all. I assume that Jen is still with you. My duplicate, Len, never comes along with me."

"Oh, Jen, of course," she replied. "Why do I keep forgetting about her?"

"That's what I would like to know," Jen said, suddenly appearing beside Jenna, but she smiled in good humor.

"I'm sorry, Jen," I just keep forgetting to include you in our adventures."

"I'm not worried about it, Jenna. I'm always with you. I can listen in and come out whenever you need me. I'm you, aren't I?"

"Oh, you sure are, Jen, but do you mind staying here and warning us if those two knuckleheads return before we do? Since the containment wizor is already compromised, you can escape if you have too."

"Or I can just become invisible and follow them," Jen replied.

"Hey, that's a great idea," Lenny said. "Maybe you can follow them after they return next time. If they don't, well I can help you locate them with my wizard staff."

"Anything you want," Jen replied. "Now get your business done while you can"

"Take my staff, Jenna," Lenny said, and then both of them vanished to reappear on the same street as the guildhall, but several blocks away. "Aha," he said, "I thought there was an eatery here. It looks like they serve mincemeat pies, and the bakery next door has fruit turnovers, black bread and apple butter."

"Let's do it quickly," Jenna replied. "I'm getting nervous. Someone could see us who shouldn't if we stay here too long."

"Come on then," Lenny said, stepping inside.

Jen, however, did as she was told. They had been gone only a few minutes when Butkus stepped inside the warehouse with a leather bag of mincemeat and raisin cakes and another jug of water.

"Where's loud mouth?" he asked, glancing around the warehouse.

Although astonished to see him so soon, Jen merely chuckled and replied, "He's behind that screen doing what little boys do, of course."

"Give me a few minutes," Lenny's voice replied. "If you've brought food, just leave it if you want, unless you have something you want to discuss."

"Actually, I do," Butkus said. "This cane, it's magical, isn't it? I saw how you sucked up food off your plate with it. I want you to tell me how it works."

"That was just an old parlor trick," Lenny's voice replied. "I do it because Brena doesn't like it. She thinks it's uncouth."

"He does it all the time," Jen said. "I keep telling him to stop doing it in public, but he won't listen. There's nothing magical about that old willow stick."

"You don't mind if I burn it then?" Butkus asked.

"Of course, I would since I need it to help me get around. If you destroy it, I'll have to find something else, that's all."

Butkus thought for a moment, but then he replied, "Come out from behind there. I want to see you face to face."

"Give me another minute," the voice from behind the screen replied. "I have to pull up my pants."

A moment later, Lenny rounded the screen fastening his belt in place.

"Well, here I am, Butkus. Is that enough for you?"

"I suppose," he replied. "There are enough groceries in that bag to last you a couple of days if you don't get greedy about it. The water should last you too."

"Thanks, Butkus," Lenny said. "You're a real pal."

Butkus nodded and ambled out the door of the warehouse, resetting the confinement wizor as he went.

"That was close," Lenny said as Jenna appeared from behind the screen next.

"You were a real lifesaver, Jen," Jenna said. "We had just purchased what we wanted when you informed me that Butkus was here. Mimicking Leonard's voice until we could get here was genius."

"Certainly, but if I'm to follow him," Jen replied, "I need to go now. He's just leaving."

"Sure thing," Jenna replied, "go to it."

Jen faded out of sight, leaving them alone. Lenny set up his wizard staff television. Magus drove the carriage himself and obviously was in a hurry. Jen appeared in the back of the carriage only long enough to wave and vanish again.

"All right, let's have one of those fruit turnovers," Jenna said, sitting on the makeshift bench. "I can hardly wait."

"Same here," Lenny replied, calling them up from his wizard staff.

CHAPTER 12

ROSINA

Rosina was indeed unhappy during this time of year when Mercilus spent so much time away from home creating his nefarious monsters. She also hated when he was home since he sat eating monstrous quantities of food before passing out afterwards. It didn't matter where he was, whether the table, living room floor or sofa. He rarely made it upstairs to his bed. Realistically, she couldn't stand his presence when he was so engaged in his trade.

She sat on the living room sofa, glad that he was still in his lab for now. She could at least think for herself and her children. Gobie climbed onto her lap and gave her a hug while Shuma and Brena sat beside her. They at least seemed to know when she needed their company, but they needed her reassurance that all was well.

"Mommy, doesn't daddy love us anymore?" She had a very grown-up awareness of her environment for a child of three years old. "I'm scared when he's home."

"I know, Gobie," Rosina replied affectionately. "You're very grown up now as are all of you. I don't know him when he's making monsters for the arena. He's under a lot stress, not that I'm making excuses for him. He knows how it affects all of you. I wish that I could just take you away from all of this, but we're prisoners in our own home."

"I want to go outside and see the city," Shuma said. The others chimed in with agreements. "We can see the people and carriages on the street from the window. Why can't we take one of them and just go someplace?"

"It's not possible, dear," her mother replied. "You know that your father wouldn't allow it. He says the city is too dangerous for us."

"Why?" Brena asked. "I've never seen anything bad going on out there from the windows. People come and go all the time."

"I'm sorry, Brena, but I don't know what's on your father's mind to make him say that."

"I think he's afraid of something," Gobie said unsympathetically. "I can see it in his face all the time."

"You do?" Rosina replied. "That's a very astute thing for you to say, Gobie. We haven't even started your formal education yet."

"I already can do some things," the little girl said. "Brena and Shuma teach me a lot."

"Perhaps you're right, Gobie," Rosina said. "We'll start with the alphabet and numbers tomorrow. How's that."

"I already know that stuff, Mommy. I can read and write. I'm pretty good at addition. I can write my name and all sorts of things."

"We taught her," Brena confessed. "She saw what we were doing and she caught on quickly. She's very smart for her age."

"You all are," Rosina said. "I admit that I should have started all of you on your formal education before I did. I enjoy doing that more than you know."

"We do too," Shuma said. "We don't mind teaching Gobie. We know how nervous you've been while waiting for the fair to start. We understand why you don't want to go too, and we don't blame you."

"Do you, dear?" Rosina said. "I have a premonition that something horrible will happen this year. I can't explain it. I think it somehow involves me, but I don't know what it is."

"Make sure Barcelis sits with you in the arena," Brena said. "His magic isn't much, but he can support you in many ways. Maybe you can convince him to talk to father to let you stay home."

"I promise that I'll keep Barcelis close, but Mercilus won't let me stay home. I'm quite certain of that. Listen, all of you, I'll be fine. I won't take any chances, and I'll sit as high up in the stands as possible. Does that suit you?"

"We love you, Mommy," Gobie said, hugging her. "I want to sleep with you tonight. House takes care of our needs, but it's still lonely in my room. House doesn't always say the right things or sing the right songs to help me sleep, not like you do."

"I understand, dear," Rosina said, kissing her on the forehead. "You may but just for tonight. Now the rest of you, off to bed. I'll take Gobienna up with me."

Barcelis arranged the wizor bowls in order and filled them with the ingredients listed in the open book on the bench beside him. Each one had to be filled exactly as planned. Carefully weighing the ingredients, he tipped the measuring cup over the bowls and washed the contents out with a water bottle. The water evaporated during the activation process when he placed it over the brazier.

Leaning over the bench, Mercilus sat wearily beside him. The activation of every wizor took much out of him, and the food he had brought for the purpose was already consumed.

His son watched the water in the wizor bowl boil until gone. Adding the activation ingredient, he said, "This one's ready."

Mercilus leaned over the wizor bowl to watch for the proper moment, but suddenly he slipped off the stool and bumped the hot wizor bowl off the brazier. The bowl crashed to the floor at their feet and exploded into flames across the floor. His robe suddenly caught fire.

Slapping at the flames, he cried, "Barcelis, help me!"

Barcelis quickly doused the flaming robe and the burning remnants from the wizor bowl with water from a bucket he used to refill the water bottle. Once the fire was out, he assisted his father back to where the air was clearer.

"You're weary, father," he said. "We should stop for tonight."

"No, there's no time!" he cried. "This wizor has to be finished tonight to stay on schedule."

"Very well, I'll clean up the mess and prepare another bowl. It's only the fifth level just to let you know. You'll have to stay awake through all of the levels."

"Just prepare the damn bowl, Barcelis. I'll worry about the mess.

Every minute counts now."

Barcelis swept the debris on the floor out of the way and off the bench before preparing a new wizor bowl. There was no point in working in such disarray no matter what his father said.

Although Mercilus was growing weaker, levels five through eight were completed without any trouble. Thankfully, the critical level nine would merely be added to the others in the wizor bottle without activation. That would happen on site when he was much fresher.

Barcelis capped the bottle and inserted it into a harness that he looped over an arm before assisting his father up the stairs from the laboratory and the main stair into the apartment above. He knew that his father would be ravenously hungry. Indeed, Mercilus clutched his son's arms as he ambled unsteadily into the dining room.

"House!" he cried. "Food and lots of it. I'm hungry, damn it!"

House suddenly came alive in the kitchen as pots and pans began to move about on their own. Easily cooked foods like eggs and sausage came first while potatoes, corn and high protein lentils that took longer to cook came later. House seemed to know exactly how much food to cook for its master, having done it many times before.

Barcelis enjoyed some of it for himself, but he lacked the hunger that came from wizor making. When he finished, he allowed house to remove the dishes, but he stayed with his father to make certain that he finished his meal without injuring himself.

After a time, Mercilus pushed his plate aside and shakily stood up. Barcelis simply followed him to the living room. Apparently, the sofa was the target, but he didn't reach it. Instead, he sank to his knees and fell onto the thick brown carpet spread out before it.

Barcelis made no effort to move him to the sofa himself. He knew that he wasn't strong enough to lift such a dead weight. Instead, he went upstairs to his own room. His was the first room on the left, and his sisters' bedrooms were on the right. His parents' room was at the end of the hall. He waited a moment to see if his mother heard him climb up the stairs or not, but she did not appear.

He sat morosely at a small table for a moment before extracting a diary from a drawer. He began to write furiously in it until he gained control of himself and slowed his pace.

If he had turned around, he would have found Cassy there admiring him. She had fallen in love with him five years in the future, but she was forced to remove all thoughts of that from her mind. She wanted to see him again, which made it difficult not to reveal her presence.

After a moment, he shoved the diary and pen into the desk drawer and stood up. He thought he saw a shadow of a woman on the wall projected by the flickering oil lamp, but when he turned, he saw nothing. The shadow was also gone.

Thinking that he was hallucinating from the late-night work, he shrugged and pulled off his shirt and pants. Capping the lamp, he slid into bed and turned away from the light that fell through the shaded window.

Cassy stood there watching him breathe for some time before tears began to flow down her cheeks. Yes, she loved him, but there was nothing she could do. He had married and died a thousand years into her past. This love was simply foolishness, but she ethereally laid herself down on the bed beside him. He would never know that she was there.

Barcelis, however, felt something odd. He rolled over onto his back and saw the thin outline of a young woman who smiled at him. He reached for her, but his hand passed through the image. A moment later, she was gone.

"What was that!" Barcelis cried, but the spirit did not return. Turning back over, he fell fast to sleep.

Cassy was still there ethereally, however. She was amazed that he had detected her. That meant that his personal magic was stronger than she realized, much stronger than when they met five years into the future. That intrigued her.

Leaving the room, she visited Brena who rested comfortably but not quite asleep. She was crying.

"House," she whispered, "I'm very lonely. Please send me someone to talk to."

House, however, could not fulfill that command, and she knew it; however, she heard a voice she did not recognize.

"Brena, do not be afraid. There is a time very soon when you'll have to be very strong for yourself, Shuma, and especially Gobie. They'll need you. Barcelis will too, but he's headstrong and will push you away. Don't let him do that."

Brena sat up in the darkness, but she could see the silhouette of someone standing in front of the window. She wanted to tell House to turn on the lamp, but she dared not lest this person leave.

"Who are you?" she asked instead. "Do I know you."

"You do, Brena. I'm here at your wish. Who do you think I am?"

"You can't be House," she replied. "Father told me that it can't generate people or spirits or anything similar. Are you for real, spirit?"

"Yes, I'm very real. Someday, you'll discover that I am your most trusted friend, but I don't exist in this time. That's why you only see me as a shadow. I came because you called for me. Does that frighten you?"

"No, not now. Can you stay for a while?"

"I'll stay for a time for you and your sisters. Your brother doesn't know it, but I'm here for him too. All of you need a friend right now. I am that friend, the one you asked for. I know that you probably won't understand that, but perhaps someday you will. Take care of your sisters, Brena. They need you now more than ever and even more once the fair comes. You'll understand what that means when it's time."

"I think I do now," Brena said. "Mother says that she expects something awful to happen in the arena. Is that true? Is something going to happen?"

"Yes, Brena, but I can't tell you what happens because it's forbidden. I'm here because you need a friend, but I can only stay until then. After that, I'll no long exist here."

"I know I should be frightened," Brena said, "but I'm not. I think I knew all along like mother that something awful would happen this time. If I could stop the fair this year, I would, but no one can overrule father. He doesn't listen to anyone, not even mother."

"That's another reason why I'm here, Brena. All I can do is comfort you. I can do nothing else."

"You're real enough for me," Brena said. "Do you have a name, spirit?"

"Cassandra, if you must call me something. It is probably a strange name to you."

"Yes, but I like it. Maybe after I get married and have a daughter, I'll name her after you."

"That would please me, Brena. I know that you'll have trying times for a while, but take heart. All will end happily for you and your siblings. I want you to understand that. Never doubt yourself and everything that I've told you tonight."

"Cassandra," Brena said, but she did not continue.

"Yes, dear, what is it you want to ask me?"

"Cassandra, are you real enough to hold me for a while? I really do need a friend."

"If you wish, but please be careful of what you wish for. I can grant only so much and so very little. I'll stay with you tonight if you wish it, but I'll be gone come morning."

"Yes, please, stay with me, Cassandra. I want you to stay."

"Very well, throw open the sheet and move over. You may not feel anything at first, but as you close your eyes, you'll know that I'm there."

When Brena complied, Cassy ethereally climbed into bed and hooked an arm over her. "I'm here now, Brena. You may cover up."

"You know, I think I really do feel you next to me. Thank you, Cassandra. I'll never forget this."

Cassy simply smiled and didn't reply. She allowed herself to become a little more real to satisfy Brena's insecurity, but she had a strong reason for helping her. She grew to love these children during the short time she was here five years into this future. It wasn't something that she could simply turn off and walk away from. No, these children deserved much more, but she regretted that she couldn't give it to them.

CHAPTER 13

CROCODILIAN

Mercilus sat at the table eating as piggishly as he did the previous night. He appeared gaunt and wistful and failed to acknowledge the presence of anyone around him. He hadn't bothered to replace the robe he had worn. The fire had burned away a patch up to his left knee, and the blisters from a second-degree burn were plainly visible on his calf. Still, it passed as though of no importance.

When he finished, he glanced up at Barcelis sitting across from him, who waited for this moment. "Barcelis, you know what to do in the laboratory," he said. "We're making one more of this monster, so prepare the wizor bowls just as you did before. I'll return as soon as I've activated this one."

"Father, you must allow me to dress that burn before it festers," Barcelis said. "You should replace that robe too. You don't want to show the others that you're not taking care of yourself."

"Practical as always, Barcelis," he replied. "I'll have my healer meet me at the stadium. He'll take care of that. As for the robe, you're quite right, but I don't believe that I can walk up the stairs to my room."

"I've already laid out a clean robe for you in the living room. If you can't bathe, you really need to change clothes."

"You are your mother's son," Mercilus replied, rising more steadily from the table.

He ambled into the living room while Barcelis made certain that his sisters were not present. Mercilus threw off his clothes without regard to anyone who might be present and donned the fresh ones. For the first time, he noticed his body odor.

Turning to Barcelis, he stated, "I'll bathe at the stadium before I return."

Retrieving the harness from the sofa, he pulled it on and made certain that the monster cannister was in place before ambling down the steps.

Barcelis watched from the window as his father climbed into the waiting carriage at the curb. When he turned back, he found his mother standing there. Her eyes were wet with tears, and the frown on her face nearly broke his heart.

"Mother, I'm sorry," he said. "If I could do something about him, I would, but he's too strong even in the condition he's in now."

"I know, son," she replied, "but I need to talk to you before the fair starts. That's only a couple of days away now. I calculate that he must have at least one more monster to make, perhaps two, or else he wouldn't be so driven to complete them."

Barcelis moved her to the sofa and sat down next to her. "Mother, I know there's something on your mind, and I believe it involves the fair. I know you don't want to go, and I don't blame you. I can't influence father's decision. He never listens to me."

"You talked him into changing clothes and to bathe," she replied. "That is at least something."

"Yes, but what is that next to all the other issues? I know that he loves you, but he won't express it. He carries around so much anger inside that it's eating him up. I know it's all because of the pressures introduced by creating bigger and better monsters, but that's all he wants to do."

Rosina dabbed at her tears with a kerchief and then smiled. "Barcelis, you're a wonderful son, and I know that you've done all you could, but there is one thing I want you to do."

"Gladly, Mother, I would be pleased to do anything you ask."

"Barcelis," she said slowly, "please sit with me at the fair. I know that you don't have any chores to do once it starts."

"Is that all, Mother?" he replied. "Of course, I'll sit with you. You have nothing to fear."

"Perhaps," she whispered. "There is one more thing. Promise me that if anything happens to me that you take good care of your sisters. They at least trust you."

"Mother, nothing is going to happen on first day besides the destruction of twenty or thirty magical monsters. Father is gruff and selfish, but he can do what he says he can do. Three days at the fair and it'll be over for another year."

Rosina took him into her arms and hugged him deeply. "I love you, son," she whispered.

Brena and her sisters listened to the exchange from the dining room, but they quietly ascended the stairs to Brena's bedroom. Brena sat on the bed while the others climbed on top of it with her.

"Mommy is sad," Gobie said. "She mustn't go to the fair, but we can't stop her."

"I have a bad feeling about it too," Brena said. "I hate this helpless feeling. We can only trust that Barcelis will bring her home safely, Gobie. There is no other choice."

"What about that spirit you mentioned at breakfast?" Shuma asked. "What is her name, Cassandra? Maybe she can help."

"I don't think I believe in spirits," Gobie said. "Father said there are no such things. Everyone says that."

"I wasn't sure until last night," Brena replied. "She promised that she would stay with me all night, and she did. I could still feel her next to me come morning, but when I told House to turn on the lights, no one was there. Her presence was so very real, though. She said that she might stay with me until after the fair. I hope she does."

"That's really weird," Shuma said. "Do you suppose that she'll visit with us too?"

"Oh, I do want to meet her!" Gobie cried. "Is she here now?"

Brena carefully glanced about and listened. Finally, she replied. "I don't think so. If she comes tonight, I'll ask her, though. Sorry, it's the best I can do."

Gobie walked across the bed and hugged her around the neck. "It's all right, Brena, if she doesn't want to talk to us too. You can tell us what she says, won't you?"

"Gobie, you're my sweet little sister," Brena replied, "and I love you dearly. You know I will, assuming that she does, of course."

Giggling, Shuma tackled her sisters and tickled them until everyone cried out in submission, but they found their mother waiting at the door with a smile on her face.

"Come downstairs, children. Allow House to make up the bed and clean the room. School is in session."

All three of them bounced off the bed and raced each other down the corridor to the stairwell and into the living room where they plopped excitedly onto the sofa.

Cassy had tuned into the children's conversation from her hiding place in Mercilus' beard while he journeyed to the stadium. Since the trip took at least thirty minutes, she had nothing else to do except to listen to the sorcerer's snores.

She wondered if she had done something she shouldn't have by speaking to Brena as she did, but she couldn't just do nothing. The children were too lovely for that. Now, however, the others wanted to talk to her too, but she couldn't decide if she should. Speaking to Brena as she did could be passed off simply as a stress related hallucination, but it would be different if all three children told the same story.

It was still on her mind while Mercilus' physician tended to the burn on his leg. She also watched while he activated the monster wizor. This was the first of the crocodilians. It had the appearance of a simple legless serpent in the beginning, but the legs appeared in only minutes and the general shape of a crocodilian only a little later. It was intimidating while growing, but it didn't take long to discover the cage and the fact that it couldn't escape. The growls and hisses became much more protracted and alarming to its captors. They all departed the caged beasts at that point.

"That's the worst one yet," Magus whispered as he and Butkus hurried across the arena to the sorcerers' private area. "Did you see that burn on Mercilus' leg before the physician healed it?"

"I wonder how Mercilus did that," he replied. "He didn't say anything to anyone about it."

"It just goes to show that even Mercilus can make a mistake,"

Magus said. "I noticed that it didn't improve his mood any. I'm wondering if we should leave here earlier than planned. He might try to take it out on us."

"Not before we're paid, Magus," Butkus said. "We'll need it to get to our destination. We may have to keep low for a year or more before he stops looking for us. I'm thinking that it was a mistake to kidnap his kids like that. If we let them go now, they'll go straight to him and spill all they know."

"We're over a barrel, for sure," Magus replied. "We still might have to bump them off before we go. I know they're kids, but they're powerful kids. We can't simply walk away and forget anything happened. Mercilus won't."

The pair soon fell silent and departed the arena in their carriage unaware that Jen sat invisibly in one of the seats behind them and that their captives watched them on Lenny's magic television.

Munge huffed and puffed up the stairs to the fourth floor of the apartment building and knocked on Lenny and Jenna's door. When she received no reply, she opened the door with her pass key. Finding the place remarkably clean and orderly, she wondered if the children were living here at all. She hadn't seen them come or go for several days. There were no personal items left lying about, and no one had called on them. Well, since they were paid up for several more days, she decided to leave it alone, but she would let it out again the moment their rent expired.

Lenny and Jenna appeared in the room the moment Munge closed and locked the door.

"Do you suppose we should let her know that we're still living here, Leonard?" Jenna asked. "She might call the police or whatever passes for them here."

"I doubt that," Lenny said. "She's too greedy. They might make her give up our advance rent or something. I don't know how that works here. Come on, we better return to the warehouse. I know that Jen would warn us if she discovers something we need to know, but we need to think about this without distraction. I'm working on a way we can get into this a little deeper. Maybe if we do escape, Magus and Butkus would have a conniption and spill their guts."

Jenna laughed. "Now what could they say that we don't already know, Leonard? They're scared to death of what Mercilus would do to them if he found out about us, but we both know that Mercilus wouldn't do anything. He knows his kids are alive and well at home."

"You have a point, Jenna," Lenny replied. "They're definitely terrified of Mercilus. I suppose that the most we can do is wait."

They vanished then and reappeared inside the warehouse where Lenny setup his wizard staff television. However, it wasn't long before he began to pace anxiously.

"What's the matter with you, Leonard?" Jenna asked. "I've never seen you so nervous."

"I'm going buggy, Jenna," he replied. "I'm really thinking about going to the stadium and capturing the wizors Mercilus used to create the monsters. Analyzing them would give me something to do."

"Are you serious, Leonard? What if we're caught?"

"We can leave before anyone knows we're there," he replied. "Since we've been there once, my wizard staff can take us to the low-level monster side in an instant. It would take only a few minutes to get the wizors. Besides, Jen can warn us in plenty of time if there's trouble."

"Well, it would give us something to do," Jenna agreed. "For once, I have to agree with you."

Smiling, Lenny grasped his wizard staff and held out his hand.

They vanished the instant she accepted it.

They appeared inside the caged area where they found the low powered monsters previously. There were more of them now.

"It looks like Mercilus isn't the only one making monsters," Lenny said. "He's been concentrating on the higher power ones, but his minions may be helping out with the lower power monsters. That makes sense."

Jenna edged up to the cage of a cute bearlike animal and smiled. "My, you're beautiful," she said. "I've never seen a bear with black and white stripes before. It looks like it's wearing a striped overcoat."

She had admired it for only moment before the beast became anxious and leapt at the cage. Magical sparks from the cage security flashed like fireworks, anxiously driving her back.

"It's an imposceros," Lenny laughed.

"It's a what?" Jenna cried. "I've never heard of such a thing."

"It's merely a name for something you don't have a name for,

Jenna, something to laugh about."

"Oh, I get it," Jenna laughed. "Sometimes I don't know whether you're serious or not."

"Don't take anything for granted here, Jenna. Remember, all of these animals were magically created to fight and die in the arena. It makes sense that they're vicious."

"You mean that we should laugh now at the absurdities and cry later when the monsters start fighting each other?"

"Something like that," Lenny agreed.

"Then let's get this over with," she whispered, anxiously sidling up to him.

Laughing, Lenny captured the residue aura from the bear first then continued on to the next cage until he had all of them. Walking through the great door into the next section, he easily captured the auras of the higher power animals there.

"That's that," Lenny said. "They must have the highest power monsters in the other half of the stadium. I really need to capture the aura of a crocodilian if Mercilus has created one. I might find a way to combat the ones in Duscany."

"Leonard, I'm scared," Jenna said. "Let's go now."

"This will take only a minute, Jenna. We can be in and out in a few seconds."

Appearing inside the entrance of the long corridor outside the cages, they were amazed by the monsters caged there. The troglodytes were already nearly full grown and eyed them with hateful curiosity. It was simple to take a snapshot of their auras.

The only crocodilian was probably no larger than a normal crocodile or alligator in Lenny's world, but it immediately went into a terrorizing frenzy by racing around the cage walls, spreading magical containment sparks everywhere. The growing troglodytes followed likewise, making an intimidating fuss.

Lenny quickly took the last snapshot of the crocodilian, but suddenly, they heard a number of excited voices approaching them. He touched Jenna and tried to transport them back to the warehouse, but nothing happened.

"What's the matter, great and mighty one?" Jenna asked giggling.

"The transport wizor doesn't work," Lenny said. He pushed her into the shadow of a massive roof support and whispered. "This is no joke, Jenna. I think Mercilus built the monster containment wizor into this corridor as a precaution. It's much stronger than the one on the warehouse. There's no time to figure it out."

"I wonder what set the trogs off," Magus said. "We're the only ones in here."

"You've got me," Butkus replied. "Maybe it's because of the crocodilian. We've never had one before. Look, it's going crazy. Smells bad too."

The crocodilian clung to the cage door and hissed at them. A thin white stream of mist shot straight for them. Only a little reached them, but then they cried out in alarm and rubbed and scratched at every spot the mist touched.

"It's some sort of poison!" Butkus cried, stepping back almost into the children's hiding place. "It hurts like hell."

"Yeah," Magus agreed. "God, it's turning my skin to stone. Run, Butkus! We have to get out of here now!"

The pair retreated down the tunnel and into the open arena.

"What are we going to do, Leonard?" Jenna whispered. "That thing is filling the corridor with that awful stuff. We can't get out of here."

Although the white mist had not reached them as yet, the crocodilian's anxious behavior was generating enough airflow to spread it through the corridor.

Lenny, held up his wizard staff to capture the aura from the mist and began to analyze it. "This is really nasty stuff, nineth level just like the crocodilian. We don't have time to sort it out."

"Oh, Jen, where are you?" Jenna tittered.

"Right here," Jen replied. "What can I do for you?"

"Jen, that mist is touching you!" Jenna said. "It'll turn you to stone."

"Actually, I can evade it," Jen replied with a smile. "Do you want me to dispel it for you?"

"Oh, Jen, of course, we do!" Jenna cried. "It's death on contact."

Jen merely giggled and began to rotate sideways like a cartwheel, creating a reverse wind that drove the mist back toward the cages. The troglodytes backed away apparently aware of the danger. Even the crocodilian leapt down from the metal door and retreated to the rear of the cage.

The fatal mist soon dissipated, allowing Lenny and Jenna to retreat down the corridor until they escaped the containment effects that trapped the monsters.

"Thanks, Jen," Lenny said. "You deserve a kiss for that one."

"Kiss away," Jen said, puckering up.

Jenna puckered and enjoyed the kiss just as much when they connected. "Thank you, Leonard," she said.

"Oh, I keep forgetting that you two are like the same person," he said. "Now let's get out of here."

CHAPTER 14

BRENA

Luckily Mercilus' physician had not departed the stadium as yet. Examining the blistered skin nodules on Magus and Butkus, he shook his head.

"I haven't seen the like," he said. "These skin nodules appear to be stone. Brontis, come over here and look at this."

Brontis had just dressed after taking a shower and was listening with interest to the dialog. "What caused that, Magus?" he asked. I haven't seen anything like it before."

"It's the croc," Magus replied. "We went to check on why it was making a fuss, but then it spat some sort of white stuff at us."

"Well, the solidifying process has ceased," the physician said. "The most I can do is clean away the stone nodules and apply a general healing wizor. You'll be fine in short order. Brontis, has the night shift arrived yet?"

"They'll be here anytime," he replied. "I think I should tell them to avoid the croc cage until Mercilus has advised us on what to do."

"I was about to suggest that. Now sit still, Magus. I'm not done with this."

The physician scrubbed away the nodules with a small gauze

dipped in ointment and then applied the healing agent. He soon repeated the process with Butkus. Both of them sat in misery until the physician finished, but the healing agent soon ameliorated the pain and healed the damaged skin.

"Thanks," Butkus said. "I've made up my mind that it doesn't matter how much that crocodilian acts up, I'm not going to investigate, too dangerous."

Magus made it clear that he was of the same mind, but the physician didn't disagree with them. He simply packed up his bag and left the stadium.

"I hope that Mercilus knows about that mist stuff," Butkus said. "Enough of it is clearly lethal, and that croc is still a baby."

"You can bet that he does," Magus replied. "Nothing he creates is accidental. I just hope he can take care of it himself during the fair. I'm certainly not chancing it. The least he could have done was to warn us about it."

"Considering how he's been treating us," Butkus replied, "maybe he did it on purpose. He clearly hates us."

"All the more reason to get out of here the moment we can," his partner replied. "I know some of the others grumble about the pay, but they haven't expressed a commitment to leave. Otherwise, I'd bring them in on the deal. Right now, the most we can do is sit and wait."

"Well, the opening ceremonies of the fair will start the day after tomorrow," Butkus said. "Supposedly all of the monsters will be ready by the time they're needed. The level nine monsters are supposed to be damn near invincible. This is sheer madness. If something happens to Mercilus, we're all doomed."

"If that happens," Magus replied, "I'm the first one out of here. It doesn't matter if Mercilus is still alive or not. He's on his own."

"I'll be right behind you, Magus. Nothing will hold me back either."

Lenny conjured a sofa from his wizard staff and fell heavily into it. Jenna fell with him and rested her head on his shoulder.

"Next time you have a great idea, Leonard," she said, "let's ignore it. I'm fine staying right here, death sentence or not."

"I'm inclined to agree with you, Jenna," he replied, "but we're here for a reason."

Holding up his wizard staff he projected the crocodilian aura up before them and then the aura of the milky mist. Spreading them out so they could analyze them, Lenny came to a single conclusion.

"They're identical!" he shouted. "How can that be?"

"How can they be identical?" Jenna replied.

Lenny thought about it for a moment before he came up with a possible option.

"I think it's because they're made from the same magic. Just touching the crocodilian mist will freeze anyone into stone. That's its magic. I'm sure that Mercilus created it this way, but why? All of these monsters are for showmanship. Why make a monster that's lethal to touch if he's not going to demonstrate it?"

Jenna's mouth dropped open in horror. "That's what he's going to do, Leonard. That thing will turn another monster into stone to increase terror and make people think it's invincible. Maybe it'll be one of the troglodytes."

"Or a person!" Lenny cried. "Maybe our friends, Magus and Butkus. They clearly aren't getting along."

"Oh my," she said, "I wouldn't wish that on my worst enemies. Clearly though, those two murderers are. I guess I wouldn't mourn them too much."

"Yes, well, it's still speculation," Lenny said, "but I'll bet those two are thinking the same thing right now. They're next. I think we need to prepare for them to show up if they intend to kill us. I'll prevent that, of course, so don't worry."

"I'm not helpless, Leonard. I can defend myself just fine, thank you."

"Must I remind you of how we were bagged and brought here, Jenna? It's best if you warn Jen to keep an eye on us too. She may be the deciding factor who saves us both."

Jenna sighed and relaxed on the sofa. "You're right, of course. You're always right."

"Don't sell yourself short, Jenna. You've had your share of good ideas, and I've listened to all of them. The fair will start in a couple of days, and we have to be prepared for it and the bad guys. Whatever goes wrong, it'll happen quite soon."

Mercilus stumbled up the stairs to his apartment and sat down at the table to eat furiously as before while Barcelis had his share. When he finished, he made it to the sofa and fell asleep the moment he stretched out on it.

Exhausted, Barcelis retired to his bedroom, but this time he kept a close eye out for any shadows he didn't understand that might show up while he wrote in his diary. None did but only because Cassy realized her mistake and stayed only until he finished.

She crawled into bed with Brena as she promised. Brena immediately felt her form next to her and said, "I'm glad you came back, Cassandra. I told my sisters about you. I hope you're not mad."

"I could never be mad at any of you, Brena. I'm here because I promised that I would return. As for Gobie and Shuma, I can't reveal myself to them like I do to you. It's best that only you know for certain that I exist for now anyway. I'm sorry, but I've already told you everything I want you to know. I don't know what else to say."

"I have lots of questions, Cassandra," Brena replied. "For instance, were you once a for real person?"

"I am still a for real person, Brena, just not here. I'm forbitten to tell you about my world."

"You're not just a spirit?" Brena replied, astonished. "That makes a big difference. I had no idea."

"My world is a someday world, Brena. I know that doesn't make much sense, but it's as close to the truth as I can say."

"You mean someday as in the future, Cassandra? That someday?"

"Yes, that someday but in a different world altogether. If you wish, I'll show you me as I really am but only for a moment. I don't want to alarm you."

"Oh, yes, please, I want to know what you look like. I so much want you to be real."

"Very well, but don't tell anyone other than your sisters. Only they will know if you're telling the truth. No one else will understand."

"Oh, please show me, Cassandra!" Brena cried.

Cassy carefully adjusted her facial features so that Brena would not recognize her as being Mata Hari in her future five years from now and stood next to the bed, her whelf wings fully extended and shining in starlight. She wore a thin white gown that covered her torso.

"You're a fairy of some kind, a whelf? I've read about those."

"In this world, yes, but in my future world I'm much like you are, Brena. I'm telling you this because I want you to trust that I've told you the truth about your future and the futures of your siblings. There will be much to fear, but you will prevail if you're brave. Take care of your sisters like a mother because that duty will fall on you. Barcelis is naïve, but he'll find his proper way too. Trust him."

"Oh, Cassandra, this is all so strange, but I do believe you," Brena replied. "Thank you for caring about me."

Suddenly the lights switched on, and Gobie and Shuma stood at the open door.

"We heard talking in here," Shuma said. "What's this all about?"

"Cassandra is here standing beside the bed!" Brena cried.

Her sisters seemed confused as they approached.

"No one is there, Brena," Shuma said, anxiously glancing about.

"Really, she's still there. I can see her as plain as day. She's some sort of whelf with wings and everything. You must believe me."

"I told you that they can't see me or hear me, Brena, but I'll help them believe that you are telling the truth."

Gobie cautiously wandered toward Cassy, sweeping a hand from side to side. Cassie took her hand when she approached close enough. "I believe you, Brena!" she cried. "She's holding my hand. I don't see her, but I can feel her touch."

Curious, Shuma approached Gobie and held out her hand. Cassy took it and squeezed briefly.

"I feel her hand too, Brena! She is real."

"Oh, Cassandra, I wish they could see and talk to you as I do, but I understand why not. Believe me, I didn't set this up for them to catch you unaware."

"I know, Brena," Cassy replied. "This is the only way I can reassure them right now because they look up to you, the eldest. They must believe in you when the time comes."

"Cassandra, I don't know why you trust me so much," Brena said, "but I appreciate it." Turning to her sisters, she added, "She said that I must take care of you, and you must trust that I'm telling you the truth."

"We know you are," Shuma agreed, but she held onto Cassy's hand as if it were a life savior. Gobie did the same, but they both cried for her to return when she released their hands.

"I must go for now, Brena," Cassy said. "I may return tonight for a time, but if not then tomorrow night, but I can't promise that. You must get your rest. Whatever you do, don't tell anyone about me.

They won't believe you anyway."

"Oh, please don't go, Cassandra," Brena pleaded. Cassy faded out of sight, but She remained close while Brena explained to her sisters what Cassy had said.

Satisfied, Cassy threaded herself through the ether and into the laboratory located deep beneath the apartment below to stand beside the queen whelf's prison.

"Why have you come, queen of the future whelfs?" she asked. "I can give you no information that you don't already know."

"I know, but I wanted to see you one last time. The fair will commence the day after tomorrow and I'll be very busy. I am so sorry that I can't free you, but I cannot change your future."

"My future is the same no matter what you do, Cassandra. I appreciate your concern, but when it's my time, I'll become a neophyte reborn in the fen. The whelfs will choose a new queen, and the cycle will continue as always. That is our curse and yours should you choose it. Go now. I do not require your company or sympathy. I'm a queen whelf and will die like one."

Since the captive queen retreated deeply within her prison and did not return, Cassy had no choice except to depart. As a whelf, she required no rest or sustenance, but she was part human too.

She appeared next in the warehouse to stand over Lenny while he slept. Taking the crumpled piece of parchment she found on the bed, she read the short list and smiled. He was obviously trying to make sense of the wizor list prior to falling asleep.

Suddenly, he awoke and sat up. "I always know when you're close, Cassy. You know that."

"Of course, but I had to look in on you and Jenna. I like your little setup here. I take it that these beds are your handiwork."

"I made my bed, and Jenna made hers," he replied. "That parchment you're holding, Cassy, can you make heads or tails of it? It's some sort of wizor. Leanne Mellot left it inside of a walnut charm. It has to be important. I was studying it to see if it's something that can point to her whereabouts. That's what got us into this mess if you recall."

"Oh yes, the bride of the Blaine," she replied. "It's sweet that he still loves her and wants to find her, but have you considered that she might be dead?"

"Do you believe she is, Cassy?"

"No, but I have to look at it realistically. We have our hands full right now, so I don't see any point in pursuing her until we return to Duscany. That's where the trail goes cold."

"I still think she's hiding out in the Bugo alternate world somewhere, but what if she went to our world? I'm not sure of what to think."

Cassy sat down on the edge of the bed and looked him in the eyes. "If she's alive in our world, we have absolutely no clue as to her identity and how to find her. To go to our world, she would have had a way to do it, but there is no evidence for that. Personally, I think it's quite unlikely. She is adept with Bugoward wood and stone magic, which suggests that she and her family were born in either the Bugoward alternate world or Duscany."

"I'm adept," Lenny countered, "and I haven't any ancestors who lived there. I'm not sure that I agree with your reasoning."

"It's a valid point," she said, "but you had a jumpstart when you absorbed some of Scapita's magic. Remember that you had to give our parents the same jumpstart before they could do magic in Duscany, and they're still not great at it."

"You're right, of course," Lenny agreed, "but it's only a theory anyway. We haven't explored her background in the alternate Bugo world."

"Then we still have some footwork to do once we return to Duscany, but first we have to find a way to destroy the crocodilians."

"I think I have a start," Lenny replied. Retrieving his wizard staff, he projected the crocodilian aura in the air and spread it out, revealing each of the nine levels. "This is the nineth level wizor that created them. We also found out that they emit a protective mist when riled, which freezes anything living into stone. The mist has an identical aura about it. That suggests that they're both integral to the whole. I just haven't unraveled the relationship yet."

"You have been busy, Lenny," she replied. "You may have something there, but you'll have to consult with Scapita on that matter. I don't know anything about wizor making. Magic is just magic to me, the way of the whelfs. I think it'll take both of us to figure this one out. I know that Jenna is quite good with wizors. She will be invaluable as well."

"Too bad we can't get Mercilus to tell us," Lenny said. "He obviously knows how to destroy the crocs. I'll try to get as close to the action as I can come fair day to see if I can capture the wizor he uses."

"That's astute of you, Lenny," she replied. "Now that you mentioned it, I'll watch for it too. We didn't see how he managed it last time we were here, but we weren't exactly looking for it then, and you've learned how to capture the wizors that created them. I think we can do this if we're smart enough," she confessed.

Jenna suddenly moved and opened her sleepy eyes. Sitting up, she said, "Oh, Cassandra, you're here. Anything happen that I should know about?"

"We've just been discussing Mercilus' monsters," she replied. "It won't be easy to defeat them. Now it's best if you two get some sleep. We don't know what tomorrow will bring, all right?"

"Give me a hug before you go, Cassandra," Jenna said, holding out her arms.

Cassy gladly complied, wished them goodnight and vanished into the ether.

"She's so perfect at that," Jenna said.

She soon closed her eyes and slept.

Lenny thought about monster wizors for a short time before doing the same.

CHAPTER 15

SUM OF FEARS

Brena and her sisters cautiously descended the stairs but only after Mercilus and Barcelis had departed for the day. Since this was the last monster creation before the fair, they left together for the stadium.

She watched them climb aboard the carriage and vanish down the street before she said anything. Finally, she anxiously began to pace the living room floor while disparate thoughts raced through her head.

"We've got to get mother out of here!" Brena shouted. "House is nothing but a cage to keep us here!"

She tried to open the door to the down stairwell, but it didn't budge. She knew that it wouldn't open although she hadn't tried it until now. Then she angrily kicked the panel and fell on the floor holding her foot in pain, and her skirt tangled around her waist.

Rising to her feet after the pain relented, she tried something else. She and Shuma dragged a dining room chair into the living room and together hurled it against the glass window, but the chair crashed back to the floor with a broken leg without harming the window.

"Well, we were told that House was inescapable," Shuma said, disappointed that the window didn't at least crack.

Glancing down at the chair, she was astonished to see the broken leg move slowly back into place. The crack in the wood sealed without a blemish.

"It's eerie when that happens," Brena replied. "There has to be something we can do."

"What are you three up to?" Rosina asked. "I heard the noise from upstairs." Spying the chair on the floor, she guessed half the truth. "Children, I understand your frustration about not being able to leave the apartment, but we must respect your father's wishes. There's nothing out there for you to see."

"It's not that," Brena replied. "Mother, we know that you expect something bad to happen at the fair this year. We just want to protect you. Surely there's a secret way out of this prison. Isn't there, mother?"

Rosina hugged the girls together. Tears rolled uninhibited down her cheeks. "I'm afraid not, my beautiful children. I'm as much a prisoner here as you are. House will do everything for us within reason, but it'll never let us leave without Mercilus' permission."

"What about Barcelis?" Brena asked. "He's allowed to come and go on his own. Maybe he can help us leave. We can find someplace to hide until the fair is over, and then we can come home."

"Listen, girls, Barcelis is a prisoner too. He can't do anything to help us leave. I think he would leave on his own if it weren't for us being stuck here. He loves us too much. You just have to accept the fact that we can't go without your father's permission. He believes he's keeping us safe, and we have to respect that. Now hurry up and get your breakfast. School will be in session as soon as you're done."

"Mother," Shuma replied, "I don't feel like having school today. I'm worried, and well, we never have school during the fair anyway. Couldn't we just have today off?"

Rosina glanced at the other children who seemed to be of like mind. "Very well, girls, but don't get into any more trouble. I'm working on a project of my own, and I must finish it for tomorrow."

"Are you making another dress for the fair with House's help?" Brena asked. "You do that every year."

"Yes, but it's a special dress. Now no more questions. Get your breakfast. I'll be down when I'm finished." She lifted the chair from the floor and returned it to the dining room before climbing the stairs.

The children hung their heads and obeyed, but they sat silently at the table without ordering anything.

"I'm hungry," Gobie said. "Aren't we going to eat anything?"

"Oh, we might as well," Brena replied, "even though my appetite is completely ruined."

"House, feed us!" Gobie cried. "I want my usual."

"Same here!" Shuma cried, but Brena soon relented and asked for breakfast too.

⸻

Assisted by his walking staff, Mercilus ambled hunched over into the stadium passageway, a clear signal that he had not recovered from the last wizor making session the night before.

Barcelis walked beside him, ready to offer assistance, if necessary, but Magus and Butkus stayed well enough behind as they approached the troglodyte cages. Mercilus was quick to notice.

"What are you cowards waiting for?" he cried. "The faster we activate this wizor the faster it'll grow to maturity. The fair starts tomorrow and on time."

"We're not cowards," Magus hazarded. Although reluctant to disagree, the crocodilian cage was just beyond the troglodytes who fussed as they passed. "It's just that the croc spat something at us last time that turned anything made of flesh to stone. You didn't tell us that would happen."

Mercilus suddenly turned to face them. "You're still cowards, but I must have missed something when formulating the wizor. Well, now that I know it, we'll just have to deal with it."

The troglodytes grew bolder as they passed, but Mercilus ignored them while Magus and Butkus cringed against the far wall.

Mercilus paused in front of the active crocodilian cage and admired the creature curled up there. Already half grown, it was twenty feet long and three feet tall at the shoulders. It had long legs and feet that resembled human hands. It gazed back with malevolent eyes, but Mercilus met them without flinching. Nodding, he moved on to the cage where Magus and Butkus opened the door of the last empty cage and stood behind it.

Mercilus paused at the door, laughed at their cowardice and then entered. Placing the cannister on the floor, he allowed Barcelis to pull the opener cord and tugged him back out of the cage.

Magus and Butkus were quick to push the heavy door closed, but they leapt back when the crocodilian in the next cage thrashed at the bars and swept a long tail about like a whip. Every contact with the cage produced a barrage of sparks that threatened contact with exposed skin.

Magus and Butkus pressed against the far wall and raced out of the tunnel, but if they had been more diligent in their jobs, they would have noticed that the locking bar had not fallen completely into place.

Chuckling, Mercilus held up a hand and made a circular motion that created a shield to protect him and his son. They cheerfully strolled past the shrieking troglodytes and out of the passageway into the open arena. Pausing, he glanced up at the warm sky and breathed the open air.

"That's the last one," Mercilus said, "but, of course, you knew that, Barcelis. You've been a wonderful help. I have every expectation of you gaining your full powers as a sorcerer one day. You already know the routine of wizor making. Power will come with mastery."

"Father," Barcelis said slowly, "I have to talk to you. Mother really is frightened to come to the fair. She really thinks something bad will happen. Even the girls are afraid that they'll lose their mother. They're beside themselves with anxiety. You really should reconsider forcing her to attend."

"Nonsense, Barcelis," Mercilus laughed. "What is there to fear when I'm in full control of the monsters? I'm feeling my old pep returning even now. I'll be fully recovered by opening day. We start out with small monsters just to make certain that I have enough energy by the third day to handle the level nine monsters. We'll pair them off with each other anyway to take the sass out of them before we destroy them. It's all in the preparations. I thought that you had learned that by now."

"Of course, but mother and my sisters don't know that. Not everyone loves your monsters, father. I thought that you understood that."

"Barcelis, you're a grown man. Showmanship is just that. I understand that not everyone enjoys the same show, but that doesn't matter. Those who do pay good money to participate in it for the thrill of the kill. I'm giving them that. Some enjoy the bloodletting, others the pageantry of the fair, but together they produce an incomparable experience. Your mother will come around once the show starts, and your sisters will stop fussing when it's all over. Now let's make an overall inspection of the monsters to see if we've made the proper precautions. I need the exercise anyway, and we've both been cooped up in the laboratory far too long. My, the sun feels good, doesn't it son?" He faced it with his eyes closed and breathed in the fresh air.

Barcelis nodded. Perhaps Mercilus was right. There really wasn't anything to fear with his father in charge. There had never been an accident at the fair in all of the years Mercilus had staged it. True, not everyone approved of the monster games, but no citizen was forced to attend them, except for mother and himself. Mercilus expected him to be there supporting him as much as he did mother. He decided that the lack of choice was what he objected to. Mother had no choice in the matter anymore than he did. When his sisters came of age, would they?

Lenny and Jenna concentrated on the projection of the crocodilian's wizor aura as they sat on the sofa that he had conjured from his wizard staff. They spread out the levels to examine each one to learn all the secrets hiding there.

"It's plain," Lenny said, "that the first level is the seed that begins the monster forming process. Most of the parameters of appearance and behavior are there, but level two enhances them and three encourages the growing process. The other levels continue that process until the creature is fully formed in level eight. Level nine simply encapsulates all the levels together into a cohesive whole. I still don't understand where all of that power comes from, though."

"Have you forgotten already, Leonard?" Jenna said. "Cassandra said that Mercilus is holding the whelf queen of this time in captivity. The power comes from the fen."

"I haven't forgotten, Jenna. It's just that I haven't identified any part of this wizor that calls for it. Maybe that's what level nine does. It must perform more than just one function. I thought that if I could turn off the power, I could reverse the process. The monster would simply evaporate as it grew weaker."

"It's a nice theory," Jenna replied, "but I doubt if it's that easy. Those crocodilians have been sleeping in the Whelf Fen for a millennium, and they haven't grown any since creation."

"True, but they gained their power from the magic found in the Whelf Fen. The wizor stipulates how the monster grows to maturity and when to stop, presumably when it can't absorb more energy. It's also the maximum level that Mercilus can control. Otherwise, the monster would keep on growing without limit, which creates a man-thrall. You would have to say goodbye to Duscany at that point because nothing could stop it, not even the Queen of the Whelfs without becoming a man-thrall herself."

"Are you saying that this is hopeless, Leonard?" Jenna asked. "I mean, if there's no way we can destroy those beasts, Duscany is toast anyway. Maybe the crocs have already destroyed it. Oh, wow, I hadn't thought of that until now. Maybe we're just wasting our time."

"Cassy!" Lenny cried. "Did you hear what Jenna just said? We're in big trouble."

Cassy slowly formed into the ghost of herself, but she didn't appear to be alarmed.

"Yes, I did, but there's no reason to worry right now," she said. "We'll return at the exact moment we left Duscany. Time is a funny thing. We're here and not here. All of this is how the Power of the Fen recorded it. It's real and not real. I don't know how else to explain it."

"You're talking time paradox again, aren't you, Cassy?" Lenny said.

"Of course, but I can't just fast forward to when the problem became a problem. We're forced to observe it as it happened. Otherwise, we probably could have skipped a few days in retrospect, but we would have chanced missing a critical detail. Tomorrow is the first day of the fair, but we don't know if the crocs escaped on that day, the second or even the third. We can't stop that from happening or any of the events following it. We can only interact in a small way that doesn't change anything. I just wanted you both to know that."

Lenny threw up his hands and nervously paced for a moment before he sat down again. "Well, I sort of understood it when you said that we had to discover how the crocs got loose and became frozen in the Whelf Fen. That's the real mystery here. I guess, I'm just a little impatient to get it over with."

"You don't have to apologize," Cassy said. "I'm just as guilty of it myself. I became attached to Mercilus' children when I was here last time, and I didn't get over it. I suppose that I shouldn't have made contact with them, but I did."

"Oh, Cassy, you didn't!" Lenny cried. "What if they remember you when we return five years from now?"

"Don't worry, I changed my appearance enough to prevent that from happening, but the time paradox may have prevented it anyway. Like I said, none of this is real."

"It sure feels real enough to me," Jenna said. "We weren't here when all of this happened before, but Magus and Butkus still kidnapped us. Why would they do that if this isn't real?"

"The Power of the Fen is helping us to interact with this world," Cassy replied. "You do have a point, but no paradox has a straight forward answer. In this case, I wish it did. We would all be much happier."

Lenny witnessed the hurt in her eyes. He understood that she had fallen in love with Barcelis when they were here before, but that worried him. "Cassy, you didn't meet with Barcelis, did you? That would be a really bad mistake. Mercilus could find out about us."

"No, but I did talk to Brena. She's only ten now, but she's smart, and I wanted to prepare her for taking the initiative to care for her sisters."

"What for, Cassy?" Lenny asked. "What about the time paradox? We don't know if it would help her relate to what really happened in her own time or not."

"Again, I can't answer," Cassy smiled, "but I had to try. Sometime over the next three days, the girls will lose their mother in a horrible accident. Brena knows it. Rosina is a clairvoyant, Lenny, a strong one. That means that she already knew that she would die when she went to the arena. I think that she expressed her reservations to her children, even Mercilus, but he didn't listen. I also discovered that Barcelis had the courage to confront his father today and explain, but he still didn't listen. As you know, he's my age in this timeframe, but at least that won't be on his conscience when he loses her."

Lenny grinned and clapped his hands. "Cassy, you're just an old smoothy. You still care for him, don't you?"

"Of course, but I know that it's an impossible dream, so don't worry about me, Lenny. I'm not going to skip town or time or anything and come back. Once we leave here, we're gone. This timeframe will no longer exist for us."

"Cassy, I know you," he replied. "Regret is already showing on your face. If you could stay with him, you would. After all, there is still five years before he meets and marries Arlie. Do you regret setting that up too, or didn't it happen because of the time paradox thing?"

Cassy chuckled and blushed, detectable even as a ghost figure. "Well, I don't know that either. I did check his ancestry registration in the archives from that time. He did marry her and had several children who have descendants living today in Duscany. So yes, I think that what we're experiencing is real to a point, but doubt will always stand in the way."

Lenny became thoughtful. "To tell you the truth, I checked the archives too. I discovered that all of our adventures in Eskeling are recorded there. We're even mentioned by name by King Gumber, who was the last king of Eskeling and the first of Duscany. I really think that all of this is real, time paradox or not. That's why you shouldn't have contacted Mercilus' children. We don't know how it'll influence the past or even the future. Something may have changed once we've returned home."

"Lenny, you watch too many Sci-Fi and fantasy movies," Cassy replied. "We've been very careful. I doubt if anything we've done here will change the future in the slightest way. I doubt if being kidnapped by Magus and Butkus has changed anything."

"I really hope you're right, Cassy," Lenny breathed. "If someone dies in the arena during the fair because of our interference, I think it would. We've interacted with Magus and Butkus because they think we're Mercilus' kids. They were already suspicious and paranoid of him, but our presence must have changed that somehow, probably for the worse. No, Cassy, all of this stinks, and I really think that we've changed something we shouldn't have."

Tears formed in Cassy's eyes. "We have no choice except to wait and see," she replied, unhappily fading away.

CHAPTER 16

FIRST DAY AT THE FAIR

Rosina sat anxiously on the living room sofa dressed in a black, ankle length gown trimmed with gold. A few rose-colored sequins formed a stylized rose on the front of her left shoulder strap. She casually sat down and crossed her legs.

"The dress is beautiful, Mother," Shuma said, sitting beside her, "but I've never seen you wear anything so plain. You said that you were making a special dress for the fair."

"It's perfect for this one, dear Shuma," she replied through a coy smile.

Her sisters sat on the sofa with them, but from their expressions, they were just as curious.

"I want you all to be good while I'm gone," Rosina said. "Brena, you are the eldest and in charge. Shuma, Gobie, don't give her any grief, all right?"

"We promise," Shuma said.

Rosina wondered why they all seemed so subdued, but they understood that she had no desire to attend the fair.

"You can tell us all about it when you return," Brena said. "We've never been outside of this apartment, so anything you say will be interesting."

Unable to hold herself back, Gobie climbed up onto Rosina's lap, crying. "I love you mother. Please come back to us."

"My little one, what makes you think that I won't?" she replied. "Is that how all of you feel?"

"We know that you do, mother," Brena explained. "You can't hide it from us."

"I suppose not," she replied, "but I want all of you to understand one thing. I love you all, and I will return if at all possible. Barcelis will be here soon to take me to the fair. Whatever you do, don't show him the same faces I see here. He's your brother, and he loves you very much, all right?"

"We understand, mother," Brena replied, attempting to put on a cheerful face. Touching Gobie's forehead with a forefinger, she added, "Don't we, Gobie?"

Gobie wiped away her tears with the back of her hand and tried to smile bravely, but even she knew that she had failed.

Rosina tried to be optimistic as she sat next to Barcelis on the way to the arena, but she eventually fell silent, and tears came to her eyes.

"I promised to stay with you, Mother," Barcelis finally said. "I'll keep my promise. There's no reason to worry."

When she refused to reply, he gave up, but the arena was now in sight. The driver dropped them off at the staff entrance and moved on.

She anxiously grasped his arm and squeezed, but she followed him past the guard station, the gate and down a corridor to the staging area.

"Wait here, Mother," Barcelis said. "I want to find out if father is here. I'll be right back."

She stared at his back as he departed, but then she was startled by a familiar voice.

"Rosina," Brontis said, taking her hand, "Mercilus said that you would be here."

Brontis was a tall, broad-shouldered man with dark complexion and laughing eyes who was a few years shy of her own age.

"Hello, Brontis," she replied, wiping a tear from her eyes with a kerchief. "Sorry, I got some dust in my eyes."

"There is plenty of it here," Brontis agreed, "but I know why you've reluctantly come. Barcelis has expressed that fact to me several times. I'm sorry that Mercilus forced you to come. I want you to know that I'll be in the VIP box today, and I'll keep watch for you. I don't perform until last day. Mercilus wants me fresh to meet the level nine monsters."

"Level nine, I had no idea that they would be so strong," Rosina said.

"Then you know what that means."

"Of course," Rosina replied, "it comes with being a sorcerer's wife."

"Very well, I just thought I'd offer you my support, Rosina," Brontis said. "Enjoy the show."

Rosina took his hand and momentarily pressed her left check to his. "Thank you, Brontis, you're a good friend."

"Mother," Barcelis said, joining her as Brontis walked away, "I told father that you're here. He wants me to take you up to the VIP box."

Mercilus stepped out of the shadows, having witnessed the affection between Brontis and Rosina. Scowling, he followed Brontis into the staging area and slapped him hard on the back.

Brontis whirled about to face his attacker, but then he smiled and asked, "Mercilus, why did you strike me?"

Mercilus took him by the shoulder and pushed him toward the great door at the end of the staging area. Pulling the cable that set the gears to open the door, he escorted Brontis inside, and closed the door again.

"I saw your touching little meeting with my wife, Brontis. Apparently, you've never learned to respect another man's property."

"I meant no disrespect, Mercilus," he replied. "I merely offered her my support during a trying time. What's wrong with that?"

Mercilus glanced at an empty cage twenty feet cubed and opened the door. "This is what's wrong, Brontis!" he cried, taking him by the back of the neck.

In agony, Brontis tried to scream as the pain wizor took effect, but he could not. He couldn't resist as Mercilus guided him into the cage and closed the door. Mercilus activated the containment wizor to the cage and stood there glaring at him for a long moment before opening a large cabinet attached to the wall. Taking a leather canister from it, he returned to the cage and smiled at Brontis.

"I keep these for times like this, Brontis. Have you ever considered what it would be like to fight in the arena from the perspective of the monster?"

"No, Mercilus, you wouldn't!" Brontis cried. "I've been loyal to you all of these years."

"Have you, Brontis? I've heard that you've complained about not being paid enough."

Mercilus chuckled sardonically and pulled the string that removed the waxed seal of the canister and tossed it into the cage with Brontis.

Brontis recognized the wizor immediately for what it was and backed away, but there was nowhere to go. Merely touching the cage wall sent him into agony. He breathed in the curling mist from the wizor and choked until he fell to the floor from dizziness.

"I would kill you if I could, Mercilus," he whispered hoarsely.

However, he began to change. His body grew longer and thicker. Scintillating reptilian scales replaced his clothing. A tail coiled about his body. Soon the serpent could not avoid the shock from the containment wizor and collapsed unconscious onto the cage floor.

Barcelis assisted his mother up a series of steps that led into the stands to a reserved box overlooking the open arena, only fifty feet above the ground. Several hundred people had already taken their seats with more arriving. Glancing about she realized that the stadium was already nearly full including the VIP box five rows deep. Rosina sat down next to a young woman she didn't know. Barcelis sat reassuringly next to her and held her hand. She squeezed so hard that he flinched, but he didn't complain.

The young woman sitting next to Rosina with Cassy's face glanced at them and smiled, but she turned her attention back to the arena.

Costumed actors soon ran into the arena, waving banners and pretended to chase and slay costumed monsters. Thousands of fans waved their arms, stomped their feet and shouted a cacophony of excited chants.

Barcelis leaned close to Rosina and whispered. "It'll start soon. Father likes to let them celebrate with the parade for a while first. He says it gives them a sense of participation. It's an illusion, of course."

She closed her eyes and trembled. Extracting a kerchief from her purse, she dabbed at the tears in the corners of her eyes.

"I have to speak with father for a moment, Mother," Barcelis said, returning her hand. "I'll be back before it starts."

She wanted to shout after him to return, but she didn't want to give the others the impression that she was nothing but a hysterical woman. Instead, she placed her hands in her lap and waited as calmly as she could.

"They say that the show is a horrible spectacle," the young woman said, "lots of blood and excitement. I see that you don't share in it."

Rosina was startled to hear the young woman speaking to her, but she smiled and replied. "I'm the wife of Mercilus. I have no choice except to share in it if you please."

"I know who you are, Rosina," Cassy said. "For the record, I don't share much faith in it myself. It pleases me to sit next to someone who feels similarly. Does that amuse you?"

Rosina looked at her more carefully. "How do you know me, Mistress? I don't recognize you at all."

"We've never formally met, but I know you by reputation. You have a son and three lovely daughters. Am I right?"

"Of course, but I'm so confused now. We've never met, but you've chosen to converse with me. Why is that?"

"I just thought that I should," Cassy replied. "I can see that you're quite distraught. You may want to hold my hand as well during the show. I won't mind."

"I don't know," Rosina said, but now that she looked, she realized that this woman couldn't be any older than her son. No doubt, she was frightened too. "Is this your first time here, Mistress? I'm sorry, but I don't know your name."

"Call me Mata, Rosina. We probably won't meet again, but at least I'm pleased to meet you this first time."

Rosina glanced about for Brontis, but he was not present. "I thought Brontis would be here," she said. "Do you know him? I think you're sitting in his seat."

"We've met, Rosina. I'm sorry, but he won't be attending the games today."

Cassy didn't know what else to say. She couldn't explain that she had witnessed Mercilus transform Brontis into an ophidious monster while she hid in Mercilus' beard.

Barcelis hurried down the stairwell to the sorcerers waiting lounge, but not finding Mercilus there, he continued into the staging room where the sorcerers prepared for the show. Mercilus was dressed in his black robe held together by a red sash. His formidable whip was coiled in his hands. The other sorcerers seemed to be just as prepared, but they were obviously waiting for the celebrating in the stands to subside.

"Father," Barcelis pleaded, "you must allow me to take mother home. She's a nervous wreck. It's cruel to subject her to this kind of entertainment."

Mercilus, however, was as hard and adamant as before. Unyielding, he replied, "She'll calm down when she realizes that I'm in full control of the show. Now sit with her and offer your reassurance. She trusts you. She's here because the other sorcerers expect her to support me. Get on with you now."

Barcelis sighed and wondered if he should take matters into his hands and take her home, but then he couldn't overrule Mercilus, who commanded an irresistible presence.

When the sorcerers began to move toward the entrance to the arena, he decided to do as he was told. Racing back to the box, he sat with her and took her hand.

Grateful, she also took the hand of the woman who called herself Mata, who smiled reassuringly in return.

Lenny and Jenna sat as high up in the stands as they could so that they could watch and talk. At least there were no seats behind them, and there were quite a number of empty seats on either side and below them.

"We're lucky everyone else wants to sit as close to the action as possible," Lenny said. "I wonder where Cassy is."

"I've been thinking about that too, Leonard," she replied, "but I think I've got it figured out. Look in the VIP box. She's sitting next to Mercilus' wife. I'm sure of it."

"I'll find out," Lenny said. Using his wizard staff, he amplified his vision and zoomed closer. Concentrating on communication, he said, *Cassy, turn around.*

Cassy turned, smiled and waved before turning back. Suddenly he heard in his mind, *I'm trying to reassure Rosina, Lenny. Please understand.*

Cassy, you can't do that, Lenny thought back. *What if the monster that kills her does it today? You can't interfere.*

139

I know, but I doubt if it will happen today. These monsters will all be low-level but lots of them. Just relax, Lenny, I know what I'm doing.

Lenny sighed and shut down the communication. "It's her all right, Jenna. I don't understand what she's doing down there. She can't help Rosina no matter what happens. If this isn't interference, I don't know what is."

"Calm down, Leonard," Jenna whispered. "People are listening."

"I doubt that, Jenna. I can barely hear you over this noise."

Suddenly a loud cheer went up from the fans seated nearest to the arena, but then everyone else in the stands soon joined them.

"Look, the sorcerers are entering the arena!" Jenna shouted. But then she whispered, "The show is about to start. It looks like the sorcerers are going to parade around and show off. There's Mercilus. He looks so large from up here. I don't understand."

"Call it a blend of illusion and ego, Jenna. He has to look like some sort of superman to this crowd. It's show business after all."

"Why are you so excited, Leonard? You sound like you can't wait until the show starts."

"You should have heard yourself a minute ago, Jenna. I guess we can't help but anticipate a show of any sort, even though we're not likely to enjoy this one once it starts. Cassy and I used to watch monster movies at home. I always cheered for the monsters. Cassy couldn't understand why."

"Yes, well, I don't either, Leonard. These monsters are very real and a piece of work for certainty. They'll kill anything living if they have a chance, and that's very frightening."

Lenny quietly agreed with her. "Relax, Jenna," he said, "Cassy is probably right. Low-level monsters like the ones being released today probably won't escape. It's the third day that we need to worry about."

"Oh, I'm tired of this place already," Jenna said. "I wish it was that last day now, so we can get it over with and go home."

"Are you so anxious to meet those crocs, Jenna? We haven't figured out how to fight them yet."

"I know, Leonard. I'm getting so nervous that I could scream."

"You might as well start now, Jenna. Everyone else is. They're releasing the first monsters. One of them is the cute and cuddly imposceros you liked so much."

Jenna stuck her tongue out at him and sullenly sat back to watch the show.

The bear was first into the arena followed by a two-headed wolf of nearly the same size, but the bear was the first to attack. The wolf went down on its back but both mouths snarled and viciously snapped at any part of the bear it could reach. The bear, however, was canny and tore out the throat of each head in short order. When two more double headed wolves appeared in the arena, the bear backed away but only to regroup and charge at them. The wolves split up and harried the bear from both sides.

A monstrous pair of lions soon joined the fight, but they didn't care who their adversaries were. They attacked everything that moved, including the sorcerers who ranged freely around the fight perimeter snapping their whips.

The crowd went crazy every time a beast almost connected with a sorcerer, but the sting of the whips daunted their attacks.

The bear was soon finished, but then the wolves and lions fought each other until a pair of serpents twenty feet long slithered into the arena. Normally, serpents are cautious and seek to escape, but these attacked at the first opportunity.

A sorcerer fell when a serpent whipped its tail, but the other sorcerers ran interference until he regained his feet.

"That's Magus," Lenny said. "Butkus is working next to him."

Mercilus, however, marched among the brawling beasts as if impervious to harm. His powerful whip instantly turned away any monster that approached him.

A steady stream of low-level monsters paraded into the arena, replacing those that perished in the fighting. It took only the snap of a whip to remove the carcasses as they fell.

"The monsters don't have a chance," Lenny complained. "Boo, boo, boo!" he cried, but the roar of the crowd drowned him out.

"Leonard, shut up!" Jenna cried. "We can't draw attention to ourselves no matter what."

"Maybe we should just leave," he replied. "This is hopeless."

"Leonard, you said you wanted to capture the wizors the sorcerers used to vanquish the monsters. Have you done that yet?"

"Oops, I forgot," he said, touching the pin on his lapel. Concentrating, he got to work.

One monster after another eventually fell either to another monster or the whip of a sorcerer. Lenny captured the auras he detected of either case. They all could be useful.

"They're selling shish kabobs down there!" Jenna cried. "I'm hungry. Do you want some?"

"Get as many as you can, Jenna. Doing this is a drain on my metabolism."

He watched her jump down the steps leading to the lower levels, but he had to return his attention to the monsters. Jenna, soon returned with six sticks of shish kabobs, three in each fist.

"This is all I could get, Leonard. These are the last ones he had, but he said he'd be back with more."

Lenny accepted a stick and pulled a strip of meat from it with his teeth. "Good, we might need more at this rate."

Jenna consumed two of them herself but passed the others one at a time to Lenny as he asked for them.

"Can you make a wizor that can block the sun, Jenna, maybe an umbrella?" Lenny asked. "It's getting really hot out here. I think it's past noon already."

"Well past," she replied. "I'm not sure of what to do, though. I wish we had come more prepared."

"We'll do that tomorrow. Right now, think of it as a Wizor Fair task. You have plenty of wood and stone stored in your wand, don't you? I'm sure you can come up with something appropriate."

"If I knew what an umbrella was, it might help," she laughed, "but I think I've got an idea."

"As long as it works to block the sun," Lenny replied, "it'll be fine. If it'll help, an umbrella is a foldup cloth shade supported by wire and has a long wooden handle to hold it aloft. It's used either to turn the rain or the sun's rays."

"Interesting," Jenna said. "I don't have any metal to make wire with, but I do have plenty of wood and stone."

Lenny ignored her efforts as he continued to record the auras left by the magic users and monsters. Since the show was indeed carefully choreographed, he couldn't help but admire Mercilus and his sorcerer supporters.

The monsters were larger and stronger now but none were above the seventh level. The strongest monsters charged the sorcerers rather than the weaker monsters, but the sorcerers dodged them by sinking into the ground and returning when the danger passed.

He had the impression that even the dangerous mistakes some of the sorcerers made were also choreographed. The strongest monsters easily took out the weaker ones, which left only the sorcerers to fight, but they intentionally delayed the finish to increase the tension in the stands. The fans constantly filled the stadium with incomprehensible noise, which made it difficult to concentrate on the recording process.

Suddenly, the last of the monsters was vanquished much to everyone's disappointment.

"I think I've got it," Jenna finally said, holding up the clumsy instrument over her head.

"It's a little late," Lenny grinned. "The show is over."

"Oh, I didn't notice," she said, noting the sorcerers who were taking their last bows. Appearing to be ten feet tall, Mercilus triumphantly departed the arena.

"Well, your idea of an umbrella looks like it'll work, Jenna."

"But you don't like it, do you? Look, I know it's clumsy and a little heavy, but it does the job."

"I can see that," Lenny replied, "and I'm sorry I couldn't have given you a better description of an umbrella. You didn't have a lot to work with either. Wait, let me try. Maybe it'll give you some ideas."

Lenny touched the pin on his lapel and concentrated. Thin ribbons of wood began to spin and bind together into a large, flat cloth top that bent over a firm frame that twisted around like living wire. A center pole bound the structure together into an astonishing likeness of a modern umbrella with a black shade, which functioned similarly. He illustrated by closing and reopening the umbrella.

"See, this is what I had in mind," he said. "I made the wire from the iron content in the stone I stored in my staff."

"That's astonishing," Jenna said, taking the umbrella and working it for herself. "Oh, I want one of these."

"I would make you one, but everyone is leaving the stadium. Here, you can have this one. I'll make another one later. Come on, let's find Cassy. I think she's still in the VIP box with Rosina. They might be waiting for the crowd to thin out."

Jenna absorbed her failed invention into her wand and proudly stepped down the stairs to the lower levels of the stands, spinning the new umbrella over her head. Her amused face beamed brightly in the shadow.

Rosina and Barcelis stood up and began to leave the box when they arrived. Rosina nearly bumped into Jenna, but the umbrella surprised her.

"Oh," Rosina cried, "what is that?"

Grinning broadly, she replied, "This is my umbrella. Today it's a sunshade. It works great."

"It does indeed look worthwhile," Rosina remarked. "My hat was somewhat inadequate for the purpose. The sun was hot today. Where did you get it?"

Smiling pleasantly, Jenna introduced herself and passed the umbrella to her. "You can have this one, Rosina. It opens and closes like this," she said, illustrating.

Although she thanked her for the umbrella, her mouth opened as she glanced at Cassy still seated and then back at Jenna. "Everyone seems to know who I am. That's quite curious."

Cassy immediately stood up. "I'm Mata, she said taking Jenna's hand. I'm sure that almost everyone here knows the name of the great sorcerer Mercilus' wife. I don't see anything strange about that."

Barcelis offered his hand to Cassy. "I'm sure you know who I am as well, Mata. I'm pleased to meet you. Oh, and you as well, Jenna," he said, taking her hand in turn. "And you, sire," he added, turning to Lenny.

Lenny shook his hand and replied, "Most people call me Leonard, Barcelis. I have indeed heard of your family, although this is the first time we've met."

"Indeed," Barcelis replied, "but we can't stay and chat. I must get mother home soon. The family is anxiously expecting her return."

Barcelis excused himself and his mother before escorting her down the stairwell to the ground corridor that would take them out the rear entrance.

"I think this meeting has given me a headache," Lenny said. "Cassy, there was no requirement to let them see us for any reason. We still don't know how our presence will affect this timeframe."

Cassy glanced about at the other guests shuffling past them before replying. "I think we need to find a much more private place to talk, Lenny," she whispered. "Don't you?"

When he realized that a passerby had turned his head his way, he realized his mistake. "Let's go, Jenna," he said, following Cassy down the stairwell.

CHAPTER 17

LOVE WILL OUT

Caked with dust and grime generated in the arena during the fight, all of the sorcerers, Mercilus first, took turns in the showers to scrub themselves clean.

The showers consisted of nothing more than elevated wooden barrels mounted on scaffolds. Water flowed down ceramic piping with small holes drilled in them to allow the liquid to eject in a convenient low-level spray.

Magus and Butkus intentionally held back to be the last ones in the showers. There was always plenty of water left. Soaping themselves down, they enjoyed it to the fullest.

Butkus sang as loudly as he could until Magus warned him to shut up.

"Look, Magus," Butkus replied, "you're my elder brother, and I love you dearly, but no one tells me to shut up in the shower."

With that he resumed his tirade of off-key tavern songs that would have offended the most casual of listeners.

Magus hefted his bar of soap for a moment, but then he heaved it at Butkus' head, who narrowly avoided contact. In retaliation, he heaved his soap bar at Magus, striking him in the buttocks.

"Ouch, that stung!" Magus cried.

"It would have been worse if you had actually hit me in the head, don't you think? It's hard enough dealing with Mercilus' monsters without having to look out for you too, so knock it off."

"All right, I apologize, Butkus. It's just that I'm not looking forward to dealing with those crocs on last day. Did you hear the ruckus they made during the show? Only the crowd was louder. I swear, the crocs and trogs are trying to tear the cages apart to get at each other. They can't wait to fight."

"I heard them all right," Butkus replied. "Mercilus says that's how he likes it. He designed them to fight, and fight they will to the death. He didn't mention if it was to our deaths or not. There's no way we could defeat them on our own. If something happens to Mercilus, we're finished."

"Not if we stick to the escape plan, Butkus. I've got to get out of here, though. I'm freezing. Mercilus' warm water wizor has worn off."

Sighing in agreement, Magus got out of the shower, toweled off and dressed in fresh clothes. Both of them were glad that today's slaughter was over with.

Cassy, Lenny and Jenna appeared together inside the warehouse. It seemed like the best place to talk since it was essential to keep up the appearance of being prisoners.

Lenny angrily slapped his right fist into his left palm and began to pace.

"I know you're hot over this, Lenny," Cassy said, "but we literally have nothing to fear by revealing our presence to Rosina and Barcelis. They won't know who we are now or five years into the future. She never met you two then, and I took care to hide my real face. I admit that Barcelis is a problem, but I've already modified his memory of your faces. He won't recognize you in the future."

"Oh, what about using that name, Mata Hari, I think it was? The children will know that name in the future."

"I didn't use both names, Lenny. Mata is actually a common name here if you haven't noticed. You really need to calm down and listen to me for once."

Lenny stared at her for a moment before he raised his hands in surrender. "You're right, Cassy. I guess I really didn't understand. It's just that this is a touchy time. Last day is approaching, and we still don't know how the crocs escaped. Mercilus must have done something wrong, but what?"

"That's a hard question," Cassy agreed. "I've observed every wizor Mercilus made, but I detected no errors. He and his son were very meticulous. I don't believe it was an error in making but possibly in judgement. He was exhausted by the time he finished the last croc wizor, but he recovered quickly. He conserves his energy during the first two days of the fair, so that he's fully recovered during the third. He knows what he's doing."

Lenny thought about her comment for a moment and agreed. "It has to be an error in judgement somehow. That's how he called the man-thrall five years from now that destroyed the city and ultimately him. I wish I knew what it was even though we can't do anything about it."

Weary of listening to the argument between them, Jenna withdrew her wand and began to concentrate. Momentarily, an apple turnover appeared in her free hand.

"Last one," she muttered and bit into it. "I still have plenty of mincemeat pies, though.'

Suddenly, they heard the click from the latch turning off the containment wizor. Cassy instantly vanished. Jenna absorbed the turnover back into her wand and slipped it into her skirt pocket.

Magus and Butkus strolled in with a bag and two jugs of water.

"What did we miss?" Magus asked. "You two look like you've been busy. You, Leonus, your face looks sunburned."

"Oh, we were just arguing," Jenna replied. "He always blushes like that when we disagree. He says that you're planning to kill us, but I think there's some honor left in you. Am I right?"

Magus began to laugh, but then he set the bag down next to the jugs of water. "Let me put it this way, little lady, I promised that I wouldn't hurt you if you cooperated. Leave it at that."

Magus and Butkus quickly departed, resetting the containment wizor as they did so.

Cassy immediately returned, but she plainly looked worried.

"What do you think, Cassy?" Jenna asked. "Will he keep his word?"

Turning to her, she replied, "Oh, yes, but he plans to leave you both here to die. Just keep up the act for now. You're safe as long as they don't know the truth. When you return to the arena tomorrow, I suggest that you both wear a disguise. If they see you there as you are, well, I'm sure you understand my meaning. Don't hesitate to call me or Jen if you have to." Smiling, she said, "I love you both," and faded away.

"She's got a lot on her plate too," Lenny reasoned. "Being prisoners here has pretty much tied our hands. We can't deal with Magus and Butkus without upsetting their roles at the fair. It could be the catalyst that sets the crocs free. We can't allow that."

Jenna placed her arms around his neck and hugged him. "All this makes me feel hopeless too, Leonard. Let's eat, and you can teach me how to make an umbrella. It'll pass the time, and we really do need them at the fair. You're right. The sun is brutal out there."

Rosina stared at the carriage driver's back on the way home, but she smiled when Barcelis took her hand.

"That's what I wanted to see, Mother. See, nothing happened at the fair. You're alive and well, and we'll be home soon. I want you to put that silly fear where it belongs and come back to us. We all love you."

"There's still two days left, Barcelis," she replied. "I knew that nothing would happen today, but it will happen very soon. You and your father can't stop it. I don't know what he's done, but his power has set this plot into motion. To say it plainly, my beautiful son, I will die within the next two days at the fair."

"Mother, you can't mean that. Father has everything under control. The monsters can't harm us."

"Whether monster or man, it doesn't matter," she said. "I don't know the exact way or time, but no one can stop my death now. Please, Barcelis, take good care of your sisters. They'll need you very soon. Be strong for them if not for me or your father. He's especially proud of his monsters, but they will be his undoing one day. Whatever you do, don't follow his path. It'll destroy you too."

The carriage pulled up to the curb outside of their apartment. Barcelis helped her step down and led her to the door.

"Mother, what you say can't be true. Every step of the fair is planned. The monsters can't escape on their own. They'll only be released if father knows that he can defeat them. He's careful about that. You have to believe me."

"I believe you, my dear one," she said, smiling at him, "but no one can stop the immediate future. It's much too late for that. I've seen it repeat many times over the last few months. It becomes clearer with every passing day."

Barcelis paused to listen to her, but he didn't reply. Could it be true? He had heard about others able to see the future, but this was his mother. She had never expressed that ability before. Why now?

His sisters rushed into her arms the moment they entered the apartment. He happily watched the loving relationship they had, but he really wanted to talk to his father. He checked the apartment first, but Mercilus was not there; however, when he glanced out the window, he saw him arrive in his carriage.

Hurrying downstairs, he met him at the curb. Mercilus tried to avoid him, but Barcelis took his shoulder and held on.

"Father, we must talk about mother!"

"What about her, Barcelis? You were there. It all happened like clockwork. There wasn't a single mistake. Tomorrow will be the same like it always is."

"Father, mother is a seer. She can see the future!"

Taken aback, Mercilus looked him in the eye for a moment. "I've known no one who could do that. She's never done it before. It's just fear talking. Anyone can see that. Now step aside, Barcelis, I require sustenance and rest. Don't bother me with such drivel. I don't want to see you until the fair starts tomorrow. Make sure that Rosina is in the VIP box on time. I won't accept any excuses."

Allowing him to pass, Barcelis shook his head in disbelief. Seers were rare, but not unheard of. How could he be so callous as to not investigate the matter?

Although Barcelis could not see Cassy as he entered the apartment building after his father, she had been there all along listening to the exchange.

Rosina could accurately see the future, but Mercilus wouldn't listen, she thought, very much relieved. *It was nothing I did to make that happen. The future is on track as it should be.*

Returning to the warehouse, she found Jenna constructing another umbrella under Lenny's tutelage.

"Very smart, Jenna," she said. "It's looking exactly like an umbrella should."

"Thanks, Cassandra," she replied. "It's not finished yet, but Leonard is a very good teacher. I didn't know I could make anything so delicate from a little wood and simple dirt and stone. This is actually fun."

"She is quite good," Lenny said. "It's more her than me. She picked up on the method really fast. I'm impressed."

"Spinning the fabric was the hardest," Jenna giggled. "Now that I can make cloth out of wood, I think I can make all my own clothes. I won't have to rely on the dressmaker at all now."

"Yes, well, I'm here because I've been listening in on some very interesting conversations," Cassy said. "I want you to know that Rosina is a true seer. She actually saw her death months ago. Barcelis is convinced now, but Mercilus isn't. The man's either a fool or an idiot. Well, I guess he isn't an idiot, but he refuses to listen to any argument. He bases his views only on his experience. No one else matters. That's the character flaw that kills her. Now we just have to find out when and how. We were told that a monster killed her, but which one? Was it a croc or a troglodyte? That's what we have to find out now."

"There isn't much to go on yet, is there?" Lenny replied. "I wish we didn't have to wait until the last moment to find out. Even we could get killed if the monster attacks us. We'll have to be very careful."

"I'll keep Jen close, Leonard," Jenna said. "Don't worry."

However, he wasn't convinced.

• ⋯⋯⋯⋯•)(•)(•⋯⋯⋯•|

The sisters sat across the table from Mercilus while he wolfed down serving after serving of food. Each sister stared at him as if he were an unwelcome visitor.

"What do you want?" he grumbled, glancing up only once.

Voted as spokesperson, Brena replied. "Please, Father, don't make mother go to the fair tomorrow. She doesn't want to go, and we don't want her to go either."

Mercilus pounded on the table with a clenched fist and shouted, "Go to bed all of you! I'm not going to take this conspiracy from my own children!"

Gobie began to cry and raced to climb into her mother's arms.

Rosina angrily sat down on the sofa while the other girls joined her.

"Father is just being awful," Brena said. "I want to go away somewhere where he isn't."

"So do I," Gobie whispered. "I hate him."

"No dear," Rosina replied, "don't say that. He is your father and benefactor. He's just suffering from the effects of using so much magic energy at the fair today. You know he'll calm down after the fair is over."

"We don't want you to go to the fair for your sake, Mother," Brena said. "It's not just us. We love you too much."

Mercilus had heard every word. He didn't consider himself heartless, but it hurt to hear the children say they hated him. He had never expected to hear that. Wasn't he a good provider? However, unable to apologize, he found his way up the stairs to his bedroom where he fell fast asleep on the bed without removing his robe.

Barcelis had waited in the hallway upstairs for his father to finish his meal, but in the meantime, he also heard the verbal exchange. Ducking into his room while Mercilus passed, he only emerged afterwards to descend the stairs to join the others in the living room.

Gobie kissed Rosina on the lips and whispered, "You can sleep with me tonight, Mommy. I won't mind."

"Thank you, Gobie," she replied. "I think I will. He snapped at me too when he came home, and I haven't quite forgiven him."

Jen wondered invisibly about the cages beneath the stands of the arena. She encountered at least two attending sorcerers whose jobs were to watch the animals to make certain there were no surprises the next day. The lowest level monster cages were almost empty, but there were still many higher-level monsters left. Most of them would be released on the second day.

Not finding anything interesting, she wandered across the arena and down the corridor to the nineth level monsters. The troglodytes had calmed down and now nervously paced their cages.

The first crocodilian, however, surprised her. It leveled a malevolent eye on her and released a long spray of white mist that passed harmlessly through her. That was remarkable, but what was interesting was that the monster could see her. She tracked its eye movements as she strolled back and forth before the cage.

"How can you do that, monster?" she wondered. "You shouldn't be able to see me, but you can. I wonder if Mercilus knows you can do that."

Suddenly, her legs froze in place. She struggled to move them, but then her arms froze followed by her torso.

"Oh no, I can't move!" she cried, but no one heard her.

She tried to think but she couldn't change locations either. She needed help, but she couldn't inform Cassy or Jenna. She remained frozen where she was through the night and into the opening ceremonies of the fair the following day.

CHAPTER 18

REVENGE

Barcelis and Rosina sat down in the VIP box next to Cassy who warmly greeted them. Rosina had brought her umbrella but was forced to fold it up when the guests seated behind her complained.

Lenny and Jenna took their usual places in the last seats at the top of the stands. They had taken Cassy's advice and modified their hair and appearance just enough to make them appear a little older to confuse Magus and Butkus should they accidentally meet.

Jenna, however, glanced carefully around the stadium and seemed somewhat perplexed.

"Something is wrong, Leonard," she said. "I can't find Jen."

"Are you certain she's not playing a prank?" Lenny asked. "That's her style."

"She wouldn't do that when this affair is so serious, Leonard. She's just supposed to look around for problems, but she's been gone since yesterday evening. It's not like her."

"It's a problem," he replied, "but there isn't anything I can do about it."

"Can you find her on your television? That worked pretty well before."

Lenny tapped his lapel pin and willed his full-sized wizard staff to appear. The steel ball on top flattened into the oval shape of the viewer. He used it like a far-sight instrument to scan the stands, the cage area beneath this side and then the other. The troglodytes and crocodilians were fussing as usual. The magic told him to hold the viewer there, but Jen still did not appear.

"The viewer indicates she's there someplace, but I don't see her."

"She has to be invisible," Jenna said. "The viewer wouldn't see her that way, would it?"

"Not unless I tune it for that possibility," he said. The viewer played about the corridor outside of the cages until it focused on the silhouette of something that had to be Jen. "There, do you see it? She's not moving. It's as if she's frozen or something."

"Look, she's in front of the croc cage. She's trapped, probably by something the croc did. It's even more formidable than we thought, Leonard. We have to rescue her before the monsters come out."

Lenny carefully scanned the area and shook his head. While the monsters were screaming at each other, none of them paid the slightest attention to Jen.

"I'm telling, Cassy," he said. Concentrating on communication, he said, *Cassy, Jen is in the cage area with the crocs. She's invisible and frozen. It looks like the croc's breath froze even her. They would have had to see her if they did.*

Cassy's reply came quickly. *The crocs can't harm her, Lenny. Let her be. We can't be responsible for releasing the crocs.*

Jenna shook her head. She had heard the communication in her head too. "No, I can't wait," Jenna cried. "She's part of me, but I can't feel her anymore."

"Jenna, be reasonable," Lenny replied. "Like Cassy said, we can't be responsible for releasing the crocs. That would defeat why we came here."

Jenna took to her feet and paced a few seconds. "They won't release the trogs and crocs until tomorrow. That means that no one should be inside the caged area. I don't understand why Jen was there, but she suspected or discovered something. We have to know what that is, don't you see? The show has started, so no one will even know we're there."

"Jenna, we must listen to Cassy. Going near the monster cages is too dangerous right now. You saw that yesterday."

"If you won't come with me, Leonard, I'll do it alone!" she cried. Folding her umbrella, she vanished from sight.

This was the one time when he wished that he hadn't taught her how to travel through the ether on her own. Sighing, he vanished and appeared beside her just inside the tunnel to the cages. While they could hear the monsters fighting outside, no one in the arena could see them here.

"I knew you would come," Jenna said through a pert smile.

He replied, "How could I not? I feel responsible for you because we're a team. I'm just worried about how we're going to get close to the crocs without encountering that white stuff they spit."

"I've figured that out already," she said. "We use the umbrellas. We might have to enlarge the top a bit, but I think it'll help us get close enough to Jen to pull her back. She'll probably recover on her own after that."

Jenna glanced out the tunnel entrance, but no one was coming. "I wish we had a backup plan, but this containment field is stronger than the other one. I haven't figured it out yet. Maybe I can improve on the umbrella idea by adding a spun layer of stone to the fabric."

"It would help if the crocs can't see us, but we can see them," Jenna said. "I can hear the trogs beating at the cages. They know we're here."

Lenny grinned. "You have your moments, Jenna. Now break out your umbrella."

He was already working on his umbrella. Turning the stone into fibrous thread that he spun over the umbrella shield, he extended it out and down by another foot. Another stored wizor rendered the structure invisible to them except for the support shaft. Minutes later, he had done the same to Jenna's umbrella.

"All right, Jenna," he said, "hold up the umbrella like a shield, and try to hide all of you. The shield should be large enough to do that now. Good, now follow my lead."

Trembling, she whispered, "Leonard, I'm so scared."

"This is your idea, Jenna. It's all or broke now."

"I know," she replied, falling silent.

The caged troglodytes soon became visible on the left side of the corridor, but they remained focused on each other. They lifted their heads and spun their long ovoid ears when Lenny scuffed a foot on a loose flagstone, but seeing nothing, they turned their attention back to each other.

Lenny used his wizard staff viewer to search for Jen. Although only a silhouette, her image soon became visible.

"She's just ahead," Lenny whispered.

The closest croc cracked its vast toothy mouth and roared such a frightful din that the passageway shook. Its huge eyes rolled directly at them as if it could see them. The second croc soon did the same.

"I'm sure that they caught Jen because they could see her," Jenna whispered. "I'm sure that they can see us."

"They have fantastic hearing too," Lenny whispered.

Reaching Jen, he tugged at her hand, but she remained frozen in place. Jenna latched onto her opposite arm and pulled hard. Jen tumbled solidly to the corridor floor and did not move.

"We'll have to carry her out!" Jenna cried. "Come on, Lenny, we're out of time. Those crocs are spitting that white stuff at us."

"She weighs a ton for some reason, Jenna," he replied. "We can't carry her. Can you let her back inside of you like you usually do?"

Jenna tried, but then she shook her head. "No, I don't know what's wrong."

"I have an idea," Lenny said, "but if this doesn't work, we'll have to leave her."

He repositioned his umbrella when the white smoke began to curl around the edges. Pointing his wizard staff at Jen, he absorbed her as if she were mere stone.

"Thank God that worked," he muttered. "Watch your umbrella, Jenna. The white stuff is growing thicker. Come on, run as fast as you can."

The troglodytes shook their cages, unmindful of the containment sparks as they passed. The freezing mist already entered their cages and amassed near the ceiling before raining down over the trogs. Suddenly, the nearest trog turned white and froze, and the second one did so only a moment after.

The children could hear the crocs lashing at the cages as they raced up the corridor, but they eventually quieted. They pressed against a wall near the outside entrance to catch their breaths.

Jenna began to laugh hysterically. Lenny glanced warily at her for a moment, but he soon did the same.

"We almost bought the farm back there, didn't we?" he said.

Coughing, Jenna covered her mouth for a moment to recover. "If you mean that we almost died, then you're right. I was never so scared in my whole life. I don't know how we're going to defeat them in Duscany. They seem impervious to harm."

"Not to mention extremely dangerous," Lenny added. "I want to know how Mercilus intended to defeat them, but we know that both monsters escaped. I guess there's nothing to do now but return to our seats and watch the show. You must admit that it is exciting."

"I'm beginning to think that excitement for you is much different than excitement for me, Leonard, but you're right. I'm exhausted. Let's go back, but maybe we ought to do something about these umbrellas. They're sure to attract attention now."

"Oh, that's easy," he replied, shaking it closed and then reopening it. "I built that in."

"You're some kind of genius, Leonard," she giggled, taking care of her umbrella. "I would just like to know what kind is all."

"Don't ask me," he laughed, taking his seat. "I just call them as I see them."

Jenna extracted two mincemeat pies from her wand and passed one to him to eat. The umbrellas twirled over their heads, shielding them from the unrelenting sun.

Suddenly, they heard Cassy's voice in their minds. *Good job, you two, but please don't do anything like that again. You almost gave me a heart attack.*

"SHE almost had a heart attack!" Jenna cried, but then mindfully lowered her voice to a whisper. "I almost had a heart attack, she means. I just want to know one thing, Leonard? Is Jen all right?"

"That's impossible to tell at the moment," he replied. "She's just a swirl of magic inside my wizard staff along with all the other things I have stored in there. If magic didn't contain the weight, we'd probably crash right down to the ground from here."

"Oh, I guess I didn't think about what happens when you suck stuff up in there. I suppose I could have done it myself, but I was so distraught, I couldn't think."

"Don't worry, Jenna, she's all magic and probably used to this sort of thing anyway."

"Likely, but could you send her to the warehouse or the apartment? Maybe she'll recover on her own. We could use her help later should those crocs break out. That idea just freaks me out because it can literally happen at any time today or tomorrow."

"Yeah, let's leave her in the warehouse. If she still weighs a ton, she would probably break the bed and floor in the apartment." Tapping the butt of his staff on the flooring, he added, "There, it's done. We'll check on her when we can."

Jenna purchased some more shish kabobs from the vender working the stands and returned to her seat. She wasn't interested in the monster fights or anything the sorcerers did, but she did enjoy the shish kabobs.

Lenny, on the other hand, used his wizard staff to record the residue auras left by the fight. Perhaps something in them would give him a clue of how to defeat the crocs after they appeared in Duscany.

Cassy remained in the VIP box. Rosina suddenly grasped her hand during a particularly violent fight that occurred in the arena directly below the box.

No one heard the roars of the crocs in the cages as they smashed to and fro. The sparks from the containment field proved to be no deterrent. They were no longer interested in the troglodytes since they had long since succumbed to the freezing mist. They remained where they were whether clinging to the cage wall or prone on the ground.

Croc number two crashed into the cage door, bending the already damaged latch. The monster repeated the bashing until the door crumbled into sharp barbs of steel. The containment wizor fell with it, destroyed. The croc tested the way as it strutted through the opening into the corridor, but finding no obstruction, it resumed its attack on the other cage door. Both crocs alternately hit it until the latch shattered, freeing the last crocodilian.

Together they silently worked their way up the corridor leading to the arena. Their stark red eyes shifted right and left, and their tongues darted in and out, searching for anything that might quench their ravenous hunger.

"Aha!" Mercilus cried as his whip destroyed the eighth level monster.

He was weary now as were his supporters, but there were only two seventh level monsters left. Their deaths would end the second day of the fair.

One of the monsters resembled a tarantula but twelve feet tall.

Venom dripped from long fangs. The second was a thirty-foot serpent, also venomous, and coated with opalescent scales. Their natural disposition seemed to be a willingness to fight, but the sorcerers drove them closer together, encouraging it.

Mercilus and his band of sorcerers failed to notice the crocs that tentatively emerged from the containment protected corridor and separated. Their first steps were cautious, but then they rushed the nearest sorcerers, Magus and Butkus.

The pair cried out in horror as the freezing mist overtook them. The strong concentration turned them white, but the crocs quickly swallowed them down during their headlong rush.

Alerted now, the other sorcerers fought back with their whips as if this were part of the show to the roaring approval of the crowd.

The serpent and spider suddenly lost interest in fighting one another. The spider fell pinned beneath the heavy body of one of the crocs, but the serpent coiled and sprang into the stands, landing directly on top of the VIP box, crushing almost everyone beneath it before racing up the stands directly toward Lenny and Jenna.

Cassy came to her senses and glanced at Rosina, but Barcelis was protectively holding her, unharmed. She then followed the course of the serpent. People in the stands raced aside, but then she spotted her friends at the top standing firm, Lenny with his wizard staff and Jenna with her wand.

No! Cassy thought to them. *Let it pass! We can't interfere!*

We know what we're doing, Cassy! Lenny thought back.

Cassy, however, vanished from where she was and appeared directly before them. Spreading her arms, she carried them over the rail to land unharmed at the base of the stadium outside. The serpent sprang through the air and landed far beyond the wall to race unhindered into the city.

"That wasn't necessary, Cassy," Lenny said. "I had a protection wizor all set up. We knew we couldn't stop the serpent."

"I'm sorry, Lenny," Cassy replied. "I didn't have time to think about it. I don't understand what happened, though. The serpent literally destroyed part of the VIP box and injured or killed about twenty people, but Rosina and Barcelis were unharmed. Come on, we have to go back."

The three appeared at the top of the stands and overlooked the panic ensuing inside the stadium. People pushed and shoved in their efforts to escape the stadium, trampling anyone who fell.

Barcelis fought the panic rising in his throat as his mother quivered hysterically at his side. Glancing into the arena, he found Mercilus and the other sorcerers fighting the crocs, but several had fallen and writhed about. He thought he saw the panic in his father's eyes as well. He had to be too weak to fight these ninth level monsters now.

"Mother," he said, "leave the stadium the way we came in and wait for me in the carriage. I've got to help father somehow."

She nodded, but she reached for him as he headed down the stairwell, anxiously shoving aside other patrons. "Don't go," she whispered, but she knew it was too late. Turning to the arena, her heart skipped a beat when she saw the croc bearing down on her husband, but he sank at the last moment into the escape tunnel.

Enraged, the croc cried out and whirled to find another target. Seeing Rosina standing in horror in the stands, the beast squealed and shot a long stream of white mist that enveloped her in seconds. Freezing into white stone, she toppled onto her back and did not move.

"She's dead!" Cassy breathed. "That's how it happened. I would have never thought that it would happen that way, Lenny, but it makes sense. When I saw her in her bed five years from now, she seemed to be just sleeping, but I was told that she had died during the fair this year. His daughters said that Mercilus couldn't bear to bury her and turned her bedroom into a shrine. I didn't know it then, but she was frozen just as she is now. I suppose in a sense, she survived in Mercilus' eyes."

The crocs, however, were not finished. They beat the sorcerers back but then leapt forty feet into the stands and escaped over the rail into the city.

"We have to follow them," Cassy said.

"Why don't we just watch where they go in my viewer, Cassy? It's too dangerous to get very close to them. They can see you even if you're invisible, and you saw how far they can shoot that white stuff."

"No, it's unnecessary." Cassy replied. "They're going to the Whelf Fen. All of the monsters are under the control of the whelf queen.

This has to be her secret revenge against Mercilus. Too bad he never learned his lesson because it eventually cost him everything."

"Does that mean that we're done here, Cassy?" Lenny asked.

Jenna pressed against him and held his hand with the same question in her eyes.

Cassy turned to them and replied, "We're done now. There's no point in staying here any longer."

Lenny grinned, but he had another thought. "What about Brena and the others? Don't you want to say goodbye to them now? You did go to the effort of revealing yourself to them. You said you wanted to comfort them. I think that they could stand a little of that now."

Cassy became thoughtful, but then she said, "I could only tell them that their mother is dead, but that chore belongs to Mercilus and Barcelis. I made no other promises to them. I have the feeling, though, that they already know. Take my hands, you two. Let's go."

CHAPTER 19

QUIMBY

Traveling a thousand years into the future in only an instant, Cassy and the others abruptly appeared in the fen standing on top of the stone croc. Nothing had changed.

"I don't think we should be standing here!" Jenna cried. "I think I can feel the croc moving."

"It's not this one, Jenna," Cassy said. "It's the other one out there. Its struggles are shaking the whole fen, but this one will do the same very soon. I don't understand why it's happening now, though. It's a thousand years since their creation."

"Oh, we forgot about Jen," Jenna said. "We have to go back for her."

"No, I came with you," Jen said, suddenly at her side. "I awoke not long after you sent me away."

"Oh, well, you could have let me know," Jenna said, hugging her. "You're just as much me as I am, and I worry about you."

Lenny had no more than turned to pick his way back through the fen, when he noticed something else moving in the swamp. "What's that?" he asked. "I thought I saw it move."

Cassy spotted it then and flew closer to examine the object. "It looks like a huge statue made of stone." But then she cried, "It's a frozen troglodyte! Both of them are here, Lenny. I bet the old whelf queen brought them here too. This is big trouble. Once all four monsters wake up, they'll destroy Duscany, and we can't stop them."

"Then we better get some help," Lenny said. "I think that Scapita is our best bet. He has copies of Mercilus' wizor books. Maybe he recorded the wizor that would destroy them."

Cassy shook her head and replied, "No, he didn't. Don't forget that I created the copies. I know exactly what's in them. In fact, they say nothing about the monsters he created for that particular fair. It's possible, though, that he had a change of heart because of his wife's death and destroyed his records. Perhaps he had no intention of making these monsters again."

"We can speculate all we want, Cassy," Lenny said, "but we better do something. Maybe there's something in the auras I recorded in the arena. I know that Mercilus was too weak to destroy the crocs then, but I recorded everything that happened. Maybe I have the answers and don't know it."

"Please, let's talk to Uncle Scapita," Jenna pleaded. "I know he can help. Let's go. I'm scared."

"Give me your hands," Cassy said, flying close to them. "I'll take us there directly. I've just sent him a message, so he'll expect us when we arrive in his apartment."

Even so, Scapita was startled when they appeared together in his living room.

Greeting them, Guena asked, "Are you hungry. It's close to supper time, and I can have it prepared and sent up in short order."

Lenny nodded. "I am hungry. I think we all are."

Jenna was crying now. She hid her face in Guena's bosom and didn't hold back. "We're in danger, Guena. We could all die."

"Child, what is all this about? Scapita, could you talk to her?"

"This news interests me too, Jenna," he replied. "Just why are we in danger?"

"I'll explain," Cassy said, making a seat of air and sitting down.

Lenny chose a chair next to the fireplace and listened while Cassy explained where they were and why. It didn't make him feel any better about the situation.

Scapita leaned back in his chair and rocked a few minutes in thought, but then he stopped and leaned forward.

"Are you sure there is nothing in Mercilus' wizor books that could solve this problem, Cassandra? What about the whelfs? You have the full power of the fen at your disposal."

"Because of Mercilus," Cassy replied, "the Power of the Fen created the monsters, but it can't destroy them without destroying itself. We have to find a way either to make them sleep forever or to reverse the ninth level wizors that created them."

"Ninth level!" Scapita cried, leaning back "That's unbelievable, but Mercilus was adept at creating the impossible. Well, I do have copies of his wizor books. I'll be glad to study them and see if I can find something that might help."

"I want to help too, Uncle," Jenna said. "Leonard taught me a lot about how high-level wizors work. I might be able to suggest something."

"As you wish, Jenna," he replied. "I believe that supper is nearly at the door now. Perhaps you should help Guena in bringing it in."

"Of course, Uncle," she replied, racing to the door.

"Scapita," Lenny said, "I managed to record the auras from every wizor Mercilus used. I intend to study them. If you don't mind, I might want your help at some point if I find something interesting."

"I would be glad to help, Prince Leonard. Everything about Mercilus' magic interests me, but for now, let's eat."

"One other thing, Scapita," he said, handing him the parchment he found in the walnut periapt. "Would you mind looking at this for me when you have time? It's a clue we found while searching for Leanne Mellot. It looks like a wizor list."

"Later," he replied, inserting it in a robe pocket. "I think better on a full stomach."

Lenny missed Jenna's presence when he traveled at Castle Leonard. He thought that being alone might help him concentrate, but Cassy soon joined him.

"I thought that I would let you know where I was in case you wanted to consult with me, Lenny."

"What do you mean, Cassy? I can find you almost everywhere you might be with my wizard staff viewer. It's pretty handy."

"Then I'll tell you what I'll be up to. I'm returning to the fen partly to watch the monsters while they awaken, but I'm also examining the timeline since the monsters arrived there. There could be something of importance we've missed. It's a tedious process since the Power of the Fen recorded it in real time. I can't fast forward or fast reverse it, but I can jump an interval at a time. I can only view it as it happened; however, I thought that if I reviewed it in reverse, I might discover why they're waking up now."

"That could be interesting," Lenny agreed. "I'm going to analyze the auras I recorded in Eskeling. Too bad I didn't bring back one of those whips the sorcerers used to control the monsters. That could be a clue."

"As you wish," she said, suddenly blinking away, but she instantly returned with one of the whips. "I doubt if it'll be a help, but anything is possible at this point. Scream if you need me."

She suddenly popped out of sight before he could reply.

Carefully uncoiling the leather whip onto the floor of the great room, Lenny whipped it up and back. The leather tassels on the end made a loud snapping report like he had heard in the arena. Visually, the whip looked similar to any ordinary leather whip on Earth, but he could detect nothing magical about it.

Dropping it on one of the tables, he sat down and arranged his wizard staff viewer. Focusing on Mercilus, he began to examine the aura produced when he snapped his whip. Spreading them out, he determined that they were only level one, but they weren't produced by the whip.

"That's odd," he said. "It doesn't look like the whip is doing anything to control the beasts."

Deciding to experiment, he focused his wizard staff on the whip and snapped it again. It didn't create a single aura.

"It should have!" he cried, but now he was at a loss. "What purpose did the whip serve in the arena?"

He snapped the whip again and again until he grew weary of it, but then the sharp echo of the whip off the stone walls of the great hall caught his attention. He had indeed heard the same echo in the arena. Adjusting his wizor staff to tune in on the echo, he snapped the whip again.

"That's got to be it!" he cried, snapping the whip one last time. "The magic is tuned to sound."

This time he examined the auras captured in the arena in Eskeling for the effects of sound on the monsters. He grinned happily when he discovered the relationship, but he still had not found the cause.

Each time a sorcerer snapped the whip at a monster, the echo changed in pitch according to the power of the monster, but he detected nothing the sorcerers did to make that change.

"I need a monster to test it on," he whispered, "a safe one."

He decided that he had no choice except to make one of his own but of sufficiently low power to manage and cause no harm if it managed to escape. However, as he diligently worked through the wizor levels of the weaker monsters, he found none less than level five. He figured that he would have to back up the power to at least level three for safety.

Looking for an appropriate monster, he soon found a level six. If level six was indeed the binding wizor, what if he worked his way down from there? Choosing level five, he set his staff and stepped behind a protective barrier he created from stone.

The powerful blast shook the keep, but the stone barrier was sufficient protection. Four went next and then three. That left levels one, two and the last one, level six. Carefully examining the wizor with his wizard staff, he decided that now was as good a time as any to activate it.

Concentrating on level six, he poured enough power into it to force the wizor to blend together and begin to grow. A globular body appeared first with rudimentary legs, head and tail emerging in minutes. Hair sprouted last over the body, which was now merely a foot in height but well-muscled. The fang filled mouth appeared as the head matured followed by the eyes, nose and ears.

He watched in fascination as the creature writhed on the stone floor of the keep for half an hour until it stood up and became aware of him. Although a grotesque creature, he thought it actually was a little cute.

"I wonder what I should call you?" he said, grinning at the creature's antics as it twisted, rolled over and found its feet again. Apparently, the monster hadn't reached maturity as yet. "I think that Quimby is as good a name as any from one of my favorite cartoons."

He readied his wizard staff and whip when the creature began to circle him with malevolent eyes focused on his every move. The creature almost surprised him when it didn't wait to attack. He snapped the whip while Quimby was in the air, but it clutched frantically at his jacket when it landed.

Panicking, he dropped the whip and pulled Quimby away with the intention of tossing it aside, but then he realized that the monster seemed more frightened than angry. The creature trembled alarmingly as it glanced around for a way to escape.

Feeling responsible, he held it close and petted it like a cat. To his surprise the creature responded in kind.

"Well, Quimby, you're more like a pet than a test subject," Lenny said. "Don't worry, I won't harm you. It looks like I'll have to make a stronger monster to experiment on."

Lenny tried to set the monster down, but Quimby refused to go. Chuckling, he checked the results of the whip snap to see if it correlated with expectations. To his surprise the aura produced was intense and immediate, producing a marked behavior alteration in Quimby.

"So that's how it's done," he said. "Well, Quimby, you won't have to worry about another monster in the house. I've discovered what I wanted to know. The whip probably produces an even greater reaction in stronger monsters perhaps to the point of destruction, but you're too cute to destroy. You could probably pass as a baby gorilla or maybe a chimpanzee in any zoo on earth. As far as I'm concerned, you can have the run of the place. My castle is pretty empty otherwise."

Quimby gazed at him as if it understood every word and leapt down on its own to explore the many nooks and crannies of the great hall.

Now that he had part of the answer, he knew that it wasn't enough to destroy all four monsters awakening in the Whelf Fen. He required a single, sure-fire answer to that immediate need. The monsters could already be marching on Kings Keep at this moment for all he knew.

Retrieving the whip, he decided to try one more experiment. First, he absorbed the whip into his wizard staff. Concentrating on it, he snapped the staff like the whip. It morphed instantly into the whip, but it still allowed access to the wizors he had stored inside of the staff. On command, he morphed it back to the wizard staff.

"I like that. It'll save me a lot of time when I need to use the whip."

Jenna opened one of the many tomes of Mercilus' wizor books that looked most promising and began to scan the index in front. If only his writing wasn't so complicated and difficult to follow. She had been at it some time, when Scapita interrupted her.

"If you can actually read those scribbles, Jenna, that's remarkable."

"What's so remarkable about it, Uncle? The words are easy, but Mercilus' usage of them is sometimes baffling. If I study them long enough, though, I can usually understand what he was trying to say."

"I can only agree," Scapita laughed. "Mercilus could have used a few grammar lessons. I've been studying the books off and on since Cassandra gave them to me, but I've found nothing particularly useful. All he has on his mind is monster making and little on how to destroy them once created. Now these crocodilians you mentioned, you said they're ninth level?"

"They're every bit of that, Uncle. They can see the invisible, and they can spit a long cloud of stuff that'll freeze you into stone. It's like they are stone themselves, but they're agile as cats and fiercer than anything you can imagine. The troglodytes just like to fight. They're super strong and just as mean. That's what's waiting for us in the Whelf Fen, Uncle. Once they awaken, Duscany is doomed. I doubt if any sorcerer could stop them. Leonard might, though. He's learned how to study the monsters' auras directly. He says if he can decipher how they were made, he might be able to shrink them back to nothing by reversing how they were created."

"Jenna, no one person is strong enough to destroy a nineth level monster like that," Scapita replied, wearily shaking his head. "We've used Mercilus' forbidden wizors to destroy monsters before, but none will suffice in this case."

"If Mercilus could do it," Jenna countered, "then so can we. We just have to find the answers, is all."

Scapita glanced down at the open tome and shook his head. "There aren't any answers in any of his writings, Jenna. There's no point in searching them. This parchment Prince Leonard gave me is interesting, though. It's in Mercilus' own hand. By the looks of the ragged edges, it was hastily torn from a bound book. He was right. It is a list. I would pursue the mystery if the moment weren't so dire."

"You have that parchment, and you understand it, Uncle?"

"Yes, of course, but why are you interested in it?'

"Uncle, you said that it's in Mercilus' own hand. Why then did Leanne Mellot come to have it stuffed inside a sixth level walnut periapt, something that most sorcerers in Duscany probably couldn't make? She was a strong Bugoward with exceptional wood and stone magic, but I wonder if she could have made it. Dame Mola said she was born in the Bugo alternate world and didn't come to Duscany until she was adopted as a young girl. That parchment makes her just that much more of a mystery, doesn't it, Uncle?"

"That it does," Scapita whispered, suddenly lost in thought. Pacing the floor, he asked himself, "Why indeed?"

CHAPTER 20

TALLIS

Tallis watched the Bugoward village until the sun hung low over the great trees and the children had returned to their homes. When all seemed quiet, he made his way through the forest until he paused at a great tree, the one Leanne Mellot had called home before her disappearance.

Touching the shadowed bark in a specific way to release the lock, he entered the home, but it was dark and forlorn. He felt the same loss the tree felt, and in a way, it felt like home. Perhaps that was why the tree accepted him as a friend.

He sat down in a rocking chair next to the hearth and began to think. Leanne had lived here for years, perhaps even happily. If only he could have had such happiness, but he was older and could not escape. Their pasts intertwined but she always pushed him away. He had read the fear in her heart. Still, he loved her. Why did she push him away when he offered her so much?

He was elated when he found her living with Blaine Kamp but devastated when he discovered their betrothal. He had angrily confronted her, but then she ran just like before, disappearing utterly. Thinking that she would eventually return to the Blaine, he altered his name to disguise his identity lest she had revealed her plight to him. Ingratiating himself in Kamp's household, he waited, but ten years had passed without a word. Where was she hiding? He thought that she would return here to the tree, but he found no evidence of that.

Suddenly, the interior of the tree began to take on a blue aura of its own. The phasing to the alternate Bugo world had begun. Standing before the hearth, he straightened his robe and stepped through the portal into the alternate world.

"Leanne, where are you?" he cried as loudly as he could, but he only drew incomprehensible stares from the throng of people who had heard him.

He stood at the end of a long street that extended into the Bugoward city. Everyday shoppers went about their business in the market place while farmers brought in wagonloads of produce from the outlying farms.

He stood there mindlessly as they marched by him. Suddenly, it occurred to him just how fruitless this search was. The Bugoward alternate world was as vast as Duscany with millions of places to hide. How would he find her in all of this diversity?

Feeling an itch in his left hand, he scratched it with his right, but then it began to itch as well. Holding them up to his face, he recognized the scales growing there. They began to rapidly multiply up and down his arms, and he felt the itch on his face.

"No, it's too soon!" he cried. "I need more time! This should not be happening so soon."

In time, he found that he could remain human for longer periods without shifting into the serpent form, but the weakening of his natural magic released the serpent now.

Frantically turning about to search for the portal, he nearly cried out in despair. The portal would not return until nightfall in this world. While this one was cloaked in sunlight, the alternate world in Duscany was in darkness. He could not change that.

Panicking, he raced toward the forest bordering the city but a river twenty feet wide barred his way. Leaping into the deep water, he swam as hard as he could until he reached the opposite bank, but his body was changing now. His arms and legs grew shorter, and he felt a long tail tear through the seat of his britches.

He had to reach the shelter of the forest immediately!

Diving behind a thicket at the edge of the forest, he frantically forced his clothes off and scooped them beneath the loose branches where no one would likely find them.

His body squirmed about itself as his arms and legs withdrew into the serpent's body, which elongated until it was thirty feet long and thicker than his human body had been.

This was truly Tallis' identity, the one he had to hide from the world, but he failed to realize that there would come a time when he could not control it in this alternate world. It was a profound mistake to come here, but his serpent mind thought otherwise. It was free now, free of the human who had enslaved it.

Tallis cursed Mercilus for making an example of him, a sorcerer of his caliber, perhaps as strong as he was. Transforming him into a serpent to fight in his games was unconscionable, but he couldn't take revenge on him now. That world had gone by altogether too quickly. Mercilus was dead, and he was delegated to this dual identity forever. He had hoped to die in the arena very quickly, but the serpent only thought to escape.

This world was an escape of sorts, but it was the wrong world. Even the serpent knew that. He could not show himself here, but he was hungry. Fully grown now, the serpent slithered through the barren undergrowth searching for sustenance, but there was no game here. Birds chattered in the treetops and rodents dug burrows in the soft loam, but they were not enough to feed a monster of this size.

Returning to the river, the serpent soon discovered that it was populated by large trout that frequently broke the surface while feeding on the myriads of water bugs that lived there. Sinking quietly beneath the waves, the serpent darted about to catch the frightened fish, swallowing them whole. It wasn't long before the monster had its fill and returned to the forest to hide until nightfall.

However, his human mind continued to ponder the hiding place Leanne must have taken. She had to be here, but he couldn't search for her as the serpent. That's what terrified her, driving her away. He promised her that he could never harm her, but she couldn't believe it. He had a short temper elevated by the presence of the serpent, but he did his best to think first of Leanne's welfare. She had taken his mirror, the one that would show her his dual nature. He had crafted it to help him find a way to break the wizor that held him in thrall for a millennium, but he knew that it was of no use. He would always be a man and a serpent bound together as one.

He cursed Mercilus, but the serpent rejoiced in its ancient life. It was strong, virtually indestructible and would live forever. However, the human part was its curse, a curse that could not be denied. It could rule this world, but the human would not allow it to do so.

The serpent returned to the river to consume more fish several times before nightfall, but when it came, he was ready. The portal to the tree that the human part of him had left became a soft glow in the twilight.

Growing colder now, the serpent slept and allowed the man to return. Tallis eagerly pulled on his clothes and stepped through the portal into the living room of the ancient tree that served as Leanne's home. He regretted that the lapse of his sorcerer powers would not permit him to return to the Bugo alternate world again.

Searching the room, he found the sewing box he knew had to be there and sat where Leanne had often sat. Preparing a needle and thread, he repaired his britches.

Glancing about the meagre furnishing, he noticed that Leanne's artwork in stone was virtually everywhere he looked. She had made several stones bearing his likeness, but he was more handsome then, and she had no cause to fear him. He wondered what could have made her change her mind about him, but he realized that it was a mistake to seek her help. Showing her the mirror was the worst mistake of all. She saw him for who he really was, and it terrified her. She couldn't see him for the gentle man that he was from then on.

He had hoped to enlist the great Scapita to not only help him find her but to separate his human half from the serpent. After all, his sorcery was legendary, but even that ploy had failed because of that great fool, Blaine Kamp, who drove him away. Of course, forgetting his temper at the store proved to be disastrous.

He required another form of help now to find Leanne and her true father. Her mother had died in the alternate Bugo world, but her father, he was certain, was still alive. Unfortunately, he could no longer return there without becoming the serpent, the one that hated his very presence. The monster plotted to take over his life. It would eventually dominate his very nature, but he had to find a way to prevent that eventuality and soon.

Tallis began to think that Scapita might be his only hope, but could he trust him to help rather than condemn? Deciding that he had no other choice, he departed the Bugoward forest and found the trail that would take him to the highway and thus to Kings Keep.

Realizing that it was a long walk from here, he flagged down a teamster on the highway.

"I beg your help," he said to the teamster. "Can you take me as close to Kings Keep as you can? I'm footsore as it is."

"Hop aboard," the old man replied. "I'm delivering these supplies there. This is a lonely road, so I won't mind the company."

"Thanks!" Tallis replied, climbing up onto the seat. "How far is it? Do you know?"

"We'll be there in a few hours, so don't you fret," the driver replied. "I'm Dever, and you?"

"Tallis," he replied politely. "I have business with Scapita. He's still the sorcerer to the king, isn't he?"

"That and much more, I wager," Dever said. "I've heard some strange stories about him and his niece. She won the last Wizor Fair if you recall. I've never seen so much power in a child before. I heard that Scapita was like that himself when he was a mere Wizor."

"Yes, I witnessed her fantastic win at the fair," Tallis replied.

He began to think that perhaps Jenna could be of help too especially if Scapita refused to help. After all, he had no gold to offer. The few silvers that Blaine Kamp had paid him surely would not be enough to attract the attention of the great Scapita. Sorcerers of his caliber greedily demanded as much as possible from prospective customers. After all, Blaine Kamp had offered him a thousand in gold and Scapita refused it, preferring to pass it off to his niece.

They arrived at the gatehouse of Kings Keep in the early afternoon. Tallis was hungry, but he decided to seek out Scapita first. If he refused to help, he would seek other means to force it from him.

"Where can I find Scapita?" he asked Dever.

Pointing at the tower, he stated, "You'll find him at the top of that. Good luck, Tallis."

Tallis thanked him and strolled to the entrance of the keep. A guard directed him up the stairs of the tower. He carefully climbed the long stairwell until he reached the landing just outside of the door, but a short personable woman opened the door before he knocked.

"What is it you seek?" she asked.

"I'm called Tallis," he replied. "I'm here because I need Master Scapita's help. Is he in?"

"Yes, but I screen his callers. My name is Guena. Specifically, what kind of help do you require?"

Deciding not to explain the whole story yet, he replied, "I'm here because of Leanne Mellot. I believe that Blaine Kamp explained that she's been missing for some time."

"Send him in!" Scapita's voice boomed from inside.

"Very well, come in. Scapita's in the living room. Just go in and sit down. Would you like a refreshment?"

"Ale if you please," he replied.

Entering the living room, he found Scapita rocking in his chair with a comforter drawn over his legs for added warmth. He pointed to a chair near the fireplace, but he did not speak.

Tallis sat down and waited for his host to break the silence, but he did not until Guena brought a tankard of ale for him and heated, mulled wine for Scapita and herself.

"Guena, call Jenna down from her room," Scapita said. "This is her case, so she should be here to listen to what this gentleman has to say."

Jenna, however, appeared next to Scapita, startling them all. "Who is our guest?" she asked.

"Forgive me," Tallis remarked, taken aback by her entrance. "My name is Tallis. I'm here at Blaine Kamp's bequest. We're concerned about Leanne Mellot."

"Yes, he said that she disappeared ten years ago," Jenna said. "What is your interest in her?"

"Well, I, um," he stammered. "Well, I'm the reason why she ran away. I've been looking for her ever since to apologize to her, and we're concerned for her welfare."

Jenna glanced at Scapita, but he only smiled and said, "This is your case, Jenna. You may pursue it any way you please."

Jenna gazed directly into Tallis' eyes as if probing for answers. After a moment, she stated, "You haven't been honest with us, Master Tallis. You aren't who you claim to be. Why is that?"

"You have the gift of far-sight," Tallis whispered anxiously.

Glancing at the others, he realized that Scapita and Guena were reading him like an open book as well. This was a family of sorcerers with the gift of far-sight! Dropping his gaze, he began to weep.

"I see a name," Jenna said. "Brontis, who is that?"

He met her eyes again and replied, "I am Brontis. What do you know of it?"

"I heard it a very long time ago in ancient Eskeling," she replied. "It belonged to one of Mercilus' sorcerers, but now here you are? Who is the serpent, Brontis? You are the serpent also, aren't you?"

Scapita and Guena glanced at each other. Even they had not seen this aspect of their visitor.

"Yes, I am the serpent," he blathered. "Mercilus did this to me, and I've suffered from it for all of these years. Oh, the serpent seems to know you, Jenna? You were there when it escaped, weren't you? How is that possible?"

Jenna grinned. "It's possible because I have powerful friends. Truthfully, I hadn't thought about the serpent that escaped Mercilus' fair until now. We found the crocodilians and troglodytes in the fen, and that's kept us busy. Now the serpent has appeared, you. Tell us why you are here. It's not just because of Leanne Mellot, is it?"

Glancing at the other questioning faces, he decided that he could not hold out any longer. "I'll confess it all. I met Leanne when she lived with the Bugos. Young and beautiful, we hit it off right away, but then I tried to tell her about the serpent. I wanted her father to help me destroy it, but she became frightened and refused. She ran from me. I found her living with Blaine Kamp, but she ran again. I think she returned to the alternate Bugo world to warn her father."

"Just how is her father relevant to his case, Brontis?" Scapita asked. "Who is he?"

Brontis glanced at Jenna and said, "You know, don't you?"

Jenna began to think. She didn't know exactly, but she realized that it could be only one of two people. "His name is either Magus or Butkus," she said. "The crocs swallowed them whole after converting them to stone. They must have recovered quite recently in fact. Is that not true?"

"Magus is her father," he agreed. "They awoke perhaps fifty years ago. Even they didn't know how long they slept in stone, but when they did, they escaped the fen. They knew that the crocs and trogs were there and could do the same in time. They sought a safe place to stay in case they did. They joined a Bugoward village in Duscany and decided to stay in the alternate world where the monsters could not follow them.

176

"As for me, I awoke much later. We were friends at first until I revealed my secret. I tried to get their help, but they said that they didn't know how. I had stolen one of Mercilus' wizor lists that I hoped would protect me from him back then, but after I awoke here, I thought it could protect me from the serpent. However, they didn't understand the formula any better than I did. I hid it inside of Leanne's periapt until I could find someone who could read it, but Leanne stole it from me along with my mirror. I've been looking for the items ever since."

"It seems that this is relevant after all," Scapita remarked, unfolding the parchment for Brontis to see.

"That's mine!" he cried. "How did you come by it?"

Jenna giggled and replied, "My very good friend, Prince Leonard, was astute enough to find it, but it was locked inside of a walnut protected by a sixth level charm. You don't seem to be that strong, Brontis. How did you do it?"

Brontis anxiously tried to hide his feelings, but then he confessed. "I was much stronger then. In Eskeling, I could keep up with magic Mercilus did up to level seven and perhaps a little more. I've weakened since I've been here, perhaps to level five. I don't understand why."

Jenna understood immediately. Since he had strayed from the Whelf Fen for so long, he couldn't feed on the magic to renew his strength, but she wasn't about to tell him that.

"Tell me, Master Brontis," Jenna said, "can you help us destroy the crocs and trogs coming to life in the fen?"

"They're coming to life?" he asked, terrified.

"Oh yes, and when they do," Jenna replied, "they'll destroy everything they touch beginning with the fen and working their way here."

"This is not good news," he whispered. "I'm sorry, but I don't have the power to do it even if I had my whip. Under controlled circumstances I might be able to help, but not now. Only Mercilus could stop them in my time. His monsters terrified even the strongest of us, but we were even more afraid of him."

"Then this might be our last hope," Scapita said. Unfolding the parchment, he spread it out over his lap.

CHAPTER 21

SURVIVOR

Cassy transported backwards in time in one day increments, but then she skipped a week and then a month. The Whelf Fen remained the same as it had always been. The monsters were there sleeping without disturbance.

She decided that she had no choice except to leap a year at a time and hope she didn't miss anything; however, her tactic paid off. She spotted the two man-sized statues imbedded in the mud of the fen and immediately recognized them as Magus and Butkus. The crocs had spit them out at some point.

Jumping a month and then a day at a time into the future she discovered when the stone melted and the sorcerers became men again. Apparently, the stone had protected rather than destroyed them for they pulled themselves from the fen unfettered. More jumps in time, proved that they had survived and prospered.

When she realized that, she had an astonishing insight. What if Rosina were still alive but encased in stone? Had that stone already melted and released her body to corruption?

Directing her whelf senses through the fen, she searched for her distinctive signature. She searched for some time without finding anything, but then a few miles from where the sorcerers recovered, she found her stone buried deep in the fen. If the stone had melted anytime in the past, then she would not have survived.

Cassy immediately jumped to the present and probed for the stone. She was relieved when she found it intact. Magically drawing the stone up to the surface, she gazed at the startled face of Rosina locked in time. However, as she watched, the stone began to melt away. Rosina suddenly blinked and stared at her in shock.

"You," she said, "you sat next to me in the stadium!"

Cassy smiled and took Rosina's outstretched hand. "Yes, it's me, but my name is Cassandra, not Mata."

"What is going on?" Rosina asked, sitting up. "What is this place?"

"I hate to say this, Rosina, but you are in my world a thousand years into your future. The spital from the croc magically froze you into stone. It suspended your life and protected you until now. I don't know if you would call it fortunate or not since your family has been dead for a thousand years."

Rosina began to tremble. "I'm so cold. It's so wet and muddy here. I don't know why, but I'm so very hungry."

"Then I better do something about it, Rosina. Don't be frightened when you see me as I really am. I'm going to do my best to save your life."

Rosina gaped in awe as Cassy spread her wings and suspended her in her arms. An instant later, they appeared in Scapita's living room, startling the assembly there.

"Who is this, Cassandra?" Guena asked. "Is she hurt?"

"Her name is Rosina," she replied. "She's not hurt, but she needs our help. If you would, Guena, please order some food for her, preferably soft to chew. She hasn't eaten in a thousand years. I'll deal with the rest."

"At once!" Guena agreed, hurrying to do her bidding.

Rosina suddenly became suspended in the air within a bright glow that cleansed and warmed her body. Her filthy black dress hazed away but Cassy replaced it with a courtly blue gown that fit her perfectly. She replaced her muddy shoes with a pair of ankle high laced shoes with low heels.

When Cassy set her on her feet, she stood there in shock. Glancing at Cassy, she asked, "It's beautiful, Cassandra, but can I have my old dress back? It means a lot to me."

"You can have anything you wish, Rosina, for the asking."

"You're so kind." When she turned to Jenna, she said, "I know you too, don't I?"

"My name is Jenna, Rosina. We last met in Eskeling a long time ago."

"But you both look exactly the same as you did then," Rosina replied. "How is that possible?"

Cassy explained. "We're from this time, Rosina. We journeyed back to old Eskeling to find out how the crocodilians escaped the fair. You see, we discovered them here in our time. They're about to wake up, and when they do, they'll try to destroy everything just as your husband designed them to do."

"Oh, I knew that his monsters would cause grief one day. I am so sorry, Cassandra."

"There's no need to apologize for him, Rosina," Cassy replied. "His monsters destroyed him and all of Eskeling five years after your purported death."

Shocked, she asked, "What about my children? Were they destroyed too?"

"No, they survived and helped to found the present kingdom of Duscany. That's where you are now."

Guena let the serving girl into the apartment and helped Rosina to sit at the table. "Take your time, dear," she said. "It might be difficult for you to eat."

"You're all so kind," she said staring at the plate of steaming vegetables. "I'm very thirsty, Guena. May I have some water?"

"She may be dehydrated," Cassy explained.

"I'll get it for you," Guena replied. She dipped a tankard into a bucket of water sitting in a corner and placed it in front of her. "There's plenty, so eat up."

Rosina eagerly swallowed half of it, but she began to cough, spitting up some that tumbled down her front. "Oh, I've mussed up your beautiful gown, Cassandra. I'm so sorry."

"Don't apologize for anything you need," Cassy said. She waved her hand over the spot, which vanished immediately.

"Are you a sorcerer, Cassandra?" she asked.

"I am a whelf as well as a human being," she replied. "You are in the company of sorcerers, however. They will do what is necessary to help you recover."

Rosina took a couple of bites and smiled. "That's very good." Pausing for a moment, she asked, "What will happen to me now? I'm a stranger here, and my family is gone. I have no place to go."

"We won't let you come to harm, Rosina," Cassandra said. "We are your family now. After you've rested, I'll give you some life choices that you might want to consider."

When Brontis stood over her, she said, "I know you too but a few years older than I expected. You worked for my husband, didn't you?"

"Yes, Rosina, I must say that I'm astonished to find you still alive. I was imprisoned in stone too, but I woke up a few years ago. I want you to consider me your family as well, but I won't criticize you if you do not."

He considered telling her the rest of his secret, but he decided that now was not appropriate. It was best to allow her to recover from the shock of finding herself in a new world. The first few weeks would be particularly difficult for her to adjust to. He returned to the living room and sat down to stare at the painting hanging over the fireplace. There she was set in paint standing next to Mercilus and her children.

Funny, he had not noticed it until now. He had seen the larger version in the Sorcerer's Guildhall in Eskeling many times. A copy hanging here suggested that Scapita was a descendent of Mercilus himself. Perhaps the situation wasn't as dire as he had first feared.

Cassy sat with Rosina until she finished eating, but she observed that the woman bobbed her head in weariness. She would have to take care of that before anything else.

"Rosina, I'm going to take you to my home where you can rest and recover. It's not here but in another world very different from this one. I don't want you to be frightened when you see it. When you're rested, we'll talk about your future, all right?"

Gazing at her, Rosina replied, "I doubt if anything will shock me now, Cassandra. I've seen so much that I never thought could exist. I'll go with you gladly. I'm so weary, Cassandra!" she cried, grasping Cassy's supporting arm.

When Rosina opened her eyes, she was sitting at Cassy's kitchen table as if that's where they were all along.

"I told you it's different," Cassy said. "I'm going to help you walk upstairs to my bedroom where you can rest. You need the exercise

ROBERT A. G. ERICKSON

anyway." Cassy then shouted, "Cass, I could use your help!"

Cass immediately appeared on the opposite side of Rosina and helped her up from the chair.

"You look exactly alike," Rosina said, "twins?"

"Yes, twins," Cass replied, "but I'll tell you about my family later. I can tell you that you're in a house of twins, so that you don't freak out."

"Freak out?" Rosina asked, as they helped her up the stairs.

"You know, get confused or upset," Cass explained. "Well, it's a long story. It'll help if you're wide awake when you hear it."

Lenny appeared at the top of the stairs just as the girls reached it with Rosina in tow. Rosina's eyes grew large when she saw him and glanced at Cassy for an explanation.

"Rosina, meet my brother," Cassy said. "You met him in Eskeling as Leonard, but we just call him Lenny. I'm sure he won't mind if you do too."

Rosina rolled back her eyes and fainted. The girls took her arms while Lenny lifted her feet. They transported her into Cassy's bedroom and set her on the bed.

"Cassy, we really have to talk," Lenny said. "Why did you feel that you had to rescue her? You said we couldn't afford to change the past because it could change the future."

"This isn't what it seems, Lenny," she replied. "I'll tell you all about it later. Right now, you have to get out of here while I remove her dress and get her into a nightgown unless you really want to watch."

Lenny looked cross, but then he went downstairs to find something to eat. He was ravenously hungry after a day of wizor making. He thankfully found some leftover meatloaf in the fridge.

Cassy and Cass sat down with him once they were done upstairs.

"Wipe that cross look off your face, Lenny," Cassy said. "I had to rescue her. That croc had encased her in stone, but she wasn't dead. I found her just in time to save her life. Otherwise, she would have died unnecessarily."

Lenny glanced at the girls and asked, "How did you find that out?"

Cassy explained how Mercilus had transformed Brontis into the serpent they saw at the fair but was similarly encased in stone when the monsters fought in the fen. He was even more astonished to discover that Magus and Butkus had also survived and were last seen hiding in the Bugo alternate world.

"That's amazing," Lenny replied. "We have to find them as soon as possible. If the monsters wake up anytime soon, we could use their help. I've discovered something astonishing about Mercilus' whips. With more of them, we might be able to turn the tide on these monsters."

"Well, I could return to Eskeling and get more whips," Cassy said. "They have a storeroom full of them."

"Either that or get some here, Cassy," he said. "They're just whips. It's the sound they make that matters. They create shockwaves that affect the monsters. The monsters are individually tuned to the sound it makes according to the power level at creation, not the other way around. There's no magic in the whips."

"You've really done your homework, Lenny," Cassy said, clapping her hands. "Nice job. I'll get the whips from Eskeling since they're there for the taking. How many do you think we need?"

"Let's see," Lenny said, thinking back to the fights in the arena. "Besides Mercilus, there were always eight others in the arena at any one time. You better get an even dozen, just in case we need them."

"You'll find them in your castle in Duscany," Cassy said, standing up. "I assume that you'll want to demonstrate how to use them there. It's the most logical place. Cass, please take care of Rosina's needs for now. Show her around if she wants to see the neighborhood. I don't want her to feel like she's a prisoner. Explain to mom and dad's duplicates when they come home. I have to return to the fen and keep an eye on those monsters."

"Whatever you say, sis," Cass replied. "I'll take care of everything, so don't you worry none."

Cassy smiled and vanished.

"You can tell when she's worried," Cass said. "Lenny, is this problem as dire as she says it is?"

"You know it, Cass. I hope you can quickly learn how to use a whip because all of us may be enlisted to fight those monsters. We will all have to learn how to work together on the fly."

"Are you serious, Lenny?" she asked. "I'm a girl. I'm not interested in fighting anyone or things like these crocs and trogs you've talked about."

"Cass, you are made of magic and can't be seriously hurt. All of our duplicates can be as strong as the Whelf Fen allows it. Mercilus' monsters are waking up as we speak, and we'll all be pressed into service whether we like it or not. Just be thankful that they can't cross into our world here or else the planet Earth would be in real trouble. As it is, Duscany could be just a blob of ink on an ancient map in only a few days. Remember where your roots are, Cass."

Cass began to cry. Wiping her tears away on her blouse sleeve, she said, "I'm sorry, Lenny, but I don't feel as strong as you or Cassy. I feel just like any other normal girl here on Earth."

Lenny leaned back and nodded. "The magic is doing that to you, Cass. It's making you what you want to be. You really do need to spend more time in Duscany, so you can keep that part of your identity intact."

Cass grinned and tried to look supportive, but tears continued to stream down her cheeks. "Really, Lenny, Cassy gave me the chore of looking after Rosina. That's something I know I can do. I just don't see myself fighting anything with a whip or anything else. Really, I don't know the first thing about fighting."

"Well, maybe you should just stay here with Rosina for now. Mom is still sick in Duscany and dad is with her, so they'll be of no use in this battle. Their duplicates, James and Mare, could be of value though. I'll bring my duplicate, Len, up to date on what I know. He's being a bit rebellious too, but he'll come around when he understands what's at stake here."

Len suddenly appeared at the table, staring at his namesake in astonishment. "What's this stuff about fighting monsters, Lenny?" he asked. Waiting until the magic informed him of what he had missed, he said, "Oh, I see you've been busy. I've had fun destroying monsters on videogames, but I never thought I'd be doing it for real. When do we start?"

"It could be at any time, Len," Lenny replied. "Just make yourself available when it does. It would probably help if you camped out in my castle in Duscany and start absorbing as much magical strength as you can. You'll need it."

"I'll be there," he replied. Taking Cass's hand, he said, "Don't worry, sis. If you have to fight with us, I'll show you the ropes. You're all magic just like me. All you have to do is let it in, and it'll

BRIDE OF THE BLANE

serve you."

"Thanks, Len, for your support," she said. "If it comes to that, I'll do my part. I promise."

Lenny took her other hand and replied, "That's all we ask for, Cass. Cassy is watching the monsters now, and she'll inform us if we're needed. Get a good night's sleep, everyone, and be ready to move in the morning."

When he realized what he had said, he felt stupid. Cass and Len were magical duplicates who didn't require sleep or physical nourishment either. However, they were in the habit of emulating human beings since they considered themselves members of the family.

Cassy watched the monsters stirring in the fen all night. All of her whelf friends watched with her. She was grateful for the added eyes of her friends: Sunshine, Winter and Misty, for they were closest to her, but even they understood the seriousness of the awakening.

All of the monsters began to thrash about in the bracken growing on the many islets in the fen. Muddy water dripped thickly from their bodies. Suddenly, the crocs' roars filled the fen with a disheartening din that startled the nesting birds in the trees. The troglodytes lifted their heads and roared a challenge of equal magnitude and began the muddy trek toward their quarry.

Seeing each other for the first time in a millennium, the targets attacked with such power and determination that the fen itself quaked beneath their feet. The battle raged on until dawn, never slackening, completely without remorse.

CHAPTER 22

LEANNE MELLOT

Cassy waited in the great room of Leonard Castle until Lenny, Jenna and the family duplicates had answered her summons. Only Cass had not yet arrived, but then she had another chore to perform.

When Cass did arrive, she sat at the table next to Len. "I did as you told me, Cassy," she said. "I left Rosina with Prince Symon in Kings Keep. He wanted to examine her to make sure that she was well."

"Very good," Cassy replied. "It's time for action. The monsters have been battling it out in the Whelf Fen for hours. It's best to leave them alone for now. They're shedding their strength at a phenomenal rate. The more they lose, the better it is for us. I think that was Mercilus' strategy to begin with. Lenny, Jenna, you have another chore to do. You must go to the Bugo alternate world and bring back Magus and Butkus. We'll need their help."

Lenny stood up and replied, "We can't go until the changeover at dusk. We'll need your help to go there now."

"I'll send you there directly, Lenny," Cassy replied. "Chances are they're both at the address Dame Mola provided. If not, then find someone who knew them then and can direct you. I'll convince

Brontis to give us his take on fighting these monsters. I don't know if Scapita or Guena can help, but I'll find out. Meanwhile we'll practice with the whips and stay away from the monsters until they stop brawling and start moving our way. Any questions?"

Everyone looked tentatively at the others, but no one had anything to say.

"We're ready, Cassy," Lenny said, holding Jenna's firm hand.

Cassy merely nodded, sending them on their way to the Bugo alternate world.

The day here was perceptively longer than in Duscany, but the sun was still high on the horizon. Sunset would trigger the transition time between this world and the Bugoward world in Duscany. Lenny decided that they had that long to find Magus and Butkus and perhaps Leanne Mellot.

"This has to be the place," Lenny said, pointing at a large two-story brick residence. "Cassy said she would drop us off at the exact address Dame Mola gave us."

"This place is very nice," Jenna said. "The owners must be quite affluent to afford this. My parent's home in Kings Port isn't nearly this nice."

"Then let's see who is home," Lenny said, "my way."

He set up his wizard staff and flattened the steel ball at the top to create the viewer they had so much success with in Eskeling. He tuned the view until the interior of the house focused. Walking through each room, he found a young woman working in the rear of the house, but there was no sign of Magus and Butkus.

"I think that's Leanne Mellot, Jenna. She matches the image we saw of her on the stone."

"Well, let's do it, Leonard," she replied. "I want to get this over with."

Lenny shrunk his staff down to the lapel pin and fixed it in place. His dragon handled cane suddenly appeared in his hand.

"I thought you left that thing in Eskeling," Jenna said. "How is it that you have it now?"

"I thought you knew me," Lenny laughed. "It returned to me the instant I called for it. I'm not interested in losing my things, especially not to someone like Butkus."

"He'll certainly be surprised to see us if he shows up," Jenna giggled.

Lenny rapped on the wooden door with the metal end of his cane and waited for a response. After a moment, he repeated the effort.

The door suddenly cracked open, and the young woman peered from behind it. "What do you want?" she said. "I don't know you."

Jenna smiled at her and replied, "We need to talk to you, Leanne. Blaine Kamp sent us.

"Kamp sent you?" she cried. "Why, how did you find me?"

"We followed your clues, Leanne," Lenny replied. "Blaine Kamp begs you to come back. He's never lost his love for you."

"No, I can't," Leanne replied as tears flooded her eyes.

"Please, Leanne, may we come in?" Lenny said. "We'll explain."

She stared at them a moment before she made up her mind and gave in. "You might as well. You don't look like you're here to harm me."

"Why would you say that?" Jenna asked as they stepped into the large receiving room.

"If you really understood why I'm here, you would know why. Oh, please seat yourselves. May I get you something to drink? There's a little wine left."

"No, we're fine," Lenny replied as he sat down next to Jenna. "I want you to know that we understand why you've been hiding here." He furtively moved his hand to hide the sudden appearance of the mirror he had found in Leanne's Bugoward tree home and held it smokey side up. "Do you recognize this?"

"Oh my God!" she screamed. "Get that thing away from me. Don't you know what it is?"

Seemingly pocketing the mirror, Lenny replied, "I am well aware of the fact that it and the walnut we found in your home in Duscany belonged to someone you knew either as Brontis or Tallis. He spilled everything when Jenna confronted him."

"Then you know that he's the most dangerous man who ever existed," Leanne said. "He's not a man but a serpent that kills on instinct. I fled for my life when I discovered that, but he kept following me. Then I met Blaine Kamp. He's the nicest man I've ever known. I willingly said yes when he asked to marry me, but then Brontis showed up. He tried to make me come with him, but I refused. I left the clues so that Kamp wouldn't worry too much and ran again. I figured that Brontis wouldn't look for me in this world because he was reluctant to travel through the portal. For a long time, I feared doing it myself after leaving here the first time, but I had no choice."

"That explains a lot," Lenny said. "There is one other thing. We're here to find Magus and Butkus. We need their help too."

Leanne shook her head and held a hand to her mouth as her tears renewed. She replied, "You're too late. Magus was my father. He died two years after my mother did. Butkus lived with us, but I didn't want anything to do with him. I allowed myself to be adopted by a very nice family who alternated between the Bugo worlds, but I wouldn't go back while Butkus was here. When I decided that I had no choice, I returned. I made him move out, but he died five years ago. You should know that he and my father were very old when they died. Their sorcerer powers had faded almost to nothing. I learned my strengths from my father. That's what I do. I help others with the magic I learned from him."

Lenny glanced at Jenna and replied, "The walnut periapt, did you or your father create it? It's sixth level magic."

"I made it for Brontis," Leanne said. "I make a lot of periapts for people who want them. Walnuts are rare here, though. There are only a few trees still living north of the city. I don't think they originated here or else they would be more abundant. They make nice periapts, though."

"Don't you understand what that means, Leanne?" Lenny said. "Very few sorcerer class people can make sixth level wizors of any kind, yet I doubt if you're registered anywhere as a sorcerer."

"Yes, well, it makes people nervous if you mention that word around here, so I mainly stuck to charms. It was easy for me to emulate Bugoward wood and stone magic, which was expected of me."

"Should we tell her, Leonard?" Jenna asked.

"Tell me what?" Leanne asked.

"I think we should, Jenna," Lenny replied. "Leanne, we need your help."

Then he explained the problem with the monsters bashing it out in the Whelf Fen.

"I'm sure you know that Magus, Butkus as well as Brontis were from ancient Eskeling. The monsters battling in the fen were from there as well. We came to ask Magus and Butkus to help us destroy them, but then we found you. Did they tell you anything about what they did in Eskeling or how they came to be here?"

"Father was especially tightlipped about that," she replied. "Butkus told me stories about it after Magus died. Apparently, my father made him promise not to say anything while his wife lived, but he wanted me to know their history. I'm glad Butkus told me, but the man was a lout, a drunkard, and never married. I couldn't stand to have him around. He kept trying to get money from me so he could buy booze. I guess I still feel a little guilty for driving him off, but I couldn't abide his lifestyle. It eventually killed him."

"Leanne, we need your help," Lenny begged. "Please help us fight the monsters."

"Leonard has found a way to do it, Leanne," Jenna added. "We have a lot of powerful people on our side who will be there. There is always a possibility of failure, but we must try or else the monsters could erase all of Duscany including the Bugoward forest and your tree there. Elder Wolsa and Dame Mola have kept it free of occupancy for your return should you require it."

"Oh, I was unaware of that. I did enjoy living in the tree, and I still have a lot of friends there. It would be a shame if the forest was destroyed." Leanne struggled to pull her courage up from deep down inside, but she made her decision. "I'll help. What do you want me to do?"

"Come with us and we'll show you," Lenny said. "If you need to do something first, we'll give you the time, just don't take too long. The battle is imminent."

Leanne thought carefully for a moment, but then she removed a wrap from a wooden peg and said, "Let's go now before I change my mind. I'm not a coward, but the idea of fighting monsters scares me to death."

Lenny grinned, glanced up and shouted, "Cassy, we're ready to return!"

Leanne jumped in surprise when she found herself inside of the great hall. "My goodness, where am I?"

"This is Leonard Keep, Leanne," Lenny said. "This is my home here in Duscany. I've been fixing it up, but a lot has gotten in the way lately. Let me introduce you to some of the others who will fight with us."

The other duplicates crowded around and took her hand as he

introduced them. He didn't explain their natures just yet, even though she was intrigued over the lookalikes.

She stepped back to run, however, when Brontis took his turn.

"There is no reason to fear me, Leanne," he said. "You already know my secret and my ancestry. I knew your father in Eskeling, but I admit that I didn't like him much. I suppose that you're saying the same about me, and I can't blame you. I wasn't especially honest with you from the beginning, but we're fighting on the same side now. The serpent was created to fight against those monsters in the fen, and I suppose that I must allow it to finish the fight."

"You seem different somehow, Brontis," she replied, "more passive. You know that I don't and can't love you, don't you?"

"I do now, Leanne, and I'm sorry I mistreated you," he replied. "I've given up on that idea. I have only one future left and that is in the fen with the other monsters. I thought I could shake off the serpent somehow, and I might have with Magus and Butkus' help, but they refused. Where are they? Why didn't they come with you?"

Tears appeared in Leanne's eyes as she explained. "They're dead. If you expected help from them, it was too late a long time ago."

Brontis turned aside, overcome with emotion. Sitting by himself, he struggled with what might have been if he had been more honest about himself.

Suddenly, he rose to his feet with a renewed purpose. Rushing from the keep, he ran toward the closed drawbridge.

Lenny followed him, but Cassy appeared and barred his way halfway across the courtyard.

"Don't follow him, Lenny," she said. "He has to fight his own battle now."

Lenny didn't understand what she meant at first until Brontis shed his clothes. Morphing into the great serpent, he writhed over the castle curtain and into the brushy moat beyond.

Sucking up Brontis' castoffs into his wizard staff, he asked, "Is he going to fight those monsters himself, Cassy?"

"That's what it looks like to me," she replied. "The serpent was created to fight them. Perhaps he can rob them of enough energy to give us a chance."

"We have Leanne," Lenny said. He had to say something even knowing that she already had the answers. "Magus and Butkus are dead. I can't think of anyone more deserving, but I had hoped that they could help. Now we don't even have Brontis to show us how to use the whips. I just hope that we have all we need when the time comes."

"I doubt if there's any mystery to it," she replied. "You saw how Mercilus and his sorcerers worked the arena in Eskeling. They mainly kept the monsters fighting against each other until they weakened enough to use the whips on them, and you discovered how to do that."

"Well, I just wish that I was as confident about that as you are, Cassy," Lenny replied. "As I see it, the biggest problem is fighting them in the fen. I think that the best thing to do is to draw them out in the open where they can't feed on the magic. Do you have any ideas about how to do that?"

"One," she said, glancing back in the direction that the serpent had taken. "Maybe Brontis can lure them out. I'll put the bug in his ear while you teach our volunteers how to use the whips."

She suddenly vanished, leaving him with his thoughts. When he turned around, he found the others outside of the keep, staring at him.

Leanne and Jenna strolled up to him with questioning eyes.

Lenny waved at the others and cried, "Bring out the whips! We have work to do."

Suddenly his cane became his whip. He impressively snapped it several times as if he really knew how to handle it.

———————◆◆◆◆◆◆◆———————

Scapita sat at his laboratory bench with one of Mercilus' books spread open on one side and the parchment Lenny had given him on the other. He carefully scanned information in the book, comparing it line for line to the ones in the parchment.

Guena sat down next to him and glanced at the squiggles in the book. "That looks complicated," she said. "I understand ancient Eskeling when it applies to our wizor making, but this is impossible."

"Probably just short of that," Scapita replied. "The parchment is indeed a list of wizors. Since there are five lines, I suspect that it would create a fifth level wizor of some sort. I'm getting some ideas though. Mercilus often wrote his multilevel wizors in shorthand like this. I'm sure that he knew them all by heart, but it makes less sense for anyone else trying to read it. I think I've deciphered the second and third lines. The first one identifies the overall effect of the wizor, the parameters if you will. I'm not sure what the last level does. If you would, Guena, get me some wine. It relaxes me and helps me think."

"Of course, but don't forget our wedding, dear," she replied. "It's planned for tomorrow."

"I'm sorry, Guena, but the situation may decide that for us. Plan on postponing it. I've already informed the king of the possibility. If we can't stop those monsters, well, there won't be a need for a wedding. No one will survive the first attack on the keep."

"I understand," she replied. Dabbing at the tears in the corners of her eyes with a kerchief, she departed to fetch some wine from the steward.

CHAPTER 23

QUIMBY'S END

Brontis realized that the only emotions he could detect from the serpent were those of freedom and hate. The very idea of fighting the crocs and trogs encouraged the serpent on to an even higher level of hatred. It undulated even faster over the rocky terrain until it entered the fen itself.

Homing in on the din from the battle taking place there, the serpent writhed its way over the marshy ground. At home in this environment, it screamed in anticipation as it approached the other monsters, crocodilian or troglodyte, which churned up the muddy soil everywhere they battled.

The serpent seemed unaware of Cassy's presence in an ear, but Brontis still had enough humanity left to hear her.

"You must get the monsters to follow you to the open meadow due north of here. They can do no harm there, and it'll get them out of the fen. You must do this, Brontis. Do you understand?"

Brontis understood and even reasoned why it was necessary, but getting the serpent to listen proved to be daunting. The creature raced to do battle, but Brontis eventually managed to pull the serpent aside just in time to prevent the initial clash. The serpent listlessly circled the monsters before pausing on the north side of the battle. It sank long fangs into the leg of the nearest troglodyte and backed off.

The trog fell backwards into the mire, spraying the miasmic soil across the fen. Sighting the serpent hissing only a few steps away, it squirmed out of the clutches of the croc and raced after it, but the serpent retreated north. The trog and croc immediately followed the other. Distracted, the second set of monsters also followed, battling each other as they went.

The serpent easily crossed the river to the meadow beyond. Once the pursuing monsters had crossed, the serpent returned to the river and purposely sank to the bottom. Protruding its bucket sized eyes and nostrils above the ripples of the current, it watched the monsters resume their reckless battles.

Brontis understood what Cassy had meant to do now. The monsters had to deplete their power reserves in order to have a chance at defeating them, and that made sense. The serpent had to wait for the right moment before attacking again, otherwise there would be no success. The serpent was only eighth power with no chance of winning a war against two ninth power monsters, but waiting was a strategy Brontis forced it to understand.

A croc set a beady eye on the nearest trog and spat. The white mist clung to its abdomen and turned to stone, but the trog tore it away, leaving a bloody gap and bare ribs. The trog howled in anguish but angrily leapt at the croc in retaliation.

Good, thought Brontis. *It's weakening. Just like Mercilus to add so much realism to wounds to satisfy the bloodlust of the viewers.*

The sight of blood even attracted the serpent, but Brontis managed to hold the monster's bloodlust in abeyance. *The time is not right,* he promised the serpent, *but I'll release you when it is.*

Satisfied, Cassy returned to Leonard Castle where she found Lenny instructing the others on tactics with the whip. Lenny had conjured a monster of wood to use as a target. Keeping their distance, the sorcerers snapped their whips simultaneously, then rotated together a short distance and snapped them again.

When she appeared next to Lenny, he called the practice off.

"That was great, everyone," he said. "I think that if we can do that with the real thing, we will have a chance to win. Let's go inside the keep and get some refreshments. It's hot out here."

He morphed his whip back into the dragon cane and smiled at Cassy. "By the look on your face, you have some news. Please, I want to hear some good news for a change."

"If you mean that the monsters have been relocated, yes, they have," she replied. "I think that Brontis has come around to our way of thinking. He's watching them for me. He'll know when the time is right to strike."

"Let's go inside," Lenny replied. "Maybe you can conjure us up some food? I haven't mastered that trick yet."

Cassy giggled, and followed him inside. "It's only a matter of time, Lenny. You've come a long way. One of these days I'll be asking you for favors."

Entering the great hall, Cassy spread her wings and hovered over the tables. Food and drink magically appeared there. Finished, she became herself and sat down next to Lenny. Jenna sat on his other side.

"What is she?" Leanne whispered to Jenna. "She's beautiful."

"Among other things, she's the Queen of the Whelfs, Leanne," Jenna replied. "If you hang around long enough, you'll get used to her comings and goings. You should know that she's Leonard's sister. He's not what he seems either. He's the King of the Whelfs."

"My goodness," Leanne said, "I never realized that there was such a thing. I've heard stories about whelfs, but this seems so surreal."

Suddenly, Quimby leapt up onto the table and then into Lenny's arms. "There you are, Quimby," he said. "Are you hungry?" He offered the little monster a tidbit from his sandwich, but he ignored it. "Well, I guess I didn't give you a need to eat."

"Lenny," Cassy cried, "what have you done?"

"Well, I needed a monster to experiment on," he said. "Thankfully, it worked. The monster I created became as docile and loving as a cat. I couldn't bring myself to destroy it, so I keep it here. Mom and dad would probably freak out if I brought it home."

"They're not the only ones," Cass said. "It's so ugly."

"Don't worry, Cass," he replied. "It won't bite you. Here, see for yourself."

He urged Quimby into Cass' arms. The beast willingly wrapped its long arms around her neck and hung on.

Although Cass resisted at first, she settled down and began to pet the little monster. It soon began to purr much like a cat.

"Well, it is kind of cute," she said. "I think it likes me."

"See, told you so," Lenny replied. To Cassy he said, "Now let's get down to the nitty-gritty. What do we have to do now?"

"Wait and see," she said. "The monsters are battling it out nonstop where they'll do no harm. I think they're of sufficient distance from the fen so that they won't gain energy from it. At least the Power of the Fen is ignoring them now. I think that the old whelf queen brought the trogs here to fight the crocs and give us a chance to survive." Suddenly, she turned to look at some distant point and stated, "I think that Scapita has some news though. Care to come with us, Jenna?"

"Oh, you know it!" she cried, touching Lenny's hand.

Cassy touched Lenny and transported them both to Scapita's living room.

Guena soon rushed in breathing heavily. "You could have given us a heads up," she said. "I came as soon as Scapita detected your presence. He's in the laboratory. He's quite busy with that scrap of parchment you gave him, Prince Leonard. I've seldom seen him so driven."

"We need to talk to him," Cassy said. "If I'm right, he's made a breakthrough of sorts."

"Well, I'm not certain of that, but come on. He does want to see you, though."

They followed her into the dining room and down the stairs to the laboratory. Scapita sat unmoving at the bench with a large book spread open. Handwritten squiggles covered the open pages.

"Come in," he said. "I may have discovered something that you'll enjoy hearing."

"I'm always up to hearing good news, Scapita," Lenny replied, sitting down on the only other stool at the bench. "I bet it has something to do with that parchment I gave you, doesn't it?"

"Am I that obvious?" Scapita asked. "Well, never mind. I've deciphered the first level, which identifies the nature of the fifth level wizor. I am at a loss as to why Leanne Mellot had it, though."

Lenny filled him in on her relationship to Magus who was a sorcerer working for Mercilus in his time. Brontis, aka Tallis, had stored the parchment in the walnut periapt and boobytrapped it, but Leanne snatched it and the mirror.

"She thought it might be relevant someday since Brontis was so set on keeping it hidden from her," Lenny finished. "Have you discovered if it's relevant to our needs or not?"

"I would say that it is," Scapita replied. "It's a monster weakener of sorts. That's probably why Brontis held onto it. He couldn't read Mercilus' shorthand. He hoped that I could, and planned to force me to make the wizor for him. You see, he's desperate to destroy the serpent locked inside of him. If he had been able to decipher the wizor, I suspect that he could have made it himself since it's only level five."

"Can we make it now, Scapita?" Lenny asked. "The monsters are contained for the moment, but we're going to have to fight them pretty soon."

"Control your exuberance, Prince Leonard," Scapita replied. "I've yet to decipher the last level."

"If I understand Mercilus' wizors," Lenny stated, "The last level is the binding agent. Maybe if you think of it in that respect, you can figure it out."

"A binding agent, you say," he replied. "Are you sure of that?"

"Of course, I've analyzed hundreds of his monster making wizors. The last level always binds the others together to set the power level. That has to be right."

"I think I remember something," Scapita replied, opening the book to the index in front. Running a finger down the list, he stopped and tapped an entry. "This looks like it."

Turning the heavy pages to the indicated location, he read the entry. "Yes, I'm right," he said. "Here is your binding wizor, Prince Leonard. If you're right, we have the answer to your question. There is only one thing we can do now, and that's to make the wizor. I believe that I have everything we need. Since it's only level five, there won't be a problem in creating it. Would you care to assist me?"

"I don't understand the names of the ingredients," Lenny replied, "since I don't have that kind of wizor making experience, but I bet that Jenna can do it."

"Please, Uncle," she pleaded, "let me do it."

"Well, you might be able to handle this one yourself, Jenna. I can read the strength you've gained while working with Prince Leonard. I would say that you are currently at level six."

"Really, Uncle?" she replied, glancing happily at Lenny. "I had no idea. Very well, I'll do it."

She set out five bowls, one for each layer, and began to fill them based on the notes Scapita offered her. She read the ingredients for the fifth level from the book.

"The bowls are ready," she said. "All they need now is the activator, but I'll need a larger container for the finished wizor."

Searching the shelf of apparatus, she found what she was looking for and set it at the far right of the other wizor bowls. Setting the first bowl on the brazier, she took down a container of activator. Dropping a pinch into the first bowl, she spoke the words Scapita had discerned from the parchment clues.

It took several minutes for the wizor to finish. When the reaction stopped, she dropped the contents of the bowl into the largest one and continued on to the second level. After an hour, all of the levels were finished and filled the largest bowl.

"This one is the hardest one," she said. "Look, everyone, we don't know how the combined wizors in the last bowl will react. I suggest that you step back while I activate it."

Suddenly, Jen stepped out from her. "I'll be here to keep you safe, Jenna," she said. "Go ahead and activate the wizor."

Jenna smiled her thanks and dropped the activator into the last bowl. She spoke the words in the book and stepped back.

The contents of the wizor bowl smoked alarmingly and trembled as if alive, but after ten minutes it suddenly stopped. All that was left in the bowl was a thick layer of black ash.

"I think it worked," she said, eyeing her handywork.

"Good job, Jenna," Scapita complimented her. "You accomplished that task perfectly and at level five too. That's more than most sorcerers can do when they start out. I think that you have just graduated from being a Wizor to a full sorcerer, congratulations."

"Are you serious, Uncle?" she cried. "I don't feel any differently."

"It never does, dear," Guena said. "I agree, you're a full sorcerer. I believe that the guild will accept you as such after they've heard our endorsements. Don't you agree, Prince Leonard?"

"I've believed that for a long time," he replied. "She's performed far better than I've seen other sorcerers perform. No offense, Scapita."

"None taken, of course," he replied. "Now you have your wizor. A pinch should be all you need, and I see a number of those in the bowl. It should be enough. A word of caution, however, you can only use the wizor once on any single monster."

"Still, I want to test it on something," Lenny replied, "but Quimby is the only test subject we have. Cassy, can you fetch him here from my castle?"

"If that's what you want me to do," she said. "I didn't approve of the monster's creation, but I have to agree that we have no other choice except to try the level reducer on it."

She suddenly blinked away but returned immediately holding Quimby who anxiously quivered in her arms.

Lenny took the wizor bowl and held a bit of the contents between his fingers. Returning the bowl to the bench, he readied his cane to record the wizor when activated.

"I'm ready, Cassy," he said. "Put Quimby on the floor and everyone step back. Jenna, are there any activation words I have to say?"

"Well, maybe I better say them," she said. "They're difficult to pronounce. When you're ready, hurl the wizor at Quimby, and I'll do the rest."

Quimby glanced curiously about from the floor, his face an adorable question. Lenny hated to destroy the little monster, but he reasoned that the beast shouldn't exist anyway. When Lenny flicked the wizor at the beast, Jenna uttered the words and threw up her hands to block the ensuing blast.

When the smoke cleared, they found no sign of Quimby. All that was left of him was a starshaped layer of ash on the floor.

Lenny wiped away a tear from his cheek. Turning to Scapita, he said, "The test was a success. I've recorded the wizor in my wizard staff, so there's no need to take any of the physical wizor with me."

"I recorded it in my wand too," Jenna said. "Now that it worked, I want to know why. What exactly happened here?"

"It's a level reducer," Scapita reminded them. "Since it's level five, it should reduce the strength of any monster by that much. Since your little monster was totally destroyed, it couldn't have been stronger than that."

"Quimby didn't stand a chance," Lenny said sadly. "It was only level three. Now assuming that we can get close enough to the monsters, we can reduce them down to a strength that the whips can handle. That's the plan anyway."

"Thanks, Uncle," Jenna said, kissing his cheek. "We couldn't do this without your help. The level reducer is the deciding factor. I think that Duscany is saved."

"Let's hope so," he replied. "I'm out of tricks. Listen, Guena and I really want to marry tomorrow. Please make it possible. I have confidence in all of you."

"So do I," Guena added. "Good luck and stay safe, all of you."

"Let's get this over with," Cassy said, taking Lenny's and Jenna's hands.

They reappeared in Leonard Keep as if they had never left.

Startled, Leanne said, "I don't know if I can get used to this family. No one I know can do what they've done."

"Like I said," Jenna giggled, "you'll get used to it."

CHAPTER 24

BATTLE ROYAL

Lenny explained the plan the best he could to everyone, but privately he wasn't at all certain that it would work.

"Cassy has isolated the monsters to a meadow on the opposite side of the Whelf Fen. The idea is to keep them there long enough to destroy them. Now that we have a level reducer, we think we have a chance, but the effort will be dangerous. Some of us are magical duplicates, but the rest of us are human beings who can be hurt or even killed."

He became so emotional at that point that he choked up and couldn't finish.

"That's a good start, Lenny," Cassy said, taking the floor. "Since only Lenny and Jenna have the level reducer wizor, they'll have to apply it to the monsters, but they have to get close enough. I'll be there to help keep them safe."

"I will too," Jen said, stepping up. "I'll keep Jenna safe. I couldn't live without her."

Len stood beside Lenny and placed a supporting hand on his shoulder. "I know I've made it difficult for you, dear brother, but I'll be there too."

Cass stepped up too with the same message as did their duplicate parents, James and Mare.

"What would we be without any of our children," James said. "You can't keep us away. I doubt if the monsters can seriously harm us anyway."

"Listen, all of you," Lenny said, "don't get in the way of the energy reducer when we deploy the wizor. We tested it successfully on Quimby, but you're made of magic too. The wizor could reduce you and maybe destroy you. We can't take any chances. It's time to deploy the energy reducer wizor before the monsters get any ideas. We can't predict how our presence will make them behave. While we're applying the wizor, the rest of you must remain in standby to use your whips. The monsters were programmed to respond to them. Your jobs will be to keep them off of us until we're ready to join you. We'll destroy them in the same way we've planned it. If anyone thinks he can't do it, speak up now. It'll be too late once we're there."

Anxious faces glanced around but no one spoke.

"Then we're ready," Lenny finished. "Cassy, get us there. Just remember to remain hidden until we're ready for you."

Cassy nodded and transported everyone in place around the meadow perimeter. She took Lenny's and Jenna's hands and squeezed them reassuringly. Their duplicate families stood by ready to assist if necessary.

Quarreling without ceasing, the monsters destroyed everything in the meadow. They ripped up bushes by the roots and smashed bordering trees into splinters, heaving them up into tangled heaps.

"They're weaker now," Lenny whispered. "I can feel it, maybe level eight. Waiting was a wise choice. Jenna, you have to pay attention. We'll strike the crocs first since they're closest. With luck, the monsters won't know we're there. We regroup back here the second it's done. If all is well, we'll hit the trogs second. That's when everyone wades in with the whips to finish them off. Ready, Jenna?" When she nodded, he cried, "Go!"

They appeared over the crocodilians simultaneously. Lenny pointed his wizard staff at the creature's head and fired, while Jenna did the same with her wand. Their return to cover was just as swift.

As predicted, the monsters appeared not to notice them, but the crocs roared in terror over the effects of the level reducer. They seemed to shrink almost perceptibly, but the troglodytes, taking advantage, waded back into the melee.

Coordinating, Lenny and Jenna homed in on the trogs and repeated their offensive. Their success proved to be phenomenal. The monsters continued to shrink to half their normal size but fought each other as if their enemy was responsible for it.

"This is better than I had hoped for," Lenny said. "Too bad that the energy reducer will work only once per monster or else we could do it again and end this."

Signaling the others to advance with the whips, he took the lead. Choosing a croc for himself, he snapped the whip, which produced a staggering effect on the monsters. They all ranged on him at first, but then the other whips came into play.

The sound of the whips seemed to hurt their ears in particular, but it also provoked them to greater anger.

"Be careful, everyone!" Lenny cried. "They're still dangerous, but I can feel the energy draining from them. This could take a while."

Jenna moved in to target a troglodyte, but she didn't count on the second one attacking her instead. She screamed in surprise as the monster descended on her, but Jen raced in to distract the beast. The trog snatched her from the air and crushed her body like a twig before chewing her down its monstrous gullet.

Boiling over in rage, Jenna snapped her whip again and again.

"Do it together as we practiced, Jenna!" Lenny cried. "That has the greatest effect on them."

Suddenly a crocodilian swept its tail at Leanne, knocking her to the ground. Cassy, immediately dragged her back to safety.

"Everyone will understand if you want to quit now, Leanne," Cassy said. "You're the most vulnerable one here."

Leanne glanced fearfully at the monsters but replied, "I just need a moment to catch my breath, Cassandra. I'll keep my promise."

"Just be careful, Leanne," she said.

Leanne soon found her feet. Snatching the whip from the ground, she took her place in the circle of attackers and timed the snap of her whip with them.

The monsters were as interested in fighting one another as much as their tormentors. Every snap of the whip drained energy from their bodies, making them even more vulnerable to damage. All of them dripped pools of blood under their feet. Even though the crocodilians tried to use their most dangerous weapon, the white mist traveled only a few feet before dissipating. Each time the whip cracked they crept back in terror but their archenemies were at their backs. Such close proximity resulted in a free-for-all brawl.

"It's working, guys!" Lenny encouraged them. "Keep it up."

Flagging from the effort, Leanne stumbled and fell. A troglodyte instantly took advantage and attacked, but it met head on with the serpent who had slithered from the river.

Brontis had watched the fight in awe, but when he realized that Leanne was in trouble, he raced to the rescue in the only way he knew how.

The trog fell beneath its momentum but in turn locked the serpent in a terrible grip. The serpent, however, bit a monstrous arm and rolled end over end, entwining the trog in its relentless coils. At its most vulnerable, the trog screamed in pain as its life drained away beneath the crushing embrace.

The second trog came to the rescue, but too late. The monster tore at the coils of the serpent, ripping away scales and amputating five feet of the tail. The serpent, however, coiled around the trog and squeezed until it no longer moved.

The crocodilians were not finished, though. No longer distracted by the trogs, they tore at the serpent, shredding away scales, muscle and bone.

Releasing the trog, the serpent sank long fangs into one of the crocs and pumped its body full of poison that soon took a devastating effect. The croc shrank rapidly in size until it vanished altogether.

The last crocodilian snatched up the serpent and hurled it into the river before advancing on Lenny. He had no choice except to back away, but he continued to rhythmically snap his whip at the croc, which visibly shrank at every strike. The croc, however, advanced toward Lenny and fell upon him.

Cassy snatched Leanne's whip from her hand and snapped it at the croc until the motion turned into a continuous blur and the sound like the roar of a tremendous waterfall. The croc continued to shrink until nothing remained.

They cheered when they found Cass and Len arched over Lenny in a protective dome.

"Thanks, guys," Lenny said. "You can let me up now. Did we

win?"

Everyone's eyes diverted to the battlefield, but even the bodies of the troglodytes were gone. The monsters were indeed defeated. Only Jen stood whole and reformed in the destroyed meadow, arms in the air, cheering everyone over the victory.

However, the serpent weakly slithered up the muddy bank of the river to lay unmoving in the meadow. Its tongue slashed in and out, and its slotted eyes locked on them.

Lenny realized that the serpent had little time left. He wasn't worried about the serpent, but it indicated that Brontis still lived.

"Careful, Lenny," Len said. "It can still fight."

"That's not what it wants to do now," Lenny replied. "The battle is won, and Brontis knows it. He can't speak in this form, but I know what he wants from me."

Lenny pointed his wizard staff at the serpent and released the level drainer wizor. The serpent instantly reacted. Rolling over and over, it began to shrink like the monsters had done. Moments later the serpent was gone, and Brontis lay naked in its place. Brontis tried to speak, but spital foamed on his lips. He reached for Lenny, pleading for help.

Lenny instantly raised his wizard staff and fired Brontis' clothes at him. They writhed in a blur about him until he was appropriately dressed.

"Cassy," Lenny cried, "can you help Brontis? The energy drainer is working on him too."

Cassy stood over Brontis for a moment before touching his forehead with a pert finger. Brontis instantly relaxed as his eyes closed.

"Is he dead?" Leanne asked. "I hated what he did to me, but not enough to wish him dead."

"No, he just has to rest for a while," she replied. "We need to inform Prince Symon that he has another patient. Lenny, you were right. The level drainer worked on him too. He's probably at level three now, but with care and hard work, he can regain his energy."

Lenny turned to the others and grinned. "Well, it's a success. I think we learned something very valuable today. I just hope we don't have to repeat this exercise ever again."

The tumultuous agreement was unanimous.

Cassy, Lenny and Jenna appeared in the hospital in Kings Keep. The ward was full now. Guena and Scapita soon joined them.

Lenny hugged his mother who sat upright and awake in a wheelchair.

"Didn't I tell you she would be all right, Lenny?" his father said. "She's looking great."

Marge did indeed look much better. She had recovered most of her youth, but a blaze of white hair combed to one side remained.

"I want to keep that," she said. "Prince Symon says it'll likely stay. The blaze is quite charming, don't you think?"

Lenny laughed. "It does look good on you, Mother, but it reminds me of the bride of Frankenstein. I'm not quite as fond of monsters now after what we went through."

"About that," Skeldon said. He sat on the side of his bed apparently fully recovered. "I feel like I've been left out of something important. I hope you'll bring us up to date on your adventure before too long."

"Of course, Skeldon," Lenny replied. "The whole thing was hair-raising for all of us, but we prevailed."

Lenny turned to Zada who had been listening from her wheelchair. She seemed to have recovered her full beauty. Not a hair was out of place. However, she returned his smile with a blank expression.

"I'm pleased that you are well, Zada," Lenny said. He knelt and took her hand, but she pulled away. "What's wrong Zada?"

"Who are you?" she whispered hoarsely.

"She's been like that since she woke up," Skeldon said. "She doesn't know me either."

"No, I do know you, Skeldon," Zada said. "It just came to me, but they called you Lenny. I don't know that name. I don't know who you are."

"What about my parents?" Lenny asked, pointing to Marge and Jim. "They've been here with you all of this time."

Zada nodded. "I do know them and Cassandra and Jenna, but you are a complete blank. I'm sure that we've never met."

"That's impossible, Zada," Lenny cried. "You've been my consort for over a year."

"No, my parents would never give me to a stranger," she replied. Tears soon fell from her eyes as she turned her face away.

ROBERT A. G. ERICKSON

"Give her some time, Lenny," Cassy said. "This could be temporary since she remembered everyone else."

"She's right," Prince Symon said. He had been standing by listening to the conversation. "She's had a great shock. I'll keep my patients here a couple of days for observation before sending them home. Check back with me then."

"Of course," Lenny replied. "How's Rosina? I don't see her here."

"She's in the next ward," the physician replied. "She's well and an excellent nurse. She's helping the last patient you sent me. Thanks for the work. You're keeping me quite busy."

"Somehow, I don't think you actually mean that," Lenny replied. "The work has taken you from your family."

Prince Symon merely grinned and replied, "You can visit them if you like. Brontis may be awake by now."

Lenny turned to Jenna and Cassy. "I think we owe them something," he said.

Together they entered the ward.

Rosina rose up from her chair where she had been sitting at Brontis' side. Brontis, however, was still asleep. Rosina smiled and took their hands.

"I appreciate your help, Cassandra, Leonard, and you too Jenna," she said. "I've been thinking about how much I miss my family, but it's too late now by a thousand years. Actually, I rather enjoy it here. The king told me that I could stay as long as I like. Prince Symon says that I can help him and his wife in the hospital. They're expecting a child, you know."

"That's part of what I wanted to talk to you about," Cassy said. "I believe that I owe you a choice. If I had done nothing, you would have been dead too. I'm not sure if I did you a favor or not."

"Oh, I would choose this life over death at any time," she laughed, "but you said something about a choice."

"Yes, it depends upon how much you desire to return to your family in Eskeling. They're long dead from our perspective, but it's possible to return you to them. You see, Mercilus kept your frozen body at home like a shrine. You could wake up from your long sleep and rejoin your family, but it could change the future. If you returned before Mercilus' death, you could change how he and the Kingdom of Eskeling dies. Both could survive, which would destroy this future. If you returned after Mercilus and Eskeling are destroyed, you would gain your children and their futures, but you would have to give up ever marrying again because your children would change the future. The choices are that you can return to your family at that time or stay here. I see that you seem to have some sort of affection for Brontis. Perhaps he can help you adjust."

"I knew Brontis in Eskeling," she said, thoughtfully. "He was always kind to me, and he resented how badly Mercilus treated me. Tell me, Cassandra, did my children grow up normally and have families? Were they happy?"

"I checked on them several times over their years, Rosina," Cassy said. "The answer is yes to all of those questions. They all became fine sorcerers and helped Eskeling to transition to present day Duscany. Many of their descendants are alive today. It's possible to meet them if you desire. You've already met Scapita. His surname is Ancellum."

"We're related?" Rosina cried, enclosing her face with her hands in surprise.

"Yes, he's descended through a brother of Mercilus, but if I'm not mistaken, you're also a second cousin of Mercilus. I'm sure you saw the painting hanging over Scapita's mantel."

Rosina nodded in agreement to both statements and smiled.

"It's me with my husband and children," she said. "How did he come by it?"

"I am responsible for copying it for him," Cassy replied. "He had long thought that he was related to Mercilus, but I actually proved it during one of our adventures. If you want a copy of the painting, I'll gladly provide it."

"Thank you, Cassandra, but I'll decide on that later. I was thinking about your first offer." Glancing at Brontis, she said, "I think I'll stay here. Brontis is an interesting man. Like you said, he needs me. Perhaps we can make something of it."

"That's a wise choice, Rosina," Cassy said. "Does that please you, Lenny?"

Nodding, he replied, "I didn't understand at first, but I think that Rosina has a right to life. I hope you have no regrets, Rosina. You've met my family. You can visit us anytime. In fact, Jenna can show you how to contact us. Isn't that right, Jenna? You're related to her too through your uncle Scapita."

"Oh my, I hadn't thought about that!" Jenna cried. "I suppose that makes you a distant cousin, Rosina, but you remind me of an aunt. Do you mind if I think of you that way?"

"I don't mind at all, Jenna. It's nice to know that I actually do have family here. I don't feel quite as alone now."

"If you need us, just ask Jenna," Cassy reminded her. "We'll help you in any way we can. You've seen our home in Seattle. You're welcome there at any time."

Rosina thanked them, but then she took Brontis' hand when he began to stir.

Lenny, Cassy and Jenna said their goodbyes and well wishes and returned to Scapita's apartment.

Jenna hugged him around the neck and kissed his cheek. "We couldn't have defeated the monsters without your help, Uncle," she said. "Well, maybe we could have, but it would have taken much longer without your help. Someone might have been hurt or killed."

"Thank you for your confidence," Scapita said. "Now that is over, what about your case? How does Leanne Mellot's story end?"

"I think we'll know pretty soon," Jenna giggled. "We left her at Blaine Kamp's home after we defeated the monsters. She was weary and shook up, but she was eager to see him. Guess what I got," she added, handing him a bag of reward gold. "This bag contains a hundred gold pieces. Blaine Kamp says it's only a down payment, and he'll pay the rest as soon as he frees up some assets. I hope I'm right in trusting him in this."

"I believe you can since he's a very rich man, but this is your case, Jenna," Scapita said, refusing the bag. "You get to decide what to do with it."

"Well, Leonard and Cassandra refused their share too," Jenna grinned. "Does that mean that the reward is all mine?"

"It does, and you can spend it in any way you desire. You are a remarkable young woman, Jenna. Perhaps you can use it one day as a wedding dowry yourself."

Blushing, Jenna glanced at Lenny and replied, "Perhaps you and Guena can make yours a double wedding with Blaine Kamp and Leanne Mellot. They seemed amiable with the idea when I asked them."

Guena smiled and glanced at Scapita. "I really don't mind, but it's awfully short notice. There is so much to do that a wedding can't be rushed. Ours is tomorrow, and all of the invitations have been sent out."

Cassy spread her wings and replied, "It's not impossible with my help. I can make all the preparation they require and make certain that their guests arrive safely and on time. Would you agree to that, Scapita?"

"By all means, Cassandra," Scapita replied. "I'm sure that a mere wedding would not tax the magic of the Queen of the Whelfs."

"Now that's settled," Lenny whispered to his sister. "I'm sure that school should have started for us on Earth, but you have more news, don't you?"

"I'm always in control, Lenny," she replied. "We'll return at the precise time we left. You won't miss a minute of precious schooling. Doesn't that thrill you, Lenny?"

"Peachy," Lenny said, but what he wanted was a nice supper and a soft bed for the night. "I really have had enough of thrills and chills, Cassy. School will be a vacation after what we've been through."

"Let's go home," she giggled, taking his arm.

CHAPTER 25

BELLA'S GIFT

Jenna had difficulty sleeping at first since she couldn't stop thinking about how much she longed for Lenny to return, but tomorrow was a school day for him. She wouldn't see him again until he returned to work on Leonard Castle. She had no idea when that would be.

When she did fall asleep, she had a disturbing dream involving one of Duscany's most unusual inhabitants. Bella the dryad lived in a great oak not far from Leonard Keep. Lenny first made contact with her when he inadvertently placed one of his portal staffs inside of her tree before he knew about her presence.

However, he often had reason to interact with her unique and formidable powers. For instance, he used her help to return to Duscany in their last adventure in *A Game of Shades and Shadows* when Night Shadow stole their memories and marooned them in the ancient past of the Kingdom of Eskeling.

The dream however seemed to be a message that included Lenny and herself. Her image floated before her like a green caricature of a human female. Since she was female by nature, she often took on the features of a human female visitor whether real or imagined.

"Jenna," the dryad whispered as if far away, "you are free.

Leonard is free. I command it."

Tossing and turning, Jenna suddenly awoke. The dream still played through her head until she was fully awake. "Is it possible?" she asked of herself.

Not bothering to dress, she ignited the wick of the wall mounted lamp with a fire wizor, which revealed the austere nature of her small room in Scapita's tower. Turning to the three-piece mirror located on her vanity, she touched a corner of the central mirror.

An unseen force appeared to grab her hand and draw her inside, but she stepped unfettered from the mirror on Cassy's vanity in her room on Earth. Cassy, however, was not there.

She's probably in the Whelf Fen doing queenly things, she thought.

Gathering her courage, she opened the door to the corridor and stepped lightly to Lenny's door a few yards away. She thought about knocking, but instead she turned the knob and rushed inside.

She found him sitting up in bed, sleepy eyed and bewildered.

"Leonard!" she cried. "I had the most disturbing dream. We were inside of Bella the dryad's tree. She said something really strange."

"Tell me about it," Lenny replied, but it wasn't a request. "I had the same dream, Jenna. I have to talk to her. You better go while I get dressed."

"You're not going without me, Leonard," she replied. "This involves both of us. I want to know the answers as much as you do."

"Okay then, get dressed and return here when you're ready. That nightgown is pretty, but it won't do to travel in it."

"Oh, right, I'll be right back," she said, retracing her steps through the portal to her room.

Throwing off her nightgown, she dressed as quickly as she could. Frantically brushing her hair into place, she returned through the mirror to Lenny's room.

She found him standing beside the bed with his wizard staff in hand waiting for her.

"That's better, Jenna," he said. "I'll use a portal and go there directly. Hopefully, this won't take too long."

They appeared hand in hand inside the dryad's tree. His wizard staff in the center was a dead giveaway of where they were. The steel ball on the top glowed gently, but there was no light or darkness here. Here was simply the magical representation of the interior of a normal tree. The greenish walls seemed close, but no one could reach them if they tried.

"Bella!" Lenny cried angrily. "Come out so we can talk!"

Bella, coalesced out of the magic nature of the tree and slowly morphed into a copy of Jenna, but naked.

"Don't forget clothes, Bella!" Lenny cried, anxiously glancing at Jenna, but she didn't seem concerned.

Before Bella had fully formed, the outline of simple clothes began to fill in with the same green as the interior of the tree.

"I am here," Bella whispered, as she finished forming.

"Bella," Lenny replied. "We have to talk to you. You sent us both a disturbing dream, why?"

"I will understand—disturbing dream," she hesitated, but she clearly did not. It often took time for her to extract the meaning of words from their thoughts.

"Never mind," Lenny said. "The point is that you contacted both of us with the same vision. What did you mean by saying we are free?"

"You are free," the dryad agreed, hesitating as usual. "You are free to make seeds."

"Wait," Jenna said, "it sounds like she wants us to marry."

"I agree," Lenny replied, stroking back his errant locks. He had forgotten to comb them. "It takes time to express herself accurately. I admit that I'm a little baffled. Why did she send the message?"

"Zada," the dryad said, and then she repeated the name several times in a row. "Zada, Zada, Zada."

"What about Zada?" Lenny asked.

The dryad continued to repeat her name. When she stopped, she repeated, "You are free to make seeds."

"Well, she only knows how trees reproduce," Lenny whispered, "but what does Zada have to do with this issue?"

"Leonard," Jenna replied, aghast. Tears wet her pert cheeks.

"What's the matter, Jenna?" he asked. "What could she mean?"

"Leonard, she's talking about Zada and us. She knows that we love each other, and that Zada stands in the way. I think she's trying to help us."

"Help us, but how, Jenna?" Lenny asked. "I really don't understand."

"You would if you could add two and two," Jenna replied. "I think she's responsible for Zada's condition. Zada doesn't remember you anymore. That makes us free to marry."

"Oh, good grief!" Lenny cried. "It's so clear now. Bella, why did you do this to us?"

"Free to make seeds," the dryad repeated.

"Leonard, Bella has no concept of marriage," Jenna explained, "but she does understand the concept of togetherness as in mating and making seeds like trees do. Don't you see, Leonard? With Zada out of the picture, we can marry when we're ready. I'm fifteen this year, but you're sixteen. I'll have to wait another year, but we can be together without worrying about Zada's interference. Don't you understand?"

Lenny stared at her in shock. "Oh, I understand all right, but how can we tell the Bugowards? Zada and I committed ourselves together in front of them. We said the oath."

"I know, Leonard. You told me all about it. Surely you remember that the oath was simply an engagement that could be broken if it didn't work out. Well, it didn't work out. We love each other, Leonard. We are free to marry whenever you are ready."

"I'm sure you're right, Jenna," Lenny groused, "but I made a promise."

"A promise that you obviously can't keep if Zada doesn't remember you or your promise. I agree that Bella shouldn't have interfered like that, but now that she has, we can make a much longer lasting promise to each other. This is the answer to our dreams, or my dreams anyway. I want to marry you more than anything, Leonard. Can't you simply accept what's been given to us as a gift?"

Lenny stared into her eyes, but then he smiled. "Jenna, you know that I love you as Crosia, but Zada's promise still haunts me, and I still love her. I don't know what to do."

"You know that I don't mind if you call me Crosia, Leonard. After all, that's who I was when you played Drwen Blubak in Cassandra's strange game to show us how the whelfs began. Loving you was the best part of it, love potion or not."

"I admit that game was so real, and I learned a lot, but I wouldn't do it again no matter what Cassy promised me. I admit, though, that I'm confused when it comes to you and Zada. I don't know what to do."

"You don't have to decide on anything right now," Leonard. "I must wait a year, but you wanted to wait until you were of legal age in your world. I accept that. I know that Zada was concerned about waiting so long when her friends were already married. Now she's free to marry someone else. We have lots of time to decide about everything. Please, Leonard, if Zada suddenly remembers you, I promise that I'll back away, but I really think that Zada's condition is permanent. Whatever you do, don't be mad at Bella. She doesn't understand human needs and behaviors. She thinks she's repaid you for saving her children."

"Of course, I understand that, Jenna," he whispered, "but this problem isn't at all simple. I've made a lot of promises to Zada and her family, and now I don't know what to tell them."

"Don't tell them anything, Leonard," Jenna replied. "Let them make the decisions. I doubt if they'll insist that you and Zada marry now that she doesn't remember you."

"You make a lot of sense, Jenna, for a princess."

"Well, you don't for a prince, so what's the problem? We have lots of time before we have to make a decision."

Lenny smiled comfortably and drew her close. His eyes locked on her beautiful, blossoming face for a long moment. For the first time he could see the love sparkling there, a love that he did indeed share and not just in the way the love potion caused Drwen and Crosia to love. Then he kissed her quivering lips, and she didn't object.

— THE END —

ABOUT THE AUTHOR

The author grew up in western Montana, a third-generation descendant of Swedish immigrants. He is a Navy veteran of the Vietnam Conflict and a retired US Coast Guard enlisted man. He is also the author of the Fluke Family fantasy series, the Wizor Fair fantasy series and other fantasy and Sci-Fi books.

Made in the USA
Middletown, DE
07 October 2022